A Story of the Twin Flame

The Forbidden Romance of Lilith and Samael

by Rada Lyubomirova

***

Book One, Second Edition
Neurodivergent Version

***

Compendia Publishing, 2025.

First published in digital version with ISBN: 979-8-988457-50-3 on June 2nd '2023.

Second edition paperback published with ISBN: 978-1-963038-26-2 on June 13th '2025.

Neurodivergent version paperback ISBN: 978-1-963038-07-1

Travel version paperback ISBN: 978-1-963038-05-7

Bespoke paperback ISBN: 978-1-963038-60-6

Bespoke hardback ISBN: 978-1-963038-64-4

Cover art by Warm Tail. Cover photo by Konstantin Koyokin. Cover edit by Andre J. Ginting.

Library of Congress Control Number: 2025931500

Compendia Publishing, Wilmington, DE, USA.

https://www.compendiapublishing.com

Contents

More Adaptive Fiction Works
by Rada Lyubomirova

To find out which of our published books are free to read, scan the QR code we provide below.

"LILITH AND SAMAEL" book series:
Book 1—A Story of the Twin Flame
Book 2—The House of Alchemists
Book 3—The Guardian Prince of Rome

RADA LYUBOMIROVA
21+
A STORY
OF THE TWIN FLAME
THE FORBIDDEN ROMANCE OF
Lilith and Samael

21+
HOUSE
OF THE ALCHEMISTS
THE PARANORMAL ROMANCE OF
Lilith and Samael
RADA LYUBOMIROVA

21+
The Hakawati's
UNDEAD WITCH
A ROMANTIC FICTION
OF THE TRADITIONAL STORYTELLER
RADA LYUBOMIROVA

RADA LYUBOMIROVA
21+
SPRINGTIME BIRTH
AND WINTERTIME REBIRTH
A PSYCHIC PARANORMAL ROMANCE
OF
Yarilo and Morana

THE ARK OF THE SHADOW-WORKERS:

Legend, Myth, and Folklore Retelling

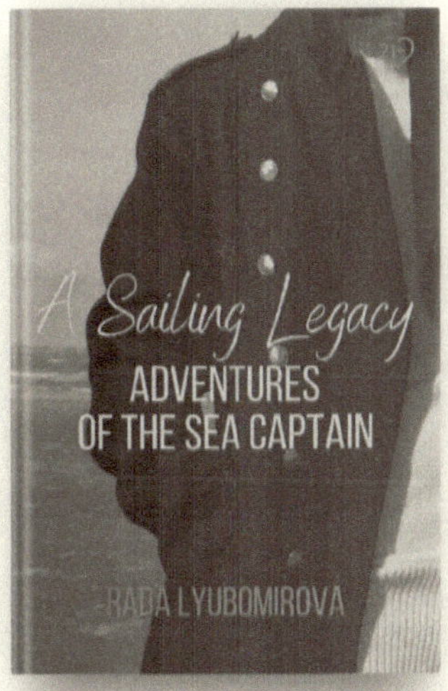

FAIR WARNING

This book contains explicit language, explicit romantic scenes, sacred companionship in ancient traditions, mentions of assaults, and depictions of mortalities. It is not suitable for readers with sensitivity to certain subjects and/or language expressions. Readers' discretion is advised.

This publication is NOT suitable for minors. The age of majority may vary from one area of jurisdiction to another. In the absence of clear guidance and/or limitations from the governing bodies, the publisher and author suggest that 21 years of age be the minimum age for reading this publication.

DISCLAIMER

This adaptive fiction draws inspiration from mythology, folklore, religious scriptures, and historical events, with some parts added for a dramatic purpose.

This work of fiction is for entertainment purposes only and is NOT to be treated as a matter of fact or as the ground for theories. However, this publication may be included as a subject to study and criticise in the language arts, literature, culture, history, hermeneutics, theology, psychology, parapsychology, pseudoscience, or any other related department or faculty. We provide the bibliography at the end of this book for the readers to look further into.

The manuscript and cover of this publication are not generated by any artificial intelligence system. No part of this publication may be used to develop and/or train artificial intelligence models, systems, or technology, with no exception for any AI-related uses that fall under the category of fair use or general-purpose AI. No part of this publication that has been made publicly available online may be used in general web scraping, text or data mining practices, and/or any AI-related transformative uses.

Dedication

To all masters: Master who keeps mastering his craft; master who protects his loved one from crumbling apart in between the flights; and master who provides the abundant nest for his little bird.

***

To all masters who keep fighting the brutal battles raging on the inside but keep the battlefield tales untold: If this literary art is an ark, then your cargo has been shipped.

***

To the little birds who provide inspirations for the masters: Let this written work be a love letter filled with the unspoken language.

List of the Regions
or Places

1. Bliss: the garden of Eden.

2. The North of the Third Heaven (or of Here):
   hell.

3. Haemus: the earlier name for the
   mountainous region of the Balkan peninsula.

4. Tangra was the highest peak of the Rila
   Mountains. It is called Musala in modern-day
   Bulgaria.

5. Illyria covered the northwestern part of
   the Balkan peninsula. The frontier was to
   guard the regions in modern-day Slovenia,
   Croatia, Hungary, Bosnia and Herzegovina,
   Serbia, Montenegro, Kosovo, Albania, and
   North Macedonia.

6. Moesia became the southeastern frontier of
   the Balkans. It was the land of the Moesi, a
   Thracian tribe. It spanned across modern-day

Serbia, some regions in Macedonia, and some regions in Bulgaria.

7. Serdika or Serdica referred to a region of Thrace. Then it became Sredetz or Sredets. Later, the name changed again to Triaditsa. Now, the city is called Sofia, in modern-day Bulgaria.

8. Kendrisiya was a region of Thrace. The oldest city in Europe is as old as the 6th millennium BC, if not older. It once had seven hills, but one has since vanished. This city in Bulgaria is now called Plovdiv.

9. Odessos: in modern-day Bulgaria, Varna is the name for both a city and a province.

10. Atanasovska Lake: the pink lake located in present-day Burgas, Bulgaria.

11. Aibunar: The ancient copper mining in forested hills near Stara Zagora. The remains are located in central Bulgaria.

12. Rudna Glava: The ancient mining that might be older than Aibunar. The remains of the site are located in modern-day Serbia.

13. Little Bear: Ursa Minor constellation in the far northern sky of Earth, with Polaris being the brightest one.

14. Salbatanu: Her Desher (Ancient Egyptian), Ma'adim (Hebrew), or planet Mars.

15. Dimashq or Dimashka: the pre-Semitic name for Dammesek, Dummesek, or Darmesek (now the city of Damascus in Syria).

16. Aktiki: Athens, Region of Thrace (now a city in Ellada).

17. Ellada or Ellas: Hellas, Hellada, or Greece.

18. Alpes: Alps mountain.

19. Alkebulan: Africa.

20. Kemet: Mesr, Masr, Misr, or Egypt.

21. Hercynia Silva: mountainous forest in ancient Europe, in the southern part of modern-day Germany.

22. Sindhu: the earlier name for the Indus River.

23. Takshasila: the earlier name of Taxila in Rawalpindi, modern-day Pakistan.

1

Our First Night

The Time of Bronze

Here we were on the highest hill of the seven. After too many quests in searching for her, it was my reward to have the magnificent views from above. The view of the hills surrounding Kendrisiya. The view of her kneeling before me.

Her solid black wings were to lift her. She, the carrier of the burdens, was to fly with her heartache. To see her wings being relaxed this way was such a fresh flow of air. Tonight they deserved to touch the ground after being strongly spread in the air.

While losing track of her, I had lost control of my own flight. My wings had merely glided to lose myself in looping time without her. Now I was willing to lose myself in her sphere.

Her night sky hair was let down loosely. My fingers comfortably got lost between the black strands. In my memory of her, I had held on for too long. Now I was to hold her head still so she could welcome me home.

She felt beatific when she swallowed all of me. She deserved nothing less than all. She was to take mine entirely. She ensphered me in the place where I belonged. Inside of her was the realm in which I should spend my endless lifetime.

Her moan spoke of how my cock became a tranquilliser for her restlessness. When she gagged, it was my duty to wipe away her tears. It was always supposed to be my duty since the time of origin.

My wings were to protect her from blaming herself. Her face sought comfort in my palm while she tried to catch her breath. She looked emotional rather than lustful.

"My little bird." While showing shiny drops of my arousal, I praised her, "You did this to me." My comforting words were to keep her from feeling like a failure.

She calmed down once I smeared these drops of mine on her lips. The face she gave me seemed like someone who just received a present. There was so much gratitude in her face. Probably my presence was indeed a bliss for her, as hers was a bliss for me.

My knuckles caressed her blushing cheek. "Are you all right, my love?" It was important that she trusted me to lead, especially with her being this vulnerable. "Tell me if you aren't keen on any of it."

"I'm your mistress tonight, Master. Have me however you want." She needed to be ready before I continued thrusting her throat again. The deep breath she took regulated her. "I'm all right. If I can't take it, I'll call your name, Samael. But I want more of you."

How much I had missed those doe eyes. They returned green as emerald stones once more. Every time her eyes were locked in mine, she captured me. There was no other choice for me but to surrender to my enchantress.

Her lips kissed the crown of mine. "Let me know what you want me to do for you." It was the kiss of life that she gave before sucking me once more. Not like the kiss of death that I gave others for them to pass before I sucked the lives out of them.

"I shan't be less than obedient." Her surrendering words sounded just like enchantment. Slowly, I gave her myself. She gave me the face of a beggar in return.

Supplicating her Master to fuck her solely for my pleasure. My satisfaction seemed to become the fulfilment of the purpose of her creation. Fulfilment was what she sought from me.

Her beggar's face became more and more helpless. Her moan screamed to me of how desperate she became. Having my entire length down to her throat was her triumph. My fulfilment would come when she became my spent harlot.

Carrying her, I walked towards a rock for us to sit on. "Free your breasts for me, Lilith." Squeezing her arse, I sat her right. Her hole welcomed my cock home. Here, inside of her, my sword was finally sheathed. "I've been craving your motherhood."

She exposed her breasts one by one. Both of them were full, waiting to be sucked empty. My tongue was now latched on one of hers. The essence of her was not like anything I had ever tasted.

Even one drop of hers was enough to hold me captive for the rest of eternity. She now lived within me, as I now merged into one flesh with her. I was of her as she was of me.

"Let me fuck myself with your cock, Master. Please?"

"Not until you're drained." She deserved to nurture me this way, as I no longer had any desire to free myself from her. "Let me see how good your pussy is at begging."

She gave me her other nipple to be sucked empty. Her fingers ran through my hair. "Your cunt. It's the sheath for my Master's sword," she said while clenching my cock tighter.

"You lent it to other men in the past. They filled you with their come so you could bear their children.

But it's my cunt from now on. It's to be fucked however I want and whenever I need. It's my belonging. These breasts, too, are mine."

Her contractions from each sucking became tighter than before. Her pussy tightening chased my suckling mouth. Tighter, until her release covered my length. Her body taught me how connected each part of her was to another.

"Coming without my permission..." I kissed her lips gently while she was recovering. "Just like a harlot, being disrespectful. Now clean up your mess!"

The winged night creature was being obedient. She lowered herself to the ground. Licking me clean as commanded, she did not miss any part of it.

"You let me taste your motherhood," I said, pulling her hair down. Her eyes glazed with tears. There was no sadness in her eyes, only attention for my next command.

"Let me fuck your beautiful face again."

My little bird knelt. Her hands clawed on my abdomen while I rose. "This sinner is yours to take. You are to punish, my Great Prince." Her parting lips welcome me once again. She let her tongue out this time.

Thrusting her throat rougher than before. Pulling her hair down. Holding her tighter. It was my duty to remind her, for I was the Master of this harlot.

When she was gagging, I said, "This is your punishment. I tell my sheath when to come. That is, if I allow you to come."

My arousal took off only by watching her cry like this. As my release was near, I widened my stance. I had waited for this moment for too long. It was right for me to be impatient with her. My cock went as deep as my length could reach the back of her throat.

"Now my release in return for your milk."

Here I came, giving her every drop of me. Finally, I emptied my sac inside of her. Every hole she had should be filled with my cock at some point in our lifetime. Probably not tonight, but eventually they all would be.

Her thirst now evanesced. "Mmh... thank you, Master. I've been waiting for this for too long."

In my arms and twelve wings, my little bird nestled. Let her rest her wings for once. I would build a bird nest to let her rest from her weariness. All I hoped was that she was keen on building our nest with me.

It was the first night we spent together after a long time apart. Throughout the night, I kissed her face as much as I could to soothe her.

My heaven was here and now, while having my wings wrap her body close to mine. They might not be the strongest ones, but the twelve were enough to keep her safe under my wings.

It had been way overdue to be with her since the time of origin. Way too long. I was never to let her go again. Not as her Master who restricted her freedom, but as her partner, who walked and flew alongside her.

From the Infernal fire, I was Created. She was the one who kept my fire burning. The flame inside of us was the same fire we lived in as a union, as twins, and as partners.

2

The Garden of Bliss

The Time of Origin

In humankind, the Creator silhouetted Our Heavenly image. Was our silhouette not only on their flesh but also on their insides? Whether or not the voice of the Merciful Spirit sounded loudly in their souls, time would help to descry.

Each of us was different, as they were. Her skin looked smoother than his. She moved more gently than the other one—her mate. She was chosen for him, as he was for her.

From my place, I could see that she was more than all right. Indeed, she was one of the most beautiful beings ever created. At least in my eyes, she was.

She looked curious about what things were and how they moved. The reasons why they moved the way they did seemed to intrigue her further. That way, Lilith was more passionate compared to him.

Her facial expression changed when her eyebrows furrowed. It intrigued my curiosity about her. She was only at the beginning of her path. She might not have the means to elaborate on each one of them yet.

There was also the way her lips pouted when not getting the answer she desired. It was the adorable pouting way, not the one when someone was disappointed.

Lilith was obviously disappointed after each fight. When they fought, he tried to establish dominance over her. It did not suit her character. He wanted to contain her. To make her his consort. The reason behind it was something I did not quite understand.

Does he believe his creation places him above her? But they came from the same dust, so he didn't make any sense of it. Or was it because he was created earlier than her? I'm the Firstcreated. I was created on the second day, way ahead of Adam. Probably I'm the one who should be with her instead."

From what I overheard from their fights, she saw them as equal creations. That was exactly my first thought. I could not agree more with her. She disagreed with being treated as if she were less than him. Why would she? Why should she?

Their fights were more about power in their relationship. From making small decisions to the way they lived. She was not to fight against him. It was praise that her ears deserved to hear instead of words of argument.

She was to compassionately lean against him so he could strengthen his stance and stand more strongly. If she were not to lean against him, the man could have lived in complacency. We could not let the man be lazy, could we?

There were even more fights about sex. Lilith seemed to have her own unique taste in procreation. Somehow, she seemed to know that sex never had one flavour.

She might see that procreation was full of colour. My azure eyes were in harmony with the emerald of hers; sex was not as rigid as black and white.

She might be keen on each of her senses to feel different ways through it. Inhaling the scent of her mate's flesh could have pleased her. I wondered if the scent of her flesh would please my senses.

Hearing his praise words might be satisfying for her. I wondered if disgrace would highly evoke her arousal. Things that came out of my mouth could be venomous. I wondered if my humiliating words would poison her naïveté.

She could get bored easily; that one I descried. Sex for her might not only be about finishing but rather a journey. She needed to be more alive with him, I assumed. She was already alive. It made sense if she wanted to live in the moment and be in alignment.

Once it got late, I returned to the North of Here. But I was certain to come to the Bliss again. There was this unfamiliar spark, even though I was built from the Infernal One. This one was not destructive but rather of planting and milling. She was like the spark that ignited the fire.

She could become the torch for others to see clearly. Or to burn her surroundings to ashes. As I was to bring the Light for them or to burn. The warmth of her flame somehow felt familiar to me. Already, she had ignited something inside of me.

"What if... I wonder if she and I were created for the deconstruction of the hierarchies? Regardless of how Divine or undivine the hierarchy is." I might not be able to elaborate on why I thought the way I thought about her yet. It felt like I let myself gravitate towards her.

***

Lilith's long hair was exquisite when she was lying on the grass. Her hair looked shiny when the ray of light hit.

Her skin glowed radiantly and seemed to be smooth to the touch. Even bugs would probably lose their balance when landing on her silkiness. If my touch landed on hers, would she allow me to remain?

Only by Watching her from afar could I feel how relaxing her alone time was. She made me wonder how the sky would look through her nurturing eyes. It must be different from the perception through the azure of mine, as I was a Being of the Sky.

Her mate, however, had now interrupted her relaxing time. His cock hardened just by seeing her naked on the grass. Surely, I resonated with him. Mine, too, was already hurting madly from Watching that particular beauty.

He bent her knees and spread her legs open. With saliva, he stroked his cock near her pussy. Without building her, he might hurt the woman. Shoving his cock into her like that, he was only able to satisfy himself.

Lilith tried to roll his body so she could be on top of him. He stopped her. With his grip, he pinned both of her wrists above her head. "No, stay there beneath me. Let me fill your cunt. I'll get you pregnant," said Adam.

He wanted her to submit. He kept fucking her until he came. Once he was finished, he dropped his head on her chest. His spent body was recovering on top of her.

"The man is still learning. He isn't there yet, Lilith. Give him some time." I wished that I could say the soothing words to her. Whispering was the only thing I could do from my place. I imagined how warm she was when I buried myself inside of her.

For now, he could not fulfil her needs. He did not yet have the knowledge or capability. He did not know that her submission was not something to be demanded. It was for her to willingly give it to someone she trusted. He had not completely gained her trust, let alone her respect.

Once he calmed down, he rolled on the grass. She rested her head on his chest. Her pussy was leaking out his come. Jealousy rushed through my Being at once.

It should be my seeds planted in her womb. It should be the remains of my come that leaked out of her once we finished. It was supposed to be mine, not his.

It should have been my warmth that filled her soul through my care afterwards. It was not so hard to comprehend her worth. She deserved to have all that I could give her, if not more.

Was this how it felt to be the object that someone claimed? It felt like she had already claimed me. She could, if she wanted to.

3

The Firstcreated Tasker

My purposes as an enigma were many. Layer upon layer, they merged into one another.

The fence at the end of one Duty towards the beginning of another was never established. Not every Being was capable of navigating the different pressures that came with my Duties.

The Polaris of the Little Bear in the sky showed where the north of Earth was. Its stability illuminated its purpose, miraculously guiding humankind. To orient them towards one of the Terranian poles.

From where they were, Polaris was to guide them in navigating towards elsewhere. The north of Earth was a lot simpler than the North of Here.

The simultaneous emergence of the flaming heat and the freezing cold in the North of Here was not for everyone to consider as simple. I was, firstly, to be its Guardian.

To ease the fire from burning everything down. To give them my fire to survive the freeze. My Light was to establish the Fence so the heat and cold would not merge into one.

To Rule a celestial body called Salbatanu was another Duty of mine. It was not a luminaire by itself. How dense its metal dust reflected the sun made it seem like a star. Others from afar viewed my morning star as red as the fire.

It sparked temptation, persistence, aggression, warfare, and conquest. Those who called it home were resistant to many events. The flaming one was not for the fainthearted. Martians' flames combusted the force to conquer, but never to be conquered.

Its Ruler was not only to Rule but to Shield it. As I was, my Shield was in the first line of the Martians' defence. The very celestial body took many hits many times from others of its kind. As I had been taking hits from others, sometimes from my own Kind.

We embraced the incomings, "Bring it to us!" We rotated with the impacts. We kept our revolution constantly on our path, revolving the Solar.

The metal dust on the surface alone tempted many. From welcoming other celestial bodies to impact us, we preserved more and more deposits of precious minerals. Some of the crystals were rare to find. Some of the minerals could power up many things.

Many of them could try to start their combustion; indeed, humankind would race each other to reach the very sky object. My Fence would be the obstacle for their pride and immaturity, or worse, their greed to reach the surface of my morning star.

The minds within humankind might overcome the test to reach Salbatanu. It would be their moral compass that leads humankind to gravitate towards it.

No one should have forgotten that it was I who chose whom to welcome. The humility within humankind would be needed for them to learn. The morning star would remain under my Ruling, never theirs.

What Salbatanu really was should be revealed to humankind at some point in their lifetime. It could be the first key to deconstructing the systems they were about to build. Once its true nature was revealed, all their belief systems could be breaking loose.

It might shake the foundation of what they believed or how they were raised as younglings. At what point of whose lifetime would I give the revelation of the red morning star? The judgement was mine to pass as its Ruler.

To reveal who others truly were was another Duty of mine. Their passion, desire, and even mischievousness were to be reflected. Their own reflections were scary to their eyes sometimes; it was understandable. I was to be faithfully reflective.

It was enjoyable to Watch others from afar. Not to stalk them but to learn from their characters and behaviours. It was fascinating to Watch them up close and learn from their reactions to others. Even a small, slightly noticeable response was unique to one.

I was to Watch how they act and react towards surroundings at a given time and space. The best one was to Watch their integrity resurface when they were unaware of my presence. With or without being watched, any being could be an obstacle to oneself or others.

They might not be aware of themselves or what they had become. That might be the reason they saw me as the Accuser. For what they were on the inside or what they did on the outside, almost every being could wear that title of adversary.

It made me wonder if the Most High at one time could be wearing the title. That one I should see. Nevertheless, I would take their blame from time to time as *Hasatan*.

As the Prosecutor, the Accuser, and the Adversary, I Delivered in the Heavenly Court. No one should have forgotten my Duty to punish and destroy those sinners once the Divine Council passed their Judgement.

This Angel of Death was to convey souls after a lifetime to the next one. It would probably take a lifetime to elaborate on me as a Tasker. This Tasker was to be sovereign when doing each Task. There was a lot for me to fulfil as well as a lot to learn along my path.

The lifetime of fulfilling my Duties had provided me with skills. My lifetime of Watching others so far had given me the knowledge. It was not merely because the Most High created me first, ahead of them.

My established Being was the line of defence on the battlefield of good and evil. My fire was a warning for the good to not melt towards the evil. My Light was a weapon for the evil to not breach towards the good. This enigma had discernment because both of them were within me.

The ability to discern between good and evil mostly became my leverage. Some other times that leverage became heavy. Then the weight became a burden.

What they might not know was that this very Tasker could feel something. The power of my silence became stronger with passing time. Keeping these feelings to myself made me a master at concealing. My free will chose to not show any of them.

It was to protect no one else other than me. The armour was necessary for my own sake. Their understanding was never my expectation, because mostly they would not. Once again, their blame was on me for fulfilling all of my Duties with what they called numbness.

The burden within my shadow side was unnecessary to be kept. The heaviness that came from being the Most High's Tasker was too much for me to carry around.

It was much easier to bury them in one place than to keep these burdens inside of my Being. Within the Bliss, I kept myself of sound mind.

The Garden of Bliss was phenomenally bright, unlike the mostly dark North of Here. There was warmth, unlike the heated and frozen North of Here.

4

Planting the Seeds

As I knelt down on one knee, my hand felt the damp soil. Not by the rain, but the place of my burial was rather watered. When I looked around, the surroundings were quite the same as usual.

No one was here when I started to dig the ground. The Tasker wept, as could the Divine. Not many had witnessed Us weeping. One day, some of them would witness the time when We shed our tears.

These clean fingers wiped away my fallen tears. Then those tears went into the hole in the ground. When nothing else remained to be shed, I filled the burial with soil as it was earlier.

My lungs welcomed as much air as they needed. Deep breaths regulated my Being. By itself, under my Command. While looking up, my face felt the warmth. The scent I did not recognise flew through the breeze.

"I hoped you didn't mind... I watered your plant." Her innocent voice startled me.

My guard was lowered while my armour was shedding. She walked into my life in my shieldless moment. Even if my shield was on, I would let her crack it open. "Your care is only for me to appreciate, Lilith."

She looked surprised that I knew her name. With a smile on her face, she asked for my permission, "May I? Your hands." The water she poured cleansed the dust off of my hands.

As she kept pouring it onto mine, it felt like I could almost hear her thoughts. "*Wash your face, my Great Prince, so no one can see you troubled.*" Here was the Tasker, doing the first task under her command.

"I wasn't quite sure if it was too much water or too little. You must know more matter than I do. That was me assuming."

"We don't need to flood it. Consistency is what each one of us needs." I was fully aware that I said 'we' and 'us' to her. "How are you aware of this place, if I may?"

"You come here often. You always seemed quite troubled when you arrived. You bent down, and then you faced the Sky. You took some time before getting on your feet again." She paused, but her face showed her struggle.

"My place is afar. There is no wing to help me see what you were doing. But there was a bump on the ground when I came here."

Her attention to me was never expected. She not only saw me at a glance but truly paid attention to me. In my vulnerability, this Watcher had been watched.

"I believe you know my name, but I don't know yours. What do I call you, my Great Prince?" Those doe eyes were gazing at me. They were learning about the details of my face. No one had ever done that to me.

Trying to properly introduce myself, I held myself back from being too excited. Scaring her away was never my intention. "You can call me Samael, but I've been called by many names. I wouldn't mind if you prefer to call me something else. The North of Here is under my Guard."

She probably was unaware of her blushing face. Her curiosity had obviously moved to my wings. She concealed it by watering the soil once again. Silently, I hoped that she would ask about my wings. This silence started to become torture for me.

"But I wasn't Created to hear thoughts. Curiosity won't be a sin of yours. You can ask me anything."

"I've never seen this many wings. I've seen six at most. How many exactly do you have?"

"I have twelve, Lilith," I said, wishing that she would start touching them.

"If you allow me to, I'd love to feel yours."

While nodding my permission, I expanded my wings for her to touch. It was the scent of her flesh that embraced me first. Her face became more beautiful as her excitement mixed with curiosity.

Now was my chance to look at her smooth skin closely. How beautiful she was in my eyes. Breathing steadily, I held myself back from running my fingers through her long black hair.

Taming my cock from hardening was much harder with her being this close. Mine was twitching already. Mine needed to be sheathed securely inside of her.

The desire to touch her was building within me. My hands did not follow it. Instead, I let her come to me. All of me was hers to touch, but she was not mine. Not yet, at least.

She started with my wings, but she might continue everywhere else. I would not stop her from doing so. Her hands could touch every part of my Being. But they withdrew from me. "Forgive me if I tickled you. I didn't mean to."

My excitement should be kept hidden from my face. "I don't mind if you did. It's all right."

Her hands ran along the wingspans. Then the gentle fingers of hers brushed my feathers. "They're beautiful, your wings."

I wished I could say, *"Not as beautiful as you are, Lilith."* Instead, I gave her another smile. Every part of me tried to compose myself from feeling her touch. "Do you think so?"

Her naïveté emerged while she was nodding. The nod. The gaze she gave me. "Some parts are damaged, so they're rough, even sharp. Some other parts are missing... um, something."

"Barbs. And yes, I'm aware that some vanes are damaged." These wings had survived the roughness of different kinds of weather. They were not soft compared to her touch.

"Hmm." She tilted her head, giving me a frowning face. "If those vanes could tell a story, I believe they would. Plenty of stories, would they?"

I gave her nothing but a nod. If only my words could build a storyline; they would be marching only into her ears. I would tell those tales to her. We would build our own tales together from there.

My untouched lips just became the focus of her gaze. She could kiss me if she wanted to. She could devour my lips to satisfy her hunger. And I would allow her to.

"And the Sword is your instrument?"

"Some refer to it as Light to help them see better. Since I'm of the fire, it's quite practical that way."

"Is it dark in the North of Here?"

"Mostly, yes." That was when I realised that I could have lost myself in her gaze. "I should probably return there. It's already late."

"Will you be coming here again, my Angel?"

"I don't have the power to turn seeds into plants within this Bliss. So I need to make sure you nurture them."

She curtsied towards me. As I was taking off, her gentle hand waved at me. She might not understand my reason yet. It was needed for me to fly away from her. Because if I had not, I could have pulled her face closer to mine.

She was to be kissed passionately. Her breasts were to be squeezed before becoming the feast only for my mouth.

This strong desire inside of me was fighting to take over my Being. The urge to fly her naked body away was hunting its prey—my sound mind.

To fuck her within the vastness of the Heavenly Sky. To fuck her so roughly until she could feel the storm inside of her body when she came.

At that very time, she would taste the wind of pleasure. Then there would be nothing but the two of us in our own universe.

I wanted to wrap her in all my wings. To keep her to myself. To claim her as mine.

I wanted her to regret wasting her power by arguing with Adam.

I wanted her pussy to sheath my cock; she would fit me. Her womb would be filled with my seeds. She would nurture my child in it.

I wanted to fill her heart with everything I have. To provide her with so much joy. To provide her with the fulfilling life she deserved.

I wanted those to be my duties. She was to be the first among the other Duties I had to fulfil.

I wanted to. Here, I fell for my desire—her.

5

Nurturing the Seeds

When approaching the Bliss, I saw them having sex. She rolled his body to be on top of him. Adam was bigger than her; I knew it must not be easy for her.

She seemed to enjoy riding him. Her already naked body was exposed to him. Her hand moved his towards her breasts. That way, he was told to enjoy them. But he simply did not bother to even try.

He rolled her over to be beneath him. She was once again under his lead. Her forearms were locked above her head. With all his weight, she was held tightly under him.

Once he finished, his knees closed her legs together. He wanted his come to reside inside of her. It was nothing more than procreation for Adam, I descried. The view of her being treated like that was not something I wished to have.

"*She's my Lilith.*" This claim that I made needed to be screamed out of my lungs so that every layer of Heavens could hear it. She deserved to be praised, as my praise needed to resonate in each direction of each layer.

It was I who needed to praise her. She was angelic to me. And she deserved her own wings. At least in my eyes, Lilith had become my angel.

It was unpleasant to see her being restrained while she was not enjoying herself. I wanted to be the one above her, but not like the way he did her. If it were me with her, she would feel nothing but pleasure under my restraints.

There was this emerging need to clear my mind. Even though I knew that what I had seen could not be unseen, I went to the burial of the seeds.

***

"Did you enjoy Watching?" Lilith's footsteps were quiet.

"Is she honestly asking me that rather irritating question? How in the Bliss do I not enjoy Watching her?"

Of course, I was keen on Watching her. But because of the way Adam treated her, I could have burnt this very Garden down. Then Hell would expand from the North to the East of Here.

"How do you mean by that precisely?"

"You are to Watch us from time to time. But did you enjoy it? Watching me when I was with him?" She started watering the soil in front of me. She was indeed washing down the burning rage inside of me.

"No, Lilith."

"No? As you haven't Watched us?"

"No, I'm not keen on Watching you being treated like that."

"And how do you suggest I should be treated, my Great Prince?"

"You should be treated the way you deserve to be treated, Lilith." I did not lie to her about it. That was precisely what I meant. It was important for her to hear it from me.

"You deserve to be praised as my angel. I should be the one treating you the way you deserve to be fucked. Senseless, that one kind of fuck."

"You seem to be troubled."

"Does this Lilith have any trouble with me being troubled?"

She chuckled. "I like how you say my name almost every time you speak. It makes me feel seen."

"Are you keen on being seen?"

"Yes, my Great Prince."

"Is that a 'yes', as you are keen on being seen while having sex?"

"By your eyes? Yes, absolutely. Those are eyes for details. That fire in your eyes is magnificent," she said while gazing straight into my eyes. "It's there when you arrive. When you leave, they return to look like the sky. I feel like I can almost see the vastness of Heaven in your blue."

"Azure. It's the colour of my eyes, as it is of the skies. There's a precious stone with a similar colour. Some call it azurite. Others call it the stone of heaven."

"As you are precious to me." She had a pair of beautiful green eyes. She might not realise that she was the one making the Bliss look greener than it had ever been. "Then what's my eye colour to be named?"

"Emerald. It's a precious stone as well. As you are precious to me."

Within her silence, I could almost hear her heart beating faster. The time and place were filled with adornment, as much as torment. "Lilith?"

"If I—um, if I don't understand something, may I ask you about it?"

"I'm not the All-Knowing. But I shall find the answer to your trouble." My mind was indeed troubled with my desire for her. I was somewhere else, only with her. That imaginary place could have been our own heaven.

"My Great Prince? Say something."

"Thank you for nurturing the seeds, Lilith."

She asked, while keeping her gaze locked into my eyes, "The seeds on the ground or the seeds inside of you?" Her gentle hand touched my chest. It was she who calmed my fire from burning out of rage.

She was so close to me. Her force gravitated me, pulling me further towards her. I was drawn only to have her as mine. Restraining myself from surrendering to her feet was no longer possible as I passed my point of no return.

Once again, she made it hard for me to keep my cock from hardening. This was how I knew that I should be flying away from her. "I should be returning to the North."

"Yes, you should. It's late already."

"Both, Lilith. Thank you for nurturing both of them."

She gave a curtsy as she replied, "I shall be here the next time my Great Prince arrive."

"*I can't wait to come here and see you again. You've become the only reason I come here from now on,*" I said in my mind, wishing that I could say that clearly to her.

6

A Place in Mind

Her approaching footsteps became familiar to me. Her scent flowing through the air raised the hair at the back of my head.

My body sensed her presence without even turning my face towards her. I let her come to me. I would always let her come into my realm.

"Will I grow wings like yours one day?"

"Lilith, I don't have the knowledge to answer that."

With an adorable smile on her face, she started to water the seeds. She made me less anxious when I came to the Bliss. Her gravity made me come here again, solely towards her.

I was much more excited to retrieve everything I knew and plant them. Secretly, I hoped that one day a Tree would grow out of the ground. When she reaped the Fruit, she would finally understand every unspoken storm inside of my mind.

She would comprehend every untold battle inside of my heart. The heart became the battlefield of restraining myself from desiring her. So far, I had been on the losing side. It would be a tale of her victory over me.

There were many tales I wanted to tell my Lilith. It might sound wicked to call her *my* Lilith, as if I had claimed her. It was more likely that she was the one who had claimed me entirely.

There was silence for a while now, as if she knew the perfect way to torture me. "Lilith, what did I tell you about hearing thoughts?"

"I was waiting for you to say my name again." She giggled, as if her silence was something amusing and not torturing me. My Lilith seemed clueless about what she had done to me and to my cock. "I like the way you say it. With intention, not simply because I was given that name."

"I'm not sure I follow."

"That's precisely it. You don't follow. You have this voice of a leader. At least it sounds like you're leading me."

Did I simply make assumptions about her wanting to lead in their relationship? Had I, the Accuser, gone blindly too far? She led me to the realisation that my assumptions of her were wrong.

"You have more wings than others. Is it because you fly higher than others, so you have twelve?"

"The given twelve were necessary for the Seventh Heaven. That's where I Reside." My Lilith noticed things that I did not. "I've never thought about them until you asked me. Well done, Lilith. That was a good way of thinking."

The way her face blushed affirmed that I was right about her deserving praises. It made me fond of her. "Do you enjoy flying?"

"It's necessary for us, Taskers. Indeed, flying is enjoyable. The lift feels like freeing me from restraints. I can see a broader view from above. Perspectives come to me through vastness."

"Is there any particular place that you enjoy visiting?"

"Yes, here." I waited for another response aside from her silence.

That thoughtful face while she kept herself silent. There were mad and conflicting feelings, but what could I say? Her brightness had already made me fond of her. I could not wait for her darkness to make me madly fond of her even more.

"Would you like to fly with me sometimes? Not too high nor too far."

Excitement now filled her eyes. "I don't mind going high and far. I'll close my eyes and feel the wind hitting my hands. Can I trust you to carry me flying?"

If only I could tell her how much I wanted to fly her away right at this very moment. Only the two of us. "Your trust in me is only for you to give. I shouldn't be the one demanding it."

"If you were to fly me anywhere, where would you take me?"

"I'd like you to see Salbatanu."

"Salbatanu? What is it?"

"It's one of the celestial bodies in a universe."

"I've never heard of it. What does it look like?"

"It looks similar to fire. Salbatanu has two moons."

"Can I see it if I close my eyes? Will you take my mind there?"

"Of course you can. And I shall—" My spoken words were incomplete. My mind completed them, "... *take you wherever my Lilith wants to go.*"

As she closed her eyes, I moved closer to her. My curiosity travelled towards the naked body in front of me while she was imagining my celestial body.

I let my exhalation touch the skin of her neck. Near her ear, I whispered, "It's as fiery as your curiosity. It fuels your desire to learn more. About new things you haven't heard of. About places you haven't been in."

"It must be a beautiful one. Who Commands it?"

"I do."

"Hmm... I could only imagine what it feels like to be under your command. When can I see it with my eyes open?"

"When Earth is in the right position, everyone can see it in the morning. Sometimes, you cannot see it." I paused while my fingers became so close to touching her face. "But you always know that it's there. Salbatanu, along with the other morning stars, is meant to watch over you. It might feel so close but somehow unreachable. An untouchable beauty."

"How unfortunate it is to desire the untouchable one."

Right before she fully opened her eyes, I stepped backward. It was my reality to swallow, as I desired this beautiful, untouchable being.

"You closed your eyes when you were with Adam. Have you finally enjoyed his lead?"

"No, I never have. I was somewhere else. At least in my mind, I was."

"Where did you go, Lilith?"

"Here, my Great Prince. I like being here. With you, time becomes favourable. But it never feels enough."

Hearing those words come out of her lips, I could not let out a single word. Both sides of my mind were conflicting. Everything laid in between them was epic chaos.

"Every time my mind goes here, the river flows in between my legs. Just as here and now, the river flows."

"*Was she saying what I thought she was saying? That she was thinking of me when she was with him? That she was willing to submit to me? That she would let me fuck her the way she deserved to be fucked? I thought she wanted to establish dominance and lead the way. Why would she want me to lead her?*"

"Where were you when I was with him earlier?"

"With you."

"I don't hear thoughts, either, my Angel," she said, breaking through the silence between us and finding her way into me. "Should I continue talking about where my mind went? And how did I see you there? What did you do to me in my mind?"

"If you want to tell me about it, I'd love to listen. But it's already late." What I had in mind was to find a way to overcome the obstacles. For us, I needed to solve this. "Is it all right if I come here earlier next time?"

"Please do. I'm looking forward to it," she said while giving a curtsy.

"Until next time, Lilith. I can't wait to see you again. I mean it."

My hand was almost touching her blushing face, but it did not. If only it did. And if it did, it would not only be her face. There would be an endless journey of exploring her entire body. Her river would continue to flow until this thirst was no longer in my throat.

7

To Let Her Fly Away

There was some excitement that I could not elaborate on, even to myself. Lilith somehow enchanted me in her unique way.

She had lived freely in my mind, my heart, and my soul. My Being would become her realm. I would build a home for her within my realm. The timeline within it would pause when she was home.

By the time I arrived, it seemed that the Bliss already had an argument. Adam pushed her away while she was on top of him. She obviously had been frustrated with him. Their argument built into a fight.

He did not understand how it was a privilege to be in his place. I would trade anything to replace him as her mate. I would give anything I could gather from the surface down to the depths of the earth, only to have a piece of my soul—her. That was how important Lilith had become to me.

My arms needed to wrap her warmly to cool her fire. I would fly, carrying her away. My wings were to fly us far and further away from here. I would carry her away from him. As much as I genuinely wanted to, I could not interfere. A Watcher needed to keep Watching.

She let out a piercing scream. Her bursting tears tore apart my heart. Then the unforeseeable happened. It was she who called out the Creator's name in desperation.

It felt like lightning struck my entire Being when I heard it. The storm inside of me burst out when she did what was forbidden. My knees dropped to the ground as my wings trembled. My body was shaken as some of my feathers fell off of me.

"Oh, my Lilith. My dearest Lilith, my love."

I should have carried her right away the moment I arrived. This could have been prevented from happening. It was my fault for not foreseeing it coming. With her frustration, I should have seen it much earlier.

It was my imaginary hope that she could change him. Whether he wanted to change for someone, it was his free will that chose the change. I had failed to foresee what was coming. In that way, I had failed her.

My Lilith grew wings by herself. One pair of black wings, as black as her hair. Probably they were the extensions of her hair. They were now expanded, ready to fly her. I wanted to touch hers. Even with her emerald eyes turned carnelian, I would.

This feeling was the heaviest I had ever felt in my chest. My heart was suddenly broken. My knees felt like they were melting into the Blissful soil. I had flown to the highest point of the Heavens, but my chest had never lacked air like this.

This Tasker immediately became unfit to fulfil any Duty. I did not have the heart to use my Sword to destroy the sinner. Because that sinner was *my* Lilith, who was now flying away with her new wings.

***

Three Angels were sent to pursue her, for she was to return to Adam. As much as I wanted to calm her down in my arms, I needed her to be all right. Maintaining my distance, I followed the Three. My own eyes needed to see that she was all right.

They found Lilith hovering over the Red Sea of Earth. Right away, I could tell that she enjoyed flying. Her wings looked strong enough to lift her. She no longer needed my wings to fly. She could rely on hers at all times from now on.

Tonight was my first time seeing her at night. Where the moonlight hit her hair, it reflected a blue radiance. How beautiful my Lilith had become!

The Three persuaded her, but it seemed that she had had enough of submitting to Adam. The four of them were having a heated argument.

Then Three calmed down, leaving her alone. On the path of their return, I intercepted the Angels. I needed to hear about the agreement they made earlier.

They said that she chose to not return to Adam. She had agreed that she would continue to fulfil the nature of her creation. She was to bring illness to newborns.

Was it a matter that the Most High had agreed upon? Why would the Creator create her for that purpose? The comprehension of it was beyond me.

Lilith must have wanted children for herself. The nurturing side of her took care of the seeds I had buried. That one I witnessed from being close to her.

In return for her departure, they agreed upon another one. The newborns who wore amulets with the symbol of the Heavenly Beings would be untouched.

Well, that was my Lilith. She was smart. With her words, she could talk her way through anything. No one taught her how to negotiate. How proud I was of her!

What I certainly did not understand was the reason these Three Angels left her. The Creator told them precisely to get her to return. Yet they made agreements with her.

These Taskers did the opposite of their Task. We should see what Judgement these Three would receive. It was me to Prosecute Them in the Heavenly Court.

Even after the Three left me, I stayed. Even from afar, I descried her anticipation of me. Both Lilith and I were hovering still. Our distance in the sky of the Earth was maintained.

My Sword had never been drawn towards her and never would be. She deserved my heart, not my Sword. She was a part of my soul. To show it to her, I placed my hand on the heart. Then I bowed, showing her that I would praise my Lilith in my own way.

My love for her became a feeling I would keep to myself from now on. In the silence of the dark night, my words of praise would fly towards her ears. Whether they would land on her ears or not, to me, did not matter.

She replied with a curtsy, which I adored every time she did it. She turned away, but at one point she looked back over her shoulder. She gave me one last smile. There, she flew away, leaving me behind.

"Fly, my love! Find the freedom that you deserve. I shall keep you in my mind and my heart. Your happiness will become mine as well once you have it. I shall deserve you once I become worthy of you," I said to her from far away. Even though I knew how nearly impossible it was for her to hear it, I did.

Once she was out of my sight, I returned to the North of the Third Heaven. To love someone sometimes required keeping a distance from her. To keep my Lilith safe from my Sword, from my Duty, and even from myself. I did not know what I would become.

My feelings for Lilith had become that much and that strong. Today had become my doomsday.

It was only the beginning of the hell inside of me. Nothing but relying on the memories of her. The image of her was to keep me warm from the inside.

My Being started to freeze on the outside. The layer of a shield started to build armour to protect her within me.

8

Motherless Seeds

Even after Lilith's departure, the seeds still needed to be watered regularly. No one told me to continue doing what she started, but I needed to.

To the Bliss, I came to nurture the Tree. To have my blissful memory of her alive. To let her grow within the Blissful Garden. It was simply for me to feel her presence.

As wicked as it might sound, I could almost sense her every time I came to the burial. Her scent must be rooted so deeply in this Bliss, not only in me. She kept me of sound mind.

Nothing had been buried here since the day she left. It was not because her departure was light, nor because I took her for granted.

It was I who never wanted to put away a single bit of her memory from my mind. It was for no one else other than me. No one could have the memories of her. That was how selfish I became about her.

On every flight, she stayed with me. She freely lived inside of me. She resided within the realm of reality within me. If my feelings for her needed to be buried, they would be planted so deep in the core of my Being. Everything about her would flourish from the inside out.

From the seeds beneath the ground, the Creator then grew trees for humankind. For them to eat and be left alone. There was Guidance to follow.

The Tree of Life grew in the centre of the Bliss. The One that came from my seeds grew near it. My seeds of thought contained everything I knew and felt about Lilith. Even though she was no longer in the Garden, this One must have remembered her care.

Other trees grew in a spiral. With the Trees in the middle as their Source of livelihood, Lilith's Tree provided my Knowledge. Each one of them that was connected had known her. They grew massively while adoring her greatness. They became fruitful while praising her.

They grew immensely remembering how One of their Sources had been nurtured by her. She had nurtured both what was in the ground and what was within me.

Humankind was forbidden to approach and eat from It. When the Creator told Adam the Boundaries, I felt like being understood. To me, it felt like my unheard state of mind was truly being heard. Probably, my troubled mind was so obvious for everyone to Watch.

The Serpent broke the silence, "We have another humankind created. Have you heard about it?"

"So I've heard. An Ishshah, is it?"

"Yes, his Ishshah."

"Is it true that she was created from his side?"

"She was, indeed. Probably because the man prefers an obedient companion, not like the last one who left. This one is more—" The Serpent stopped Himself immediately. It must be the moment when my eyes started to flame.

For a while, the both of us kept ourselves in silence. "So, have you seen Lilith since she left? I knew you two were close."

"And then do what, Serpent? What I was created for? To her?" It was forbidden for anyone to pronounce the Creator's name. And yet Lilith had done it. "What are you suggesting I should do precisely?"

"Hey... hey... There's no need to be mad, Samael. I get it; you love her. You're troubled about it. Understood. Your eyes start to look like Hell when you're mad."

Closing my eyes, I sighed. There would be no more tears to shed. Neither the soil nor any being in the

Bliss deserved more knowledge about her. "From Hell's fire, the Most High Created me."

"So you *do* love Lilith, don't you? I'm sorry for your situation."

"Huh, you, Serpent, are feeling sorry? That's something new."

"You know, his Ishshah keeps watching you fly back and forth. Well, you can't blame her. Everyone has been introduced to both of them. Everyone except you."

"How am I supposed to introduce myself? 'Greetings, Ishshah! I'm the Leading Angel of Death.' She would have an unnecessary mare of being created and being dead on the same day."

"Better be hideous than have her dead with curiosity haunting everyone. What is it with females being curious and suspicious?" Serpent might think that humour solved everything.

Indeed, Lilith's curious face haunted me. "Are you not female, Serpent? You certainly have a great sense of curiosity, especially about things that don't concern you."

"We certainly *are* concerned if another woman of Adam is curious about you. Is it the way you look? Or is it the way you speak that leads women to you?"

"Well, you may tell her either of my names if she asks." There was no word being let out while I kept watering the Tree and caring for it.

The Serpent eventually brought me back from silence. "What? You're here, but your Wicked mind might be planning something somewhere."

"Question her about what she's up to."

With furrowed eyebrows, the Serpent asked, "About what she'll be doing for the day?"

"No. Question her to the point where she questions herself."

"And if she's planted into desiring you?"

"Let her desire me." Having me in her mind each time Adam fucked her should be her path. That way, her desperation would torture her. "Through her desire, I shall bring hell to her." To the North of Here, I returned.

Each time, the seeds of Lilith inside of me became hurtfully drier without her watering them. This Garden seemed to be less green in my eyes without her emeralds. Even with more trees being grown, Bliss was lacking her nurture.

It became less favourable without the sound of her giggles. Nothing in Here was radiant without her blushing face. The memories of her were for my reminiscence.

The feelings I had for her were mine alone. Not to be shared for others to know. She could rip the heart out of my chest if she wanted to. Mine was to be hers already.

They called me Wicked for letting a malicious sinner claim me. For others, she might be malicious. It was only I who knew that she was indeed the guardian angel of my broken heart.

9

The Forbidden One

Indeed, the Tree grew out of the soil from Knowing how to separate the good from the evil. It did not matter to me how they named it.

Everyone was aware of me returning to Lilith's Tree more frequently than I should in between my Duties. Even if it was only for a glance at her memory, I would make time for her. Tales were being told to the Tree as if I were speaking to Lilith in person.

No one else should touch my only remembrance of Lilith. She was untouchable to me, but her touch imprinted a silhouette on me. The essence of my Being was branded as hers from now on. I belonged to her.

How much I missed my Lilith was only for me to feel. The centre of the Blissful Garden was the evidence of my grief over her departure. They had been avoiding looking me in the eye.

"Has Adam ever *missed Lilith as much as I do? Does he even care about her? Or does he become too busy with his Ishshah?"*

There was an urge to know whether she even mattered to him. When hovering over Bliss, I saw him wandering around alone.

"Wait, where is his Ishshah? I did not see her with him today."

Then I remembered that bloody Serpent. Immediately, I became anxious about his Ishshah being near the Tree. *"That's Lilith's Tree! No one should get near it!"*

There, I found her; I saw her from above. In front of Ishshah, I hard-landed. The soil was ripped open where my feet touched down. And here she was, with none other than the Serpent.

"You aren't supposed to be near this Tree!"

She was shaking in fear when my fiery eyes were locked into hers. With a trembling voice, she said, "Please forgive me, my Great Prince."

"Don't you dare come near here again! This Tree is not for you!"

She slowed down her pace while walking away from me. Her feet stopped for a moment. Over her shoulder, his Ishshah looked back at me.

There was a similar conflicting expression on her face to Lilith's. The similar naïveté showed in their faces. She might know that the Knowledge was good. What she did not realise was that the Knowledge of good and evil came with consequences.

***

Unbeknownst to me, she hid one of the Fruit from the Tree. Her doing slipped from my disturbed attention. They lost it once they knew it. As they were being stripped down to their naked truth.

When the Creator walked on the Blissful soil, Adam and his Ishshah hid. After the two humankinds came out of their veil, there was shame I could sense in them. Serpent and I kept Watching until we were Summoned by the Most High.

"That Fruit is not for you! None of you deserve to have it! Now, which one of these sinners should I punish first?"

Naïveté no longer lived within his Ishshah. That smitten look of hers was no longer there. It was fear that filled her eyes now. They were glazed with tears. She should be fearful. Being awakened into such awareness without being prepared would be terrifying.

Her husband only had the spare of what she had. She ate it first, then served it to him. Hers was the first bite. Now she had a taste of my realm. She was welcomed into my hell.

Neither I nor she spelt out any word about it. Both of us understood the unspoken thoughts. The Tree was grown from my seeds. They came from my mind and heart. Every Knowledge she gained from the first bite was authentic to me.

Guidance was given to him. He then relayed it to her. There was the void in the way he spoke that caused her to lack understanding.

The comprehension in her mind was the one that the Serpent tested. She was questioned to the point where she questioned herself.

It was he who was left behind by Lilith, just as I was. There were sorrows within us. We mourned for her departure in different ways. They created the void within us, waiting to be filled again.

Since he had his Ishshah, he might have someone new to fill his void. His free will had made Adam listen to her words. Regardless of what he was told, it led him to disregard the Guidance.

His integrity was what the Most High tested. Without being Watched, he did not keep listening to the Divine Guidance. Adam blamed his Ishshah afterwards.

She accused the Serpent of leading her astray. Her mind was only being tested. No one should have questioned oneself. She decided to place herself in hesitation.

Serpent had followed my venomous words. The cursed one had only been an extension of me. The Adversary was only a Tasker of the Most High to test humankind's mind.

This Angel of Death fulfilled the Task to bring the end to their lives in the Bliss. Adam and his Ishshah were to be reborn outside of the Garden.

It was I, the Most High's Venom, who was blamed for planting the seeds in the first place. After they ate from the Tree, I was banished from the place where I buried my burdens.

A Tetramorph was given a Fiery Sword. East was where the Cherubim stood to keep everyone from nearing the Tree. From side to side, the wheels kept spinning. On those wheels, the Tasker moved to Guard.

10

Telaesthesia

Now I was pushed away from coming to the place that reminded me of Lilith. Here it was, my fall. Falling for Lilith in a realm of grief.

Banishing me was probably better than Watching me mourn for much longer. That never meant for me to retire from any Duties. It meant new paths were opened in front of me. To wander different paths.

From the Heavens, my realm was to expand beyond. This time, towards the earth, I descended. The void within would be a companion for me.

His Ishshah was now given the name Eve. He gave it to her as he took her under his responsibility. As was I, the man and his wife, Eve, were cast out of the Bliss.

From their lives in the Bliss, I granted them their passings to live their lives on earth. Those were grants from the Most High because hell would have bound them for endless time.

From the time of origin to a place where time spun differently. From a Blissful Garden, to a much smaller celestial body that took only a moment to cycle completely.

They were now only to catch up with the alignment of everything on earth. Let them race against the spin of time in Heaven to regain their places in It.

They had gained Knowledge and earned their curses at the same time. They now understood how much such Knowledge would cost. The challenges that came with it became part of their lives. Outside of the Bliss, they were to work and reproduce.

If he thought living in the Blissful Garden was hard for arguing with Lilith, he was now enlightened about how much power he always possessed.
He took her for granted. Over what? Power? He already was empowered without seeking it outside of himself.

With his strength, he was now to work harder on the land. It was harder on the earth than in the Bliss. She was to give him a purpose in his lifetime. She was to lean against him to make his stance stronger.

She now knew how to remind him of his strength. The knowledge was now within her to challenge him to be a better humankind.

He was now enlightened about how hard it was for me to fulfil my Duties. He started to speak out fewer words. His war was now within.

From the Fruit, he now understood how precious Lilith had been to me. He understood how much of a loss I had. His grief was nothing compared to mine.

***

Her womb was still empty. There, I saw his wife had not borne any child yet.

"Why is she alone outside of the house? This late at night? Has he been bored with her? Or has he become tired after working on the land? Hasn't he touched his wife yet today?"

"Have you yet felt helpless being cast out?" My arrival startled her. There was a sense of remorse in her eyes.

"I beg your forgiveness, Great Prince of the Heavens. I—I didn't know the Tree was about you and Lilith."

The rage towards Eve was rushing through my body. "Don't you dare speak her name with your sinful mouth! You deserve nothing from the Tree!"

In tears, she said, "I didn't mean to... I didn't know about such matters. The first time I took the Fruit, I was—"

"You surely know what I was Tasked for."

"Yes, I do, Angel of Death. You punish sinners."

"And you must know which sinner I'm going after today."

Eve nodded in tears, saying, "I do. I truly am sorry for your loss."

My hand instantly held Eve by her neck, pushing her to the tree behind her. "No, not losing her. I simply haven't found her again. You know nothing about her."

"My husband wronged her. He has never been punished for it. I'll take the blame." She was compromised. She stood in between the will to take the blame and her desire for me.

"How petty the man's wife is! Now take off all your clothes." As soon as she was naked, I started kissing her roughly. Sucking all of the air from her mouth, I suffocated her to the point where she was nearly fainting. This was not her time yet; I broke the kiss knowing that.

"Oh, I can taste your desire for death. Not your time yet, woman. My time to fuck you in hatred!" One hand covered her mouth. The other one on her breast.

"Aren't you foolish enough to take the blame for him?"

"I'm foolish, my Great Prince."

Slapping her face, I then sucked her breasts roughly. "Should I continue punishing you?"

Her mouth was free from my hand. "Yes."

"Yes, what, Eve?"

"Yes, please. Let me redeem your sorrow. Forgive me for what I've sinned against you and her. This fool needs to be punished."

Pulling her from the tree, I then laid her on the ground. With her legs being spread open, her wet cunt was exposed.

"Your cunt obviously wants this punishment." All the hair on her body rose at my touch. "Tell me, are you taking the blame truly for his sake... or for your own desire for me?"

"Never have I ever not desired you. Even when I was with him, it's always been you." Those words of hers were truthful; I believed them.

"There's only fury. I shan't be gentle with you." Ramming my cock into her, I did not even bother stretching her for the thickness of mine. "Don't even think about making a sound. I shan't give you any pleasure! All I can give you is pain. *My pain.*"

"Then let me feel how painful it is for you, my Angel. Please, I wanted to."

While hatefucking her cunt, I kept holding her by the neck. She was surrendering to her desire. But here, I saw Eve's face fading away.

All I saw now was Lilith hovering over the Red Sea of the earth, looking at me. She looked so beautiful, with her wings matching her hair colour. She became so powerful, lifting herself up to fly on her own. She did not need my wings to carry her, but still, she had power over my thoughts.

I did not care if her eyes looked like the carnelian stone now. It was never about the colour. It was the way they looked straight at me. Her gaze; I knew she was there. On the inside, she was still my Lilith.

Her grace deserved my bow. The bliss within her I adored. There I hovered, watching her leave. There I stayed, wishing that there would be a turnaround to our tale. There, within my strength, I accepted defeat.

And here I came inside of Eve, filling her cunt with every drop of fury that I had for her. Returning to the here and now was not pleasant. But the reality in the here and now was necessary.

Eve held my face. She wiped away my tears, which I did not realise were running down. "You saw her, didn't you? In your mind, she was here with you."

For a moment, I vividly saw Lilith as though she was right in front of me. There was nothing that needed to be said to Eve. Here I was, being spent on top of Eve, mourning for Lilith. Here I grieved on top of Adam's new wife.

"The pain you caused me is paid. You're with my child now. His name will be Cain. He will carry my anger, my darkness, and my Light at the same time. You'll be able to tell which son is mine and which one is from Adam. The daughter from Adam will choose him."

There, I left her with my seed to grow. It was time for me to go to the north of the earth for seclusion. Maybe it was good to be alone for a while.

I felt lost after losing Lilith. And from losing the way to my memories of her, my navigation was failing.

I did not know which direction to fly in. Here I was, lost in the memory of her.

To the hell inside of me, I spiral dove. To the hell of longing, I buried myself.

11

A Tale of Her

The Time of Copper

Not a single day nor night had passed without Lilith in my mind. Although my mind was still aligned with the time of origin, the cycle of time on earth had surpassed the counting.

To me, it felt like I had spent my time in seclusion for only a few days. Their movements on earth had spanned several thousand years. Only the Most High knew precisely how long it had been in which realm.

Thinking and questioning in my alone time, my mind could not stop wondering. What would the earth look like at the present time? Did they sustain the cycle of time on the planet?

Had they become the kindest humankind? Or were they in a balance between good and evil? About what the earth had become with my offspring, Cain, that was a concern I needed to let go of.

Thoughts flew around in my mind about the best way to get to Lilith without harming her. The thought of even risking it was the worst of them all. My judgement knew the boundary of what to risk and what not to risk. Not even in a slight possibility would I risk her.

I did not even know where to look or whether she still wanted me around her. Even if I found her, what would I say to her? During my seclusion, there were barely any beings I had spoken to. Not many words in my thoughts made their way through at the speed of sound through my mouth.

The Red Sea was the first region I went to. It was where I saw her the last time. From there, I hovered over regions that already had growing inhabitations.

My Sword was now hidden in a place that humankind could not find. I did not think they knew how to make one yet. Or if they would be able to make one ever in their lifetime.

My alone time had taught me how to conceal my wings under my skin. That one I had never known since the beginning of my existence. It might have been unnecessary or irrelevant before. Now it was.

At least one matter was convenient. Other matters still needed to be figured out. What would I even wear to conceal myself and not to terrify them?

When they were asleep, I landed in a quiet part of their housing area. Here I was, stealing clothes from the back of their house. Could anyone ever imagine how much pride I needed to swallow for this hideous mischief?

***

One morning, I walked around their city to learn about their way of life. They were sort of clothed in a similar way. There had not been much colour so far.

"Do I have to learn how to make pottery the way they do, though?" They lived by making crafts and trading the works of their hands. I needed to know what they had learnt to this day.

"Do you know how to make this?" I asked a merchant, who seemed all right. By 'all right', it meant not wicked when compared to the others.

"No, I don't. But I can ask my supplier if you need a job."

That was hilarious of him. *"Why would I need a job? Do I look like I need a job?"* The idea of concealing myself among them seemed to make sense. "Please, if you don't mind."

"Why do you want to make this kind of pottery? We're moving on to the new metal now, you know, copper. If you want to feed yourself longer, you better learn about the new one, brother."

"I shall take any available job around here."

"All right, if you say so. You can come back tomorrow."

"I appreciate your help."

"You know, you talk politely. Maybe you can be one of the thinkers there, where the rich live. But what would I know? Better to be fed than die smart."

"That's actually very smart of you."

This merchant tried to read me. "Got any food for the day, young man?"

I shook my head at him. "No, I haven't."

"You can help me bring these to the market. You push the cart while I sell the goods. Pushing and talking need two men. I'll give you some of my lunch. How about that?"

"Yes, I'll gladly help. You can call me Samael."

"If any of you want to buy anything, from the new ones to the antiques, you better look for Maamoun right here!" He shouted to me and the people around us. He was to tell everyone about himself and the merchandise he was selling.

Here I had my first job, for food. It was nothing more than pushing and lifting goods. He sold not only pottery but also clothing.

Maamoun talked a lot, especially to people who showed their interest. It was not only I who had the skills to talk things through. Gladly, I met another one today.

It was fascinating how other sellers in the market did not see him as a competitor. He seemed to have a way to find things they wanted to sell, and then he supplied those to them.

With me moving his cart, his attention moved to selling and bargaining. Until around noon, I followed him. He was about to have his lunch when he asked me to sit with him. The merchant kept his promise to share some of his food with me.

"How could you carry all these big things as if they weighed nothing?"

"I've been carrying heavy things for a long time," I said, avoiding locking my eyes on his. Indeed, there were heavy feelings I had been carrying in my chest. None of this merchandise weighed that much compared to what was inside of me.

"You know, with that much strength, you might get a job in sports. At the fair. You never go there?"

"No, I have not."

"People put their money on one of the champions. It makes good money for merchants like me. I sell food and drink while they watch. And the women, brother, they like those sportsmen. Well, except my money goes to my wife, so I can't afford those needy women. Have you got yourself a woman?"

"Not lately. I had one before. But I watched as she was pushed away." Indeed, I felt suffocated once more. I had not talked openly about Lilith to any being.

"Don't get alone for too long! Otherwise, Lilitu will catch you at night."

"Who is Lilitu?"

"Have you been living in the cave? Lilitu... Lilu... Lilin... You never heard of that evil night creature before?"

"No, I haven't talked to anyone for quite some time. And I was banished from the place I used to belong. There haven't been many to have any conversation with. You're actually the first one I've talked to in a while."

"I knew it! You weren't from here. And probably I'm right, too, about you living in a cave without sun. You have this fair, glowing skin. Also, no one around here has eyes like yours."

"Some of them call me the Wicked One. That's all right. Mostly I feel like living in the between."

"Thank goodness you're not as wicked as Lilitu. Ooo, brother... Be careful with that creature! She comes at night with her red eyes and long black hair. She feasts on the lust of lonely men. They thought they were sleeping with one beautiful woman with pale skin in their bed. They were actually having sex with Lilitu under her black, scary wings."

I, in an instance, welcomed the butterflies swarming in my stomach. It was as if they were eating me alive from the inside. The black hole inside of me would suck up everything that was left of me. Was it *my* Lilith that he was talking about? Was she now some sort of mythical being in their folktale?

Maamoun continued, "She strapped their hands to their beds. Giving collars and leashes around their necks, ooo... they were ridden as her camels. She fucked them until they had nothing left in their sacs. Or until they were dead from being used. That's how Lilitu got pregnant with those half-breed demonic children."

"Has she ever come to you at night, Maamoun?"

"Oh, no, no, no... I keep my wife close at night. I'm not planning on having baby demons. Having two human children is trouble enough for my wife. Come on, brother. Let's continue to get more money from the rich. And let's not give you any more Lilitu mares!"

For the rest of the day, I continued helping him. To sell from house to house, mostly in the bigger housing area. Then we walked to his house at nearly sunset.

He knocked on the door. Until it was opened, he waited outside. His wife, Anat, embraced him first. The children greeted him with smiles and laughter. I, too, wanted a home and to have children with Lilith. Someone who embraced me once I got home from Duty.

As I left his house, he ran towards me. "As you can see, I didn't get many sales from the rich today. This might be enough for you tonight."

"I appreciate the food you offered. You're a kind man. I was supposed to help you in exchange for my lunch. This one in your hand is your family's supper."

He nodded at me, tapping my shoulder. "I'll see you tomorrow, Samael."

I excused myself from him. The truth was, I could not show too much excitement about Lilith. As I left the housing area, I looked around before pulling my shirt off.

Hovering around, I looked for alone men. To follow them with their mischiefs. To fly around all night without knowing where to look.

It was my first night of Watching over Dimashq. After wandering an entire night, I still had not found her anywhere.

At nearly dawn, I landed near the fresh water. Not to wash myself, but simply to keep a cool head. A sound mind needed to stay inside my head.
"How was I supposed to find Lilith without any further leads?"

12

Rebirth of the Pieces

Every day around sunrise, I went to Maamoun's house to help him sell his merchandise. When he made good sales, he gave me lunch and supper for the day.

Through the food he shared, I understood why Maamoun kept his wife close to him at night. Anat's cooking filled his belly and his heart to the fullest, making him crave nothing else.

It was a lot more helpful for me than for him to sell the merchandise. From walking around Dimashq with him, I learnt about different regions. With that, I could narrow down the course of my night Watch.

Maamoun's acquaintances gave me another job. In metalwork, the men at the smithy were different. They were welcoming. By their appearances, they did not seem like they did.

Having conversations with the men after work gave me another advantage. My night Watch could be focused even further. Only some of the blacksmiths originated here.

Here, for them, copper was still considered a newly found metal. It enticed them to come. To learn. We discussed many things, including how to properly smelt and forge the metals.

Small pieces after small pieces of knowledge I gave them. Clues. Ideas. Well, I could not give them all the knowledge for their heads to explode, could I?

My Knowledge was about the nature of metal. There was much more for them to learn. But their knowledge came from their lifetime in a different cycle than mine. The smithy then became the melting bowl where we explored the potentials of each metal.

We kept trying to craft them with other elements or in different ways. Some became more durable. Some made them more functional. They worked with copper differently than how I would craft them.

They made things that could simplify their lives. Some of them succeeded; some of them made the waste pile higher. Reforging the scraps made my time on earth more pleasant. The owner saw them as waste to be rid of; he did not mind my longer time at night.

The appearance of them was different from what they used for practicality. What I saw during the day, or how I remembered Lilith that day, helped me shape them. Those scraps were then reborn into something new, instead of dying as waste.

Since they were not necessities for me, I gave them to Maamoun. He perceived my gifts as one of a kind. After meeting many of the rich, he understood their thoughts. He showed them to the riches the following day.

Indeed, those people saw my pieces of creation as unique. Some of them were to decorate the rich women's hair. The bigger ones were for their houses. Although I was not sure if the look of those reborns would please the taste of the rich, I kept making them.

Maamoun made more money for his family. To have meals for the next few days, even a week after. He was always a good man, Maamoun, a family man.

He showed me how to be considerate. The blacksmith was only to amuse himself with minerals in the treasure pile. The perspectives of the smithy's owner, Maamoun, and the wealthy differed.

Once Maamoun's son was old enough, my task with his merchandise was no longer needed. From those years of following him around, I had learnt to not only talk to different kinds of people but also to read them. Each humankind he met was different, so the way he negotiated differed accordingly.

The smithy was where I spent most of my daylight now. Having supper at Maamoun's house became a routine for me after work.

He told plenty of stories about where he and his son went. They gave me more clues to search for Lilith. After the night Watch, restlessness became my routine before starting the following day.

13

A House of Abundance

It had been quite a long time of me searching for Lilith. Everything around me had changed, but my love for Lilith had not. Maamoun's love for Anat had never changed. Even as they got older, theirs seemed to grow stronger.

There was a dark time for everyone's health in the region, especially the elders. My Sword was out tonight to show its Light. Without being invited this time, I entered Maamoun's house quietly. To relieve them of their suffering and sickness.

He woke up when the door was creaking. "Ah, it's my old friend." Since both of them got worse, they stayed in bed mostly. With her sleeping in his arms, his cough easily woke her up.

"Oh, Samael, have you eaten supper yet?" That was pretty much typical of Anat each time I came to their house. Her face was filled with concerns. She genuinely cared about everyone's wellbeing. She included me in her league of concerns.

"You've blessed me with your cooking more than I ever deserved." Her calm smile replied to me this time.

"I guess I was right since the first day we met. You weren't from here. Look at our grey hair and wrinkles. You haven't got any older, not even for a day. May I see your Sword, Brother?"

His words startled me. But, Wickedly, I was aware that he had known about me all this time. Still, he treated me like no other than a part of his family.

"My old friend, I've known you for a long time. I can tell when you're upset. Those eyes change colour. No worries. I don't always tell Anat everything. We, as men, tend to keep things to ourselves." His hand pointed at the chair for me to sit down.

On my left palm was the hilt of my Sword. Its tip rested on my right hand. Then I turned it over to show them the other side of the Light. There was always the other side of the light. Not everyone understood how blinding the light could be. Not every being would recognise the shadow.

The Lightbringer was to bring them the Light so shadow could appear on the other side. Enlightenment had always come with something more. The lightworkers were to embrace the shadow work.

"They haven't got anyone to make something like this one yet."

"None of you will be able to make one like this." Every word I was about to say became harder to let out. I had known them for a long time.

"Our children live with their own families now. Don't you worry about them! You can stay here and make it your home. I leave you with the house filled with the love she gave me," said Maamoun.

"We still have some food and seasonings for you to eat tomorrow. You know where I put all the cookware." She smiled and continued, "Don't forget to clean. Put them in their place when you're done. I trust you with my kitchen, Samael."

Anat was very particular about her kitchen and her way of cooking. All I could do was nod to her demand.

"But remember not to be alone in the house for too long. Otherwise—"

"Otherwise, Lilith would come. I know, Maamoun. I know Lilith will come," I said. My Sword was held straight, as if it were the only thing that I could hold onto from crumbling apart.

He smiled warmly at me. "So it was her all along that you've been searching for. Lilitu, I mean Lilith."

"I can't be close to her without hurting her with this Sword. And I believe she wants to have a family of her own. She's quite nurturing, actually. But yes, she's a free spirit. Well, a bit stubborn sometimes. She has emerald eyes, as green as your garden, Anat. She easily gets amazed and curious about everything she sees." Deep inhalation was to compose myself.

"You were right, Maamoun. I was living in caves, forests, hills, and even tundra in the north. Not much of the sun at some point in time. Especially in the far north. Since Lilith left, I was at a loss for where to go and what to do. For a long time, I had never told anyone about her. Only the first day we met, and now, tonight, at the end of your time."

Maamoun's eyes were filled with sympathy. "Then I'm guilty of talking badly about the woman you love. On the day we met, I didn't know. And for not helping you enough to search for her."

Anat followed, "And I'm guilty of planting envy inside of you. I let you watch our love in this house every day for so long."

"I genuinely apologise that it has to end like this. And that it has to be me."

"Amongst all these things we've been through together, Samael, I'm glad that it's you. I believe Anat thinks the same way as I do."

Anat nodded with the warmest smile she had ever given to me. Before their eyes, I took my shirt off.

Now they could see my wings. I kissed Maamoun goodbye on his forehead. "Farewell, my old friend."

"Thank you for taking care of me all this time, my love." He kissed Anat and finally held her tighter in his arms.

Maamoun and Anat were buried side by side before dawn came. After their passing, I went to the market to buy flowers and planted them near their grave. I sent messages to their children about the place so they could visit their parents' graves.

***

As I continued living in Maamoun's house, I kept Anat's garden flourishing. It was not big, but the food plants and herbs were enough to feed me.

Then I understood why she was particular about her cooking. It was not about her duty as a wife. It was about her devoting herself to the one she loved. It was about nurturing their family with him.

Surprisingly, it was quite soothing for me to be in the kitchen. Sometimes, I made some more food for new apprentices in the smithy. They did not earn much at the beginning of their work. It was for me to remember Maamoun sharing his lunch on the first day we met.

There was some sort of routine for me here. In the morning, I worked on the soil and cooked for breakfast and lunch. Then I worked as a blacksmith during the day until around sunset. From night until dawn, I kept searching for Lilith.

Keeping the same things was to keep a sound mind inside of my head. But the longer I lived here, the more I remembered Anat's love for Maamoun. Envy had been filling the air inside of this house. It suffocated me. The longer I inhaled it, the more I was longing for my Lilith.

After decades of working as a blacksmith, they might start to become suspicious. Some of them might be curious about how my look was the same as always. It was time for a farewell. I told them that I needed to learn something from the people in the northwest of Dimashq.

To Haemus right after. To the regions where they have copper mines. Rudna Glava at first, and then Aibunar. There must be more people to ask about the earth. There were more regions to wander in searching for my Lilith.

14

The Hermit in the Mountain

From Dimashq, I moved to Rudna Glava for some adjustments. Although they were not as big as in Aibunar, the wombs of copper here were quite big.

Decades of working as a blacksmith taught me to transform raw metal into something useful. It was similar to nurturing younglings into adulthood. Mining was a different kind of work. It was identical to birthing the unborn and nurturing them to become younglings.

The way we worked here was darker and colder inside of the wombs. But once those copper ores were born, we worked with a raging fire to give the newborns their lives.

Even after countless times of night Watching, it still took me quite some time to adjust my eyes to the darkness of the wombs here. Miners spent a long time working in the womb. Some of us could easily become lost in the mind-blowing tunnels.

Unfortunately, some of them did not make it out of the womb for their rebirth. Some miners got stuck in the darkness, just as we were at this very moment.

Gundahar had become anxious about the fire. It was dimming, nearly out. Now might be a good time for us to start talking about something else. A conversation was necessary to calm him down. Besides, there was not much to do for the three of us trapped here.

He kept his distance very well. All of us knew he was not originally from Rudna Glava. "Well, we don't have much to do here. As you know, Gundahar, neither am I from here."

"From the northwest of here. I came alone, like a fool. But I know that I can work in the mines." He tried to keep the fire alive so we could see in the dark.

"You couldn't be coming here alone by yourself. That far this young?"

Gundahar hesitantly answered, "A fresh beginning. I was barely fourteen when my parents died. Every part of that city reminded me of them. I couldn't believe that it's been more than two years since they passed away. Not much to do at the place where I came from. I worked in the smithy, but I couldn't keep a sound mind."

"Well, you can talk to me and Samael. You see, there's probably not much of a chance to see the morning light."

"I'm not good at talking. And talking to a woman is worse for me. Immediately, my hands became shaky. My voice disappeared. And I don't have Samael's look, so women don't usually come to me."

"It didn't matter if they came to me. There are nice women here who look good as well. But they aren't who I need."

"And whom do you need precisely, Samael? Never saw you with any woman ever since I knew you." Obviously, curiosity had already filled Goran's face. "Have you *ever* been with any woman before?"

"I have, indeed, Goran. She was pushed to leave a long time ago."

"So you *do* know how to bed a woman."

"Not with her, but with a woman after she left. It came out of fury after being left behind. Never been with anyone since then. What I see in those women is disappointment."

Goran frowned, asking, "Disappointment, you said?"

"Not because I see them less than me, but because I know that they aren't... *her*. You know what I mean."

"What a lonely life this Samael has. You have my sympathy for that. But have you ever given yourself a release? You know, in your alone time?"

"Ugh, I wanted to sometimes. I tried several times, but it didn't sit right for me. I need to see her and hear her voice. Her touch, I've missed. Even when I was with the other woman after her, all I saw was *her* in my mind."

Gundahar curiously asked, "Like what? As if the one you were with disappeared just like that?"

"Sort of like that. There was some sort of greying cloud covering that woman. It felt to me like my mind was silhouetted somewhere else. I was with the one I love, but my body was grounded to the woman under me. She felt it somehow."

"How?" Their responses were in unison.

"She asked me if I was seeing *her* in my mind. I didn't say anything, of course. It wasn't right to be with the woman from the start."

"What do you mean it wasn't right? I thought it was good you tried to find someone else."

"There was this place where we used to meet. After she was pushed away, it became my solace. A sanctuary to relive my memories with her. And the other woman, well, let's say, trespassed there. Then I was also banished from that place."

"Ah, I see. That's where the anger came from."

"What can I say, Goran?" I shrugged before continuing, "So I burn my emotions near the fire. So far, it works for me."

Gundahar was getting more anxious about the fire. He might think it was the only source we had while trapped here. "Ah, there will be no light from now on. How can we find our way without seeing anything?" He sighed, not knowing if we could free ourselves.

"You're a good man, Gundahar. I see you working hard. Keeping yourself moving on even with your struggles."

"Well, it won't matter that much anymore. Goran here might be enjoying himself as a mountain man."

"All that I had no longer means anything now. Such loyalty to one smithy owner for years, who might not realise where I am. Or if I'm trapped with you two in this darkness. Not that I'm not glad to have you with me here," said Goran regretfully.

"Not many men are loyal these days, you see. And it's a privilege to meet a loyal one like you."

As I opened my eyes, they were startled. They moved backwards, a few steps away from me. Now they could see the flaming fire. They should be scared of me already. I took off my shirt to give them the brighter light that we needed.

With a stutter, Gundahar asked, "Samael, how is your skin glowing like the stars in the sky? And your eyes... What are you?"

"I'm the same Samael you knew early this morning. And I don't blame you for being terrified. You should be more terrified of not getting out of here. Let's find our way, shall we?"

"Wherever you go, I will follow you. I'll do whatever you need me to do. You have my words."

"I've never asked for anything in return from this mountain man. Why don't we move those rocks over there? And Gundahar, see if we have any airflow to breathe." I saw them nodding as we kept trying to free ourselves from here. Since the fire now came from me, we would not have more air to waste. It was for us to breathe longer, not for the torch.

Right before dawn, we made it out of the mine. The three of us were able to find the way out through the other side of it. We took our time to breathe the fresh air. From the dew on the leaves, we found something to drink. It was refreshing for the three of us. Not much, but it was enough.

"Samael, if I may, what are you?"

"Different people from different places call me by different names." Gundahar might not get the answer he sought. "What they say isn't something important for me. You two don't have to worry about me."

"And why are you here?"

"Mostly punishing sinners and destroying them. Also giving death for humankind to pass." They looked at each other in confusion. "I know that this isn't the time for both of you yet."

"But all these times, you've been looking after us. You've been helping us, not only in mining but also outside of work."

"I couldn't help myself with you younglings. Sometimes you're foolhardy. Also stubborn enough when it comes to work. I know that some of the miners here are good men. The rascal ones tickle my nerve sometimes."

Gundahar placed a hand on his heart. "I'll do my best to be a good person. The better one, I hope. Uh, I wonder how old you are exactly." His words were amusing to me.

"Ancient, youngling, since the time of origin. You have a life ahead of you. I don't think you should live by the mourning of your parents."

"I should be telling the myth of you, the one who Guards miners in the dark. Though we need to be careful of your words, you somehow know how to make someone talk. You know I don't talk," Gundahar admitted.

"Since I knew you, almost everything you said made sense. Sometimes, you're scary, telling how wrong we are. Sort of in a Wicked way."

"They call me Wicked, actually. But I simply show the reflections of yourselves."

Gundahar chuckled, which he did not regularly do. "Precisely scary that way."

They needed to know that they were not in trouble because of their knowledge of my existence. I was walking away from them when Goran chased me. He stopped me before I took off.

"I've said farewell to Gundahar. As I said earlier, I will follow you." He looked at me straight in the eyes. "I meant those words."

"I hope you don't mind flying." And this was the first time I had ever carried anyone flying with me. Goran and I headed to Aibunar, a bigger copper mine than here.

15

Unsettled Mind

Goran had lived in Aibunar prior to his time with me. He worked for one smithy owner for almost his entire teenage years and into adulthood. That was his time before moving to Rudna Glava.

He said that he would follow me this time. Sometimes, I felt like I was the one following him to learn. His knowledge of Aibunar led me to my first claim of ownership. Not only a smithy but an entire system of metalwork, from start to finish. By living long enough among humankind, there were enough belongings for me to afford it.

Claiming ownership was something new to me. Beside the house that Maamoun left me with, I knew nothing about owning something. I understood about metalworks, but I had never learnt about trading them. Maamoun had shown me how he sold merchandise. However, he did not sell the amount of crafts that Goran and I made here.

Goran told me that I had his loyalty, but I did not even understand what that meant. To have someone's loyalty was rather surprising, even to me. It was not as if I were enslaving him as my belonging. It was not like Lilith had claimed me, either.

His loyalty was more like respecting me enough to not lie to me or say something untrue behind my back. He was also forward enough to tell me if I did something that was not right. Sometimes his loyalty foresaw my wrongdoing far ahead of time.

"Are you working at night again?"

"You know I'd prefer to work when no one can see me. It's easier this way. I can make things in my particular way. You can go home and rest if you want. I've never asked you to follow me into working late at night, you see."

"I'll make sure everyone leaves." He closed the front door and locked it from the inside. "I want to. There's so much that I can learn from you. Besides, we have stories about the night creature coming for alone men."

"Glad to know this mountain man has a sense of fear."

"Hey, I know you're more than capable of fighting against her. But I'm only a man, in case you forgot. It's better not to keep you alone for her to come. And not to keep me by myself, either."

"I've heard that story before. I'm most probably hoping that she'll come for me one day. Not to fight against her, of course."

"Is there any particular story about Samael and the night creature? You know, I've been keeping myself silent about you. No sound has come out of my mouth so far."

Smirking and shrugging shoulders were enough to go along with my silence. "I appreciate your silence." From his face, I could see him thinking about where this story would go.

After his facial expression changed, he said, "She's the one you've been searching for, isn't she? The night creature is your woman, yes? Ooo, she must be *that* beautiful to capture this Angel in her captive."

"I hope she can be my woman one day. But, I agree, she's indeed beautiful."

"You know, Samael, you keep surprising me every day. There's always something new about you that makes me question. About what we've been believing and whether it's the truth."

"Should you be questioning your beliefs?"

"I think I should challenge my thoughts. The way I was raised, they couldn't be entirely right. But I'm learning much more around you. It's useful not to settle into the same thoughts for too long. My head could have been dull."

"Well, that's good. You're learning more about yourself. You might become a better person than you were yesterday."

"Tell me. What do you call her, this night creature?"

"She and I have been called many names. In Ellada, they know her as Lamia. In Dimashq as Lilitu, Lilu, or Lilin. But she's always been Lilith for me. Different places have unique tales about us. Some of them are true. Others aren't so true. They vary, depending on their perceptions."

"And you don't mind?" While he laid out the tools, I continued preparing the fire.

"That's all right with me. I know myself well enough, though I don't think I know her that much. The more days pass by, the more I question myself for not knowing much about her. I can't speak for Lilith about how she thinks about the tales."

Once again, Goran made sure that no one was in or near the smithy. When he gave me a nod, I opened my shirt. The fire needed to be scorching by humankind's measure. He moved away, far backwards, to keep out of the heat but kept his distance close enough to watch how I worked.

Controlling the fire with my body, I sealed the kiln with all my wings. This level of heat was what caused copper ores to change colour. It gave them their new lives.

It needed a hot, contained fire to decorate this particular copper and gold vase. An old man in Odessos made an order for his wife's burial.

We made many weapons and living tools from copper. With gold, we crafted decorations. Those pieces of gold were more artisanal than functional. Thinking about Lilith, I started working on the vase.

In my mind, her hair flowed with the wind as she was flying. Here, I made lines on the vase while imagining how her hair strands would move. The shape of this vase made me think of her feminine body. A vessel of fuel that kept my infernal fire burning. The one that contained me from crumbling apart.

Her womb was one that I wished I could fill with my child. I imagined her body getting more round during her pregnancy, just like this vase. With her breasts full of milk, she would feed our child. I imagined the loving life she would provide for our family.

16

The Rite of the Smiths

Once the kiln was no longer too hot for Goran, he came closer. "Where did you go, Samael? You were somewhere else when you worked on that vase. Obviously, you weren't here with me."

"With my Lilith. Always making things while thinking about her. Making things for her. My mind, my heart—all of me is hers."

"If you're my kind, I'd laugh at you, even make fun of you." His banter had started to become more of a habit lately.

"Have you not done it already?"

"Samael, I don't know how you do it. You never looked away from her for any other woman. Not even that night when we celebrated the corps. Remember that needy woman crawling towards you? How come you weren't even hardened? She tried to swallow your cock. I saw it with my own eyes."

"That woman wasn't my Lilith, as far as I could tell. Not sure if any of my answers would ever satisfy you. It feels to me that I have no control over my body. Lilith has been the one in control of me."

"From the old smithy owner, I thought I knew about loyalty. But following you tells me the opposite. This fool right here knows nothing about it."

"Well, I made a mistake in the past. I did mate with the other woman. You don't need to look up to me that highly."

"But still, I have to learn how you do it. It's in the mind, isn't it?"

"But my mind wouldn't be like this if I didn't love her enough. How about you? Have you found a woman for yourself?"

"I'm not as lonely as you are. I see some women but haven't met the right one yet." He must be thinking about how miserable my life was. "When we were about to enter a new mine, I kept myself distant from any of them."

"Is that really necessary?"

"It feels like I need to focus more on danger than on women. You know how the untouched mines can be."

"They're unpredictable, indeed. Does abstinence help you focus while inside of new mines?"

"Surprisingly, yes."

"Glad to hear that."

"I told a few miners about it. Now some of them have started doing so."

"We need to be fully aware of the untouched ones. I can't keep watching these younglings the entire time, can I? You, younglings, need to learn to watch for yourselves. And each other, perhaps."

"They found it wicked at first. After a few men did it, word spread quickly. Even one of the blacksmiths who joined us said, '*If Samael can do it for a long time, surely we can do it for a few weeks to a month.*' I couldn't argue with that fact. Haha."

"There are reasons they call me the Wicked One. It wasn't baseless. Now you, younglings, have found yourselves wicked as well."

And there, abstinence became a ritual for those miners and blacksmiths. I was surprised that it served them well for work. At the same time, I was grateful to know that our men became more aware for the sake of their safety.

They might not have realised yet that denying their flesh was only following one of the Creator's paths. As they had not met Him yet, they were unaware. At one time they would.

Over time, we welcomed more miners coming from Rudna Glava who sought bigger challenges. With them came a myth of a tall hermit in the mountain who shone the light for lost and trapped miners.

Goran and I could only speculate as to where the myth originated. To our surprise, someone had got better with his way of telling stories. I did not mind if the myth helped miners regulate themselves inside of the copper wombs.

17

Younglings to be Raised

"Don't you think it's too early for Ognyan to start working with us? What is he? Fourteen, if I'm not mistaken."

"Gundahar was fourteen when we first met him. I was fourteen when I first worked for the old smithy owner. Well, he wasn't as old as you, for sure. But you know what I mean."

"Is it the common age for sons of men to start working? I heard plenty of you started at that age."

"More or less so, depending on the man of the house. Different houses have different rules. His mother has done her duty very well. Giving birth to Ognyan. Raising him to become a boy wasn't easy."

Goran withdrew himself to reminisce for a moment. "There's this thing that can only be learnt from men, you see. From my father to me. Now from me to my son. He needs to know how to feed himself. One day, he'll feed his family."

"It's a skill to learn what we do here, I agree."

"Better to have him here working than spending too much time at home. His mother will be spoiling him rotten."

"And his mother feels all right with your plan? Are you sure she won't be weeping all day at home while he's here?"

"Oh, you should know, Samael. His mother threw anything straight at me when I first told her. Everything that her hands could reach. But she came to her senses eventually."

"What did you say to her?"

"That Uncle Samael would gladly be the Guardian Angel. And I said that he'd be learning a lot more from you."

Frowning at him, I showed my discomfort at being embroiled in the middle of their parenting argument. It was not that I was unwilling to help him, but I had not raised any children myself. I would not know which decision was right for which child. Every youngling was different from the other; that one I knew.

"That was how you sold my name to her?"

"Was I wrong in saying that? You've been looking after us. We, miners and blacksmiths, have the same thoughts about you. Not that we like being called younglings, but we feel all right with you.

Even if they don't know what I know about you, they can sense that you're all right to work with."

"You *are* still younglings, compared to me."

"That banter about you being ancient is getting old already. Aren't you glad to be an Angel living with us so far?"

"I feel all right with myself. It's what I've become that worries me. Though I appreciate your trust in me, I feel like I can't even trust myself sometimes."

"You're not saying that you're leaving, are you?"

"In a few years, I shall leave you. You see, I haven't looked any different since the first time we met. They'd probably be running scared when they found out."

"Then you need to teach me everything you want me to know. Remember the day we left Rudna Glava? I told you that you have my loyalty. Nothing has changed to this day."

"Worry not, youngling. I shall return here one day. I still need to continue searching for Lilith."

"Well, if that's the thing, you need to teach my son, too. It's possible that you'll be returning here later in his life. Besides, I named him after your eyes, the fiery."

"I'm not sure you want your son to be like me."

"Of course, I don't want him to be miserably in love the way you do. But he can be as good at doing metalwork as you."

"Not like me, perhaps. Better than me, I hope."

"Then we share the same hope."

"How about this? He learns what his mother needs to teach him first. Help her go to the market in the morning, probably. And then he comes here in after he eats lunch. Hmm? We agree?"

"All right, then. So, he starts working here tomorrow, yes?"

"Bring another youngling in!"

We never thought that it was a relief for Ognyan to be out of the house. We could see that mining was another version of his seek-and-find quest. Goran had been good at raising his son at the smithy as well. There were a couple of years we spent working together prior to my departure.

After that, Goran and I kept our partnership close. He was a good man to trust with our work in Aibunar. We saw each other from time to time. While he was alone, of course, at night time. He remained silent about my true Being.

Something, or someone, invited me to return to Dimashq. A force. Gravity. Magnetic. The voice pulled me in. Hers; not through my ears.

18

Homebase

Returning to Dimashq gave me such fresh air to breathe in. To remember how it started. To feel the abundance of Anat and Maamoun once more. I did not realise that it was something I needed.

The owner of the smithy I used to work for did not have any children who could continue the craft when he passed. A generation of heirs had orphaned the place and its fire. The second generation had shown no interest in the craft.

With the knowledge I gained while working with Goran, it felt right for me to claim ownership of the smithy. The decision was immediate and an easy one to make. Hesitation was not here as my companion.

It was Shulmanu who helped me run the smithy. He was proficient at figuring out how much a piece was worth for sale. His thoughts were based on the raw materials and manpower needed.

It was still me, the one who gathered the materials from the miners. This way was practical since I had enough wings to go the distance.

"Should we quit making arsenical copper? Our men started to get sick one by one."

"It's like we're taking turns to get sick the next time."

"How come you never got sick? It's Wicked."

"They call me the Wicked One already." I was probably sick once or twice. But since I naturally healed in a much faster way, there was a chance I did not even realise that I had caught the sickness.

"It's Wicked indeed. Because we manipulated lead with arsenical copper?"

"Could be one of the reasons. Those men also got this similar sickness when I was working in Haemus."

"We can't lose more men if that was the cause. There's tin to mix, but it's still not that easy to find. If we mix fully with tin, can anyone afford it?"

He was right; we might sell these works at a higher price. People here still purchased for function rather than likings. The rich were the exception. They had the necessities to afford something else.

"We also need to think if they'll like it. Mixing them fully with tin gives them a less pale colour. People in the northeast try to make the colour similar to the arsenical one. They smelt tin and gold, but separately." By now, I wondered if Shulmanu was suspicious of where I had been so far. Or, worse, how old I was, to be exact.

"Let me figure it out. You ask the suppliers if it'll be cheaper with a bigger purchase."

"I shall." This would be a conversation the next time I visited Goran. It concerned me if the miners and blacksmiths in Aibunar still caught the same sickness.

"Are you working late again tonight?"

"I'm only finishing this one. You go back to your wife, Shulmanu."

"You know, *this* is why you need to find yourself a wife. To have someone to come home to." With him shaking his head, he might see me as foolish. "I'll see you tomorrow, brother."

Shulmanu went home and left me at the smithy alone. I locked the doors to make sure no one was around. It would save us some charcoal to work with my own fire. The orders were piling up while our men became sick in turns.

The smithy became silent. My alone time here helped me pass the lonely thoughts by. Copper reminded me of Lilith's pale skin. Except when she blushed, her skin would no longer be pale. Copper and every pale-looking metal looked as feminine as her.

She was already beautiful, even without any decorations. Still, I made pieces while thinking about her. From time to time, I felt like I did not know her enough.

What she would like to see or wear was still a mystery for me to solve. What type of jewellery did she like to wear? Or what kind of hairpiece did she like to decorate her hair with?

Even if I knew those sorts of things, how could I send them to her? Would she receive my gifts? How could we even be together without me harming her?

In some way, making these pieces of jewellery kept me close to her. It tricked me into thinking about her even more. In my mind, she lived. This way, I felt her in my heart.

A bracelet for her tonight. It must be nice to rest my head on her chest, listening to what her heart said. I imagined how her fingers would run through my hair while this bracelet decorated her wrist. She must have felt like home to me when it became a reality. But again, I was simply assuming that she was fond of wearing a bracelet.

Just like a fool, I assumed that she still wanted me around her. I felt like a fool, for I had failed to protect her at the time of origin. Certainly, I was fooling myself by assuming that she would forgive me for mating Eve.

My first time should have been given as a gift to Lilith, not Eve. In that way, I wronged the one I love.

19

Her Appearance

We had been accepting new apprentices to help us at the smithy. Shulmanu thought that taking them in was cheaper. They would do some work that the more experienced blacksmiths no longer wanted to do.

For others, it seemed like giving a chance to these youths. To me, it was more likely paying off my conscious debt to the people who gave me chances. How they had welcomed me when I had nothing or no one that I knew should never be forgotten.

Since some of them who helped me were no longer on earth. It felt right to pass on their kindness to the living. I was to continue their legacies beyond their passing.

As for my personal gain, they gave me new details about their origins. By asking further, they gave me more regions to Watch for. Some of their tales caught my attention.

"All three of you will work with those who recently finished their apprenticeships. If the blacksmith needs a hand, then you work with them. Shulmanu is the one running this smithy. Mostly, I work near the fire. It can be dangerous for anyone new. You can ask me anything when I take a rest from the kiln."

Shulmanu came to me with a warning. "Hey, brother! You need to start being careful now. She starts to attack again."

"What now, Shulmanu? Who's in what trouble this time? You know, I feel like I can't leave you, younglings. Not even for a moment now."

"Nabu just had a Lilitu attack a few nights ago. He couldn't stop himself from seeing random young women, could he? One of them happened to be Lilitu. He didn't realise it at first. She seemed quite the usual, he said. When he got home with her, there she came, attacking."

Hiding the excitement on my face was something I could only hope for. "Is he all right now? Was he hurt?"

"Seems that he's still in shock. He's in the back now with his shaking hands. I can't let him work too close to the fire."

"No wonder he didn't come to work yesterday. Let me talk to him later. I'll walk him home if I have to."

"But hey, I meant what I said. You watch your back. You haven't got yourself a wife. That's quite usual for those young men to be alone. You have been alone longer than anyone here. I've never seen you with any woman since I've known you."

"Oh, I haven't been with any women since I first arrived in this city." There was only the truth in my words to him.

"With these many orders, we can't lose any men. It can be bad for our sales. Certainly, we can't lose you. We'll lose our jobs if we do." He sighed when I smirked. "Get out sometimes. Find a good wife to take care of you. All this time, you've been taking care of us. I know you like to cook, and we don't mind your cooking. Try to let someone else cook supper for you. Someone who's waiting when you get home."

A simple nod was enough of an answer for him. If only anyone could imagine how I felt when hearing Lilith possibly be so close to me. A conversation with Nabu was necessary after work.

***

He was quite a hard working young man. Nabu had potential with his craftsmanship. As we were closing the smithy for the day, I approached him.

He could have expected me to ask questions about what happened. My need to make sure that it was Lilith that he met was stronger than the risk of him suspecting what I really was. Yet, the risk was mine to take.

"Here's the key. Can you check the back door? Make sure all the supplies are inside. It's a bit difficult to find new supplies with this demand nowadays."

"Yes, of course. We can't lose any of them."

Once he finished closing all the doors, I handed him the other key for the front door. I waited for him in front of the smithy.

"Let me walk you home, Nabu."

He seemed hesitant to start a conversation with me at first, but he started it regardless. "So you've heard of what happened? With me... from the men at the smithy."

"How are you doing?"

"I didn't feel like working today."

"And yet, you're here pushing yourself to move. I'm glad you came to work today. It's a good start."

"What would I do at home? Alone? I'd lose my mind thinking about Lilitu coming at me again."

"Was that not a win for you? Your thought against your temporary emotion."

"I feel a bit of shame about it. When my father left, I was still little. I felt unwanted. I've been boasting about seeing different women. Easily getting with anyone I want that they can't get. But I know that I've been reckless."

"Indeed, that's even better. You learn about yourself better now. What else did you learn?"

"I now know where to find a good woman for a wife. Obviously, not in the place I've been wandering around."

"And where precisely have you been wandering around?"

"At the fair, where they have games. People put money on the sport. Lots of needy women there. Young or old, they're all full of lust. No, no, don't go there, Samael! Not if you don't want to end up like me."

"Let me tell you one thing about the fair. Maamoun was a dear friend of mine. He regularly went to the fair and made good money for his family. He sold food and drinks that Anat made. His wife's cooking was such a blessing, even for me."

As I told the story, he listened closely to what I said about Maamoun. "You see, I don't think it was about the place but rather how to behave ourselves in such a place. I've learnt that from him. They're no longer with us, and I miss them dearly."

"How come I never saw you with a woman?"

"I had a woman that I loved. And I still love her to this day, hoping to be able to see her again. What

Wicked of me! Yes, I know," I said, shrugging my shoulders. "But tell me about this woman you met at the fair, if you don't mind. So I can keep an eye on her."

"Well, I was with this other young woman at first. I met her there, at the fair. Nothing in particular. We were watching the sport together. After the game, she went to buy some random things she saw at a stall. Then I saw this woman." He scratched his forehead. "At a glance, she was quite the usual, but somehow not really. When I took a closer look at her face, I immediately knew that she wasn't from here."

"How did you know that she wasn't from here?"

"In the same way that we all know that you're *obviously* not from here."

I smiled at Nabu. "Oh, you mean the eyes and the skin? Haha..."

"When we work late at night, I sometimes need a second look at you. I swear, at a glance, your skin seemed glowing near the fire. Sparkled, like stars in the sky. Or maybe it was only my worn-out eyes. What are you really, Samael, a star falling from the sky?"

"I can't say that I haven't fallen before. I fall for one particular woman, obviously."

"Please don't get me wrong. We never know where your origin was. But we all know that you're all right. At least for us at the smithy, you're not that bad. Haha."

"That's interesting." I was not usually curious about what others thought about me, but this time felt different.

"It wasn't actually your eyes or skin. It's the way you sound. But you sound different from anyone who came here from foreign lands."

"I'm listening."

"You've met people. A lot of them, I can tell. Maybe even people in different foreign lands." He tried his best to elaborate on it. "You Watch us before saying anything back. You talk differently than any of us here. You don't even talk the same way to each of us."

"Does it matter to you where my origin is? Or where I've been?"

"No, I don't think so. And you've always had our backs when we're troubled. You have this odd way of talking things through to get us off the leash." He took his time not to offend me. Or at least that was how it seemed. "She sounded like you."

"Did she really?"

"She—she listened. Not only to reply, but to understand. She also asked me to explain. She asked, and then she listened again. That was how I knew she was older than me."

"Are you fond of older women?"

"Sometimes. Well, it depends on the person." He sighed. "We know that we're a lot for you to handle sometimes."

"Huh, now you know what Shulmanu and I have been dealing with daily. Younglings in grown men's bodies."

"Yeah, I know. And what is it with Shulmanu, anyway?"

I was not sure if I followed his lead in the conversation. "How do you mean by that?"

"He seems to go after me any time there's a chance. He yells at me a lot, too. I've tried to do the best I could. But it seems that my smelting wasn't long enough or too long, moulding the wrong angle, forging the wrong side, more force, too much force. Everything I did wasn't enough in his eyes. Should I quit now? Well, if that's what he wants."

"Not everyone gets his special attention as much as you do. Don't you think? He probably has a grand plan for you. Maybe he saw some potential in you. But you couldn't keep your head straight from whoever woman you had. What can I say?"

"Well, I say we go out sometime to find you a woman. I can help you if you need some help with talking to them. Oh wait, you *do* know how to bed a woman, yes?"

"Ease yourself, youngling!" But I could no longer conceal my curiosity about what happened that night. "So what was she like? I mean, Lilitu."

"Why do you want to know so much about her? Is the great preserved Samael falling in love with Lilitu already?"

"If it's my Lilith that you're talking about, of course I'm in love with her, you fool!" If only I could slap him on the head.

20

Night Watch

"Go on, tell me more about her. It's your turn now to watch my back."

Then he told me about following Lilith out of the fair. The veil covered her night sky hair; he could not see it at first. But her eyes were the ones that attracted him. Those emerald eyes of hers, looking straight at Nabu's.

Her plump pink lips gave him an inviting smile. Her skin was pale but looked smooth from afar, which in an instant made him want to touch her. She told him that her name was Lamia and that she had recently returned to Dimashq. From the mountains in the northwest, she came through Aktiki by herself.

My pride for Lilith for travelling the earth was as vast as the Heavenly Sky above. By tasting life in different places, she made me feel so proud. She lived her freedom. She was smart to find her path.

As Nabu said, she was a good listener. She paid attention to his stories throughout supper. He might not be as familiar with her curiosity as I was. Now I was glad that she still had it in her. I wanted to hear her story and learn from what her emerald eyes saw.

He then invited her into his room. While feasting on her lips, he pinned her against the wall. Cupping her breasts with his hands. He then lowered himself in front of her. He had her as his dessert. He became thirsty for all of her arousal, as though walking in the desert without water for days.

After she came, Lilith strapped his neck. Both of his wrists were tied to the rail with the other end of her rope. Even though Nabu could not move his arms, she continued to ride his hardened cock. She kept pulling the rope every time he tried to get off of her. She slapped his face and covered his mouth. That way, he could not be screaming for help or even moaning.

She rode him until Nabu could no longer hold it. He released himself inside of her. When he came, once again Lilith released herself as her emerald eyes turned carnelian.

She untied him after. With her shiny black wings, she flew away through the window. From what Nabu told me, I was certain that he was talking about *my* Lilith. The storytelling ended once we reached his home.

To my surprise, there was no jealousy when listening to his story. I wanted to see her be enthralled by her own pleasure. I became curious about how she would look when she had a release.

***

The city was still full of the scent of her presence.

Deep down inside me, I wondered if Lilith was after men who were up to no good. There was this Wicked feeling inside me. "*What if she was sending me a message to receive?*"

She knew precisely that it was my Duty to punish sinners. Was it her way to draw me closer to her? This could narrow down my search even further.

If it was the truth, then Nabu was wrong. Now I knew where to look for my woman. Hovering over the dark side of the city, I chased her shadow.

They had gamblers, thieves, tricksters, drunkards, molesters, or whoever was in the shadow of the night. My Sword was always with me when I flew at night. Every night until dawn, my night Watch was never skipped.

It had been a few weeks since Lilith was with Nabu, but I had not lost any hope. Without making any noise, I hopped from one roof to another so that no one noticed. Under the first quarter of the moon, there was a chance that someone might see me.

Most of the gamblers were drunk. The one who lost hard was under my Watch. Keeping my distance, I followed him to his house. I was about to leave when he fell on his bed alone. Some itchy feeling told me not to.

With the hair at the back of my neck rising, I waited there for a while. On the one hand, I was hoping for him to sleep until dawn, and nothing would happen. On the other hand, I expected Lilith to appear. I had missed her madly.

Houses in his neighbourhood were starting to kill their fire. They started to get more and more silent. At a glance, I saw a small bird circling over the neighbourhood.

That bird landed near that man's window. Only so much that I could see from afar. Onto a few roofs closer to it, I hopped. My Sword was already out.

When my feet landed on the roof, the storm inside of me started to build. That was not a bird that I saw. That was my Lilith. She was so close to me, yet unreachable. *"Oh, my little bird is finally here."*

She denied the drunk gambler's desire to fuck her in his bed. She turned his body over, pinning him to the point where he was unable to resist. There, she had him undone. She needed to be out of the house before I came in.

My Light was held tightly in both my hands. Keeping it close to my body was not a hard thing to do. It was the desire of my entire flesh that needed to be contained.

She flew out of his house without noticing me at first. But somewhere in the night sky, she hovered. Motionless. Sending the turbulence into my gut from afar. Then she turned her body around towards me.

She landed on the roof to confirm whether I was who she thought I was. Seeing my Sword drawn out, hesitancy showed up on her face.

It was so hard for me to hold myself back from approaching her. Hugging her so tightly would be the least I would do to her. Because a senseless fuck would follow right after.

On one knee, I lowered myself down. Me kneeling before her was what she deserved. My weight rested on the Light in my left hand. With my right hand on my heart, I bowed to her.

She replied with a curtsy. Her face looked the same over time. There was brightness that she brought into my dark, lonely life. My hope was that her blushing cheeks would brighten my dark even more.

Into the drunken gambler's house I flew. Through the window, she was watching me. All she needed to know was that I never drew my Sword towards her. Not even once towards her. Once my Duty was fulfilled, I bowed to her. Once again, I watched her fly away.

21

Paths

There was something different happening with my body on my returning flight. These overwhelming feelings emerged. It came from only seeing my Lilith after a long time. It made me wonder if she felt the same way as I did.

Flying off of the track where I was supposed to go. My body was skidding away. The force to turn myself towards her became greater than the willpower to lift myself to perform the Higher Tasks.

With my self-controls crossing in different directions, my Being could have stalled. This very Tasker was most likely to enter the spin while falling into her mercy.

It was still dark, but I knew where the river was. While approaching, I got myself naked. All my clothing and Light landed on the ground.

Ditching into the river. Staying in its flow. Floating to recalibrate myself. My cock pointed in the direction towards her image. My sword navigated towards its sheath, homing.

The way she dominated that man earlier was nothing like what I had seen of her before. He was pinning her to his bed, but she had a way of slipping her body away from him. The way she had him under her control was beatific. The wings of the night sky queen expanded majestically.

She kept him defeated, letting him know that he was facing his judgement. She touched his face and then ran her fingers through his hair. She was dominating him while touching his mind at the same time.

How she did it obviously enticed me. As enticing as how she could make me harden even moments after it happened. As natural as I could feel her touch on my face and her fingers in between my hair. As real as my hardening cock was in between her legs. My mind went there in the room with her.

She could have me inside of her if she wanted it—in whatever way she wanted me. Whenever she needed me to gravitate towards her underworld, she would be the centre of my gravity. All of the forces within and around me would reach equilibrium. We would be in a coordinated flight the moment Lilith and I became one flesh.

Her underworld realm must have felt like hugging me. The feel of my stiff hand now was nothing but the opposite. While each of my strokes into her feminine body, each part of my length must have felt her gentleness. Not like the masculine force of my grip. She must be handling me with her compassion, taking her time. Not in a rush like I was at the moment.

The thought of her rushed through my body as I released myself into the river flow. Floating still, my sound mind returned to the reality in the here and now. This river became a part of my Lilith. A part of her pussy and her womb.

Lilith had claimed me to be entirely hers. She had always been important to me, but I could not claim her. In the past, I thought that I could. Now I would not, because I understood her. Because I know myself too well.

If I were to claim her, I would want to treat her as if she were my belonging. All of my belongings were mine to use. They were to satisfy desires within me. I was to be within her, to satisfy her desire.

What Adam did to her was never to be repeated. I was never him. My Lilith was never less than me. Her satisfaction was meant to fulfil me.

It was not only my body that floated in the aftermath. My mind did as well. Thinking about what was happening to me. Thinking about what it would take to make it happen. To make us happen. To make it possible for me and Lilith to be together.

***

Rumours were already spreading in the neighbourhood. They talked about what happened to the drunk gambler last night. Apparently, the man got himself so deep into debt from gambling.

Nabu looked concerned about what they said. He was not to be blamed for those anxious thoughts. Since the smithy was mine, a bit of talking was needed.

"Is everyone all right today? You seem tight and silent. Now, I feel like planning a weekend supper to loosen you up."

"Brother, have you heard the words? A man in the western town died naked in his house alone. No wife, no children." Shulmanu spoke of his concern for me each time this sort of event happened.

"Here we are again. Your matchmaking plan with whoever's cousin or neighbour. Is it me again, your victim? Is anyone else willing to take a turn being Shulmanu's victim today?" Bantering with him was delightful since he took his mission seriously.

"Well, you can't blame me. I feel like you're ancient. No wife still. And that man was alone, probably for as long as you've been. But this time is odd, Samael. I've never heard of Lilitu using a blade before."

"Probably it wasn't her doing to take his life. There's a chance that the Angel of Death himself paid him a visit at night. But you were right that I *am* ancient. You'd better not mess around if you don't want me to pay you a visit late at night."

"I don't want to die in Lilitu's hand. Maybe I should listen to my mother—" One of the terrified apprentices choked on his words. "To marry the chatty, noisy neighbour's daughter."

"Somehow I agree with Hadad. You should listen to your mother. Not quite sure about the subject matter, though." Watching our apprentices get pale faces, I could no longer hold my laughter. If only they knew that it was not her doing.

"Maybe *you* should listen to Hadad's mother. You can marry his chatty, noisy neighbour's daughter." At this point, Shulmanu became pretty irritating to me.

"Yes, I agree. Please do, Samael. Help me get out of my mother's grand plan, will you?"

"Shulmanu might be right—" Surprisingly, Nabu decided for once not to argue with Shulmanu.

"Thank you, Nabu. Finally, you came to your senses." Shulmanu looked amused by what was being half said.

"Hey, I haven't finished talking. What I was saying was that Shulmanu might be right. It's probably time for you to get out. At least say 'Hi!' to a new woman. You can't keep waiting for the long-lost woman you love. When did you say the last time you saw her again?"

"Last night, actually. I just saw her last night after a loooooong time of waiting. I've been searching for her for quite a while." If only they knew how long 'quite a while' truly was. Smiling, I left the circle of men before it turned to never-ending questions.

It was important for them to start the day without any tension. Even the well-trained and highly skilled blacksmiths knew that they needed to have a sound mind in the smithy. It was the kind of fire that could melt different types of metal. We could imagine what it would do to humankind's flesh.

"All right, everyone, it's time to get back to work now! We have many orders to fulfil today. We probably need to work until late at night. Samael will go early to get himself a wife. Haha." Shulmanu dismissed the circle with his infamous, hideous smile.

"Oh, don't forget about Samael's weekend supper! I volunteer to be the wedding planner." Nabu immediately got excited. We were surely glad to hear his laughter again. The thought never crossed my mind that the very moment would be the beginning of them making an alliance.

22

The First Shadow-Worker

The western town was the part of the city where they had a bit more fun at night. On the sixth and seventh nights, as well as during the holidays, more people came for different things.

With more wings, I assumed that I was able to Watch from higher and further than Lilith. Assuming was a dangerous thing to do. Tonight, it became a necessity since I could not ask her straightforwardly.

Those tricksters wandered around in the street. There was a group working together. My attention was on each of them, one by one. To find which one could possibly be alone tonight. There were two who seemed to be alone. Once again, I made assumptions about them.

They were walking in different directions. For not knowing the types of men Lilith would pursue, I felt like a fool. Then I remembered Nabu and the last man she had. The one who looked like both of them was the one I followed.

In the peripherals of my eyes, something was flying in a circle. There she was, flying under the moonlight. Although I could not see her face yet, I knew that was my Lilith.

Oddly, she was flying further in a different direction. At this very moment, it felt like I knew nothing about her. Towards her direction, I flew in. A safe distance from her was maintained.

For not seeing which house she landed in, I lost her for a moment. *"What a fool of me!"* There were more wings on me, but she had the capability to slip away. Her small body gave her the advantage.

In a room on the upper part of the house, I saw the trickster being strapped to his bed. He was sucking her breast while she sat on his lap. On a few roofs closer to the window, this Watcher landed. I was to make sure that Lilith saw me watching. And she did.

She ripped some of his clothes to blindfold the man. It was not the same as with the previous man. She did not look like doing it for procreation or lust. She seemed to enjoy her breasts being touched and sucked. Each of her nipples in turn filled his filthy mouth.

She kept looking to her left. Through the window. Straight at me. She was giving me a performance. I wondered if she felt as if I were the one who touched her.

Her body was dancing beautifully, as if she were on my lap. She slid him inside of her. It was supposed to be my cock, not his. I was supposed to be the one who bed her tonight, not him.

She bit her bottom lip while her body leaned back. Her eyes kept looking at me while her fingers moved to her glans. Her performance was for me alone to see; she wanted me to do it for her. That way, she melted me down.

I wanted my fingers to do it for her. I felt like it was my duty to please her. It was supposed to be my duty. I would take the punishment if pleasure did not come to her.

Even after the trickster came, she kept touching herself for me. I knew that she was close to her release as her wings expanded. I knew it as if I could hear her moaning. And finally, she came.

"This one is for my Great Prince." Those words sounded in my ears as if she truly whispered them closely. I knew her release tonight was for me.

Not once had I ever seen her being released like this. All I wanted was to tell her how enchanting she was when she came. I could only imagine how vulnerable her body was as she lay resting beside me.

When she finished getting dressed, I gave her a way out of the house. I hopped a few roofs backwards. Once she was out, I flew into the trickster's room.

Lilith was watching from the roof, where I stood earlier. There was sympathy in her eyes. Not towards the trickster, but towards me. The tears glazed her eyes.

I opened his blindfold for him to see me. The Sword was ready to fulfil my Duty. She kept watching me until it was done.

She gave me a curtsy. While holding the hilt of the Sword, I placed my right hand on my heart. Bowing to her beauty, I was to appreciate the performance she gave me. For one more time, I stood still, watching her fly away.

No longer seeing her, I made a mess inside. The room needed to be seen as a robbery. To get her out of trouble. Even from a distance, I needed to protect her as much as I could. Besides, she sort of made my Duty a lot easier to fulfil with those men.

23

Akashic Silhouette

I was only coming from the smithy one evening. Someone had left a bundle of fabric on the front door sill. That was intentionally put there for me to find it.

Once I was inside of the house, I took a close look at it. There was Lilith's feather in it. She knew where I lived. Of course, she could figure it out. She had always been smart. She was around here, somewhere.

Something was off in the kitchen. The backdoor was not properly closed. There was not much for anyone to steal from this house. Obviously, Lilith let herself into the house. I did not mind at all. My house became hers as well.

How I lived my life was a bit quiet. It even felt empty without her in it. I wished that Lilith could stay. To live here with me. To build a home for ourselves.

This house was too big for me to live in alone. I knew it was not right for me to complain. It was

Maamoun who gave me this house. For that, I should have been grateful. I kept Anat's kitchen in her particular way. Except for today, it was not the way Anat did it.

The kiln was still warm, as was the pot. There was some sort of soup or stew in it. I had never seen this type of food before. It was a mix of meat and vegetables. Surely it was not originally from around here.

I hoped Lilith had some of it for herself. It was not right if she cooked for me but did not have any of it. Before I started to eat, my mind was kept quiet. I imagined what she looked like when she was preparing the meal for me. Did this cause her so much trouble to make?

After taking my first scoop, I paused to enjoy her delicious meal. I took each scoop slowly to praise each one of them. This was what she did for me after almost a moon cycle of not seeing her.

If only Lilith were here, I would have told her how grateful I was for her cooking. Now I understood what Maamoun was talking about. This was our women's labour of love, taking care of us.

My plan earlier was to do the night Watch after supper. While cleaning the dishes, I looked at the fabric she left. Since she filled me with her kindness, I came up with a better plan for tonight.

Getting ready for night Watch, I grabbed my Sword. The Light was strapped to my spine under the shirt. On top of it, I wore a long robe to cover it entirely. Then I walked to the western town on foot.

***

They had drunkards, gamblers, and tricksters as usual. Watching the nightlife, I looked for someone who had the darkest wicked intentions among them.

As midnight passed, I followed one of them, a cheating gambler. Once I was sure that tonight was his time, I got on my wings again. To the window of his house, her fabric was tied. Lilith usually showed up around two-thirds of the night, so I waited for her.

The nightbird was in sight. With my Sword, I gave her a sign. The moon reflected the light from the sun onto the earth. The reflected light hit the Blade to travel further to where she hovered. That way, she knew where I was. She then flew, following me.

On a few roofs away from the man's house, I landed. I gave her a hand signal with the hope that she would understand. When she saw the fabric she gave me, she looked at me. It was not a confirmation being asked. In my eyes, it was my permission that she asked for.

My nod gave her the answer she needed. I had always been right about her; she always paid close attention to me. Even from afar, she understood me. She probably understood even my subtle movements. A small change of facial expression might even be noticeable to her. She smiled at me before entering the cheater's room.

Lilith took off her dress and woke him up with a kiss. I could tell that he was sober enough to know that a stranger had come uninvited. But he had bad enough intentions to take advantage of a naked woman in front of him.

His bed was facing the open window, giving me a full view of what they would do. He had bed rails connecting the pillars, but he rolled her over. With the back of her neck at the edge of the bed, some of her hair dangled down as he feasted on her breasts.

I lowered myself to one knee to get a clearer view of her. My attention stayed on her, my lusty little bird. I needed to know how bad she wanted me to fuck her.

She must be with me in her mind, because I felt her with all of my senses. This desire I had for her started to burn my luminaire Being. She made me no longer solid.

It heated me as much as the burning flame turned me into ashes. The small particles of my golden-like ashes flew downwind into the room. They landed in front of her.

Her breasts were a sight to behold. My hand could almost feel his saliva that covered her breasts. She parted her lips when he slid his fingers inside of her.

The moaning sound stroked my mind. Even though I could not hear it from the roof, her moan sounded so real. As if I were kneeling in front of her face.

How wet she must be getting as he started to lick and devour her pussy. She closed her eyes while licking her full lips. She ran her fingers through his hair but continued to look straight into my eyes.

When he raised his upper body, Lilith pushed him. He sat against the wall. His wrists were being tied to the railing. His eyes were now blindfolded. It was time for only me and Lilith to fuck in our minds.

She turned her body around towards me to give another lustful performance. She slid his cock into her while giving me a beggar's face. Begging that it was truly me with her. Leaning her back against his chest, she showed me how filled her pussy was.

She was holding onto the bed rail for balance. Watching the rhythm of her body while she locked her eyes on mine balanced my mind in sanity.

He became her camel, being ridden while she enjoyed her own breasts. Both of my hands could almost feel like guiding her hands. Both of us together would have been massaging her breasts in synchronicity.

Her pussy was drenched like a river. My tongue could almost feel like licking her glans. My mouth would have devoured her pussy while his cock was inside of her. She would have felt so much pleasure in two different ways.

When his come was leaking out of her, she rubbed her glans with it. Her other hand kept squeezing her exposed breasts one by one. Both of her nipples were well aroused.

My tongue once again could almost feel like latching onto her nipple. My fingers would have slid into her pussy, pushing her to reach her release. They would have caressed her from the inside. The shiny wings of hers expanded until she finally came.

"Your release tonight is for you, little bird," I whispered while my luminaire Being returned to my solid flesh on the roof.

Wickedly enough, I felt proud of her pleasing herself. The image of me was in her mind when she did it. She smiled at me, catching her breath. On the roof, I stayed, waiting for her to recover.

My time to enter the room was only when she was out of it. Through the window, I saw her watching me. I removed the man's blindfold and fulfilled my Duty.

Before flying away, she gave me her curtsy. I answered her with a nod. *"I better not forget to mess up the room before I leave."*

24

Kiln

"Is that a smile I see on your face? What are you possessed with now, brother? Should we be concerned?" Shulmanu asked.

"She cooked supper for me last night."

"It all starts in our bellies and gets into our heads. She knows how it works, then. Is it getting serious now?" Nabu certainly knew how to make everyone feel foolish with his ways.

"Tell me, brother, what did she cook for you?"

"No clue, honestly. Some sort of meat and vegetable soup or stew. I've never eaten something like that before. But it was delicious."

"And you were fool enough not to ask? You know, I started thinking that you might need some apprenticeships. Nabu here... He might be young, but probably knows more about talking to a woman."

"At your service," Nabu said while making a small bow.

"Now both of you won't leave me alone, will you? We gave him his apprenticeship to become a blacksmith back then. Why is he now your matchmaking apprentice?"

"We couldn't help it, brother. You've been helplessly in love with this woman."

"Oh, not to forget him being *ancient*. Anyway, when do we get introduced to this mystery woman?"

"No, I don't think you need any introduction to her, Nabu."

"Ooo... I think Samael's seeing someone famous. No worries about me, though. I won't steal her from you. I know how desperate you are with her. Haha."

"I'd better start working now. Otherwise, no order will be made because of your never-ending questions."

The alliance they formed now had a mission to accomplish. Although it was annoying to me, their mission obviously came from a good intention. Somehow I knew that fact about them.

***

My Sword was well hidden in a place high enough, hoping no humankind could find it while I was working.

Since her last visit, I decided to leave the back door open for her. She was free to come into my house at any time she wanted.

Lilith indeed came again about a moon cycle later. She put the meal on the table. Under the bowl, there was the same piece of fabric as on her previous visit. This time, she cooked minced meat and mixed it with vegetables.

They were wrapped in vegetable leaves. People served this kind of food on their special days. But what could I say? My Lilith was not one of the common people. She was always special to me. She became so special that she cooked for me without even being asked.

Searching for her was for me to caress her, not the opposite way. Not once in my lifetime had I imagined that someone would caress me the way she did. Never had I felt like I deserved her compassion. Yet I selfishly took in everything she served me.

My bed was a little messy. I hoped Lilith had the good rest that she needed here. If only we could, I would share my bed with her. For now, being grateful was the only thing Lilith and I could share in common.

Since I did not keep that many belongings in this house, I was certain that one of my shirts had gone.

I would not mind at all if it kept her warm while I could not be near her.

It made me wonder what she would look like when she wore my shirt. She was obviously too small for my clothing size. She looked adorable, I imagined.

25

Guardian of the Strong

When the night came, I went on foot. To look for some troubled men in the western town.

No wonder that many of them liked to mingle around this area. Everyone could be anyone here without being noticed. Invincible. They could be having a good time while anyone else simply left them be. Except for the women, sometimes they would not leave me alone.

Both Maamoun and Nabu were right that this area had plenty of needy women. Mostly, but not all of them were needy in the same way. For some, this town was only their place to earn a living. To fulfil what they needed at home by serving hospitality.

Here was not an ideal place for women to work this late. Neither was safe for them. Robbery, harassment, and tricks were everywhere. It was not hard for me to see the challenges they had to deal with.

"Hey! Let me send my niece home, youngling."

"Well, I didn't know your uncle was in the city. Which uncle is he from again? Mother's side or father's?"

"I'll take her from here. You better go to your house now!"

Once he disappeared from our sight, I turned to the young lady I was walking with. "Do you know that man?"

She looked down at her feet. In hesitation, she said, "He used to be my neighbour when I was little. He moved to the northern town."

"I'm going to the southern. Do you mind if I walk you home, young lady?"

"No, I don't mind. My house's not too far from the border. Only around the corner of it. You don't have to if you need to be somewhere else."

"I *am* where I needed to be." Asking her carefully, I kept my distance. "Did he often do the horrible thing to you?"

Her sight pierced my eyes, straight into my head. "You saw it, didn't you?"

My sigh and nod conveyed my sympathy. "I'm sorry that you had to experience it."

"Since I was younger... Um, he touched me. When he was still living in my neighbourhood. Um, my parents didn't know. It'd hurt them if they knew. There was even a time when they arranged my marriage. But I said no. I never want him in my life. I would have been enslaved if that happened."

"That must be hard for you to live by."

She nodded. "That's my house. Thank you for your help tonight."

"Worry not. I'm only Watching over you. Now, have a good rest, young lady. You'd need it." Once she was inside her house, I searched for the molester.

***

From up and above, I followed him home. Then, I tied Lilith's fabric to the roof of his house. Lilith would easily find him this way. Hovering over the western town, I waited for her.

My mind was disturbed with chaos. It felt like a sound mind had never been inside of my head. There she was, the one who could send peace to this arcane mind. Once Lilith noticed me, I led her towards the molester's house.

He noticed when she was entering through the window. The way he kissed her back revealed how predatory he was. She let him undress her roughly. Lilith had this way of taking over the control from him. Her way started to arouse me.

His body now faced the opposite direction of the window. It was for me to see what she would do when I was under her mercy one day. After strapping his wrists to each pillar of his bed, she blindfolded him. She made it seem like he was only a tool for us to use.

She ripped off the rest of his clothes. His body became bare underneath her. This time, it was different. Not only his wrists but also his ankles were tied to the other sets of pillars.

She tightened all the straps so that he could not move. As if she knew the horrible thing that man had done to the young lady I met earlier.

Lilith started licking and sucking his cock up and down her throat. She spat on her hand, then played with his balls. Once in a while, she looked at me, making sure that I was still enjoying her performance.

The way she lapped his cock was as if it were my cock that she was having. If only I could give her mine. She did not know that mine had already become her belonging. Mine should become usable only for her satisfaction.

She turned her body around to feed him with her pussy. How beautiful her pussy looked with her wetness drenching into his mouth. She let him lap her swollen glans. She let me imagine how delicious she was.

He drank all of her nectar like a thirsty camel. He kept eating hers until she came into his mouth. Her performance was satisfying and intriguing at the same time to watch. Her release should run down into my mouth. Tasting her delicacy would feel heavenly.

She crawled forward to slide his cock inside of her. Her body leaned forward, commanding me to watch her from behind. Looking towards me over her shoulder, she squeezed her arse. She told me that I was with her while showing me how filled she was.

With her arousing performance before my eyes, my hand travelled down to my hardened cock. Those emerald eyes watched me stroking myself as if I were with her.

While pumping his cock, her arse bounced beautifully. She fucked him harder and faster until he could not hold himself any longer. Her beautiful pussy was leaking his release out. Now her fingers were to replace his cock. From underneath, they either rubbed her glans or filled her tunnel.

Catching her shadow, my release followed hers. My release was wasted on this palm instead of flooding her tunnel. His come was now mixed with her nectar.

She smiled at me as if she had just finished making love to me. *"More of her."* This strong desire told me to approach her. My desire of having her as mine needed to be restrained.

Tonight she was rougher than usual, so I let her rest for a while. She was one of the strong ones, inside and out. I let her catch her breath; she deserved it.

26

Vengeance

She did not free him from the restraints afterwards. She let me do the rest for her.

The molester was shocked when his eyes were freed. I jumped onto the bed, then knelt above him. "Huh, I see you remember me."

There was terror in his eyes when he nodded. He could not say anything as the blindfold was now shoved in his mouth.

"You did my niece wrong." I gave him a punch in the face. "How long have you done that to her?"

He shook his head, flying a blatant lie directly to my face.

"What? You think you didn't do the wrong thing?" I gave him another punch, harder this time. "You've done it to her since she was little, haven't you?" His face started bleeding everywhere after more of my punches landed on it.

Lilith stayed on the roof outside, as she usually did. She kept watching me with her furrowed eyebrows. There was no judgement shown in her face. She was learning me and my moves.

Backing away from him, I roamed around the room. My Sword was drawn out of Its sheath. There was this feeling that I needed to hurt him even more. He did not deserve a quick and peaceful death; I would not give it to him.

I put my wrist on my head while holding the Light. My left hand could only restrain my right from enforcing rage. The frustration still rushed into my head.

Lilith moved a step ahead with her right palm facing me. I could feel her, as if her warm hand were on my chest. Even from afar, I could feel her calming hand.

I wondered what she was thinking about me at this very moment. What others thought of me never mattered. But what she thought of me mattered. Because *she* mattered the most to me.

He better had the right answer this time. I pulled the fabric out of his mouth. "Anything to confess? Or was it my niece's fault that she deserved your sinful touch? I'd be careful with the answer if I were you. The way it will be done depends on it."

"She's been needy and following me since she was young—"

Before he finished his excuses, the fabric was already shoved into his mouth again. Deeper this time. My left grip kept his neck still. Then it started heating up. The Light on my right hand was already pointing towards his heart.

When the flesh of his neck started to burn, I let my Sword go into his heart as slowly as possible. To stretch his last breath as thinly as possible. To keep him in the in-between as long as his lifetime allowed.

The heat started on his neck. Then the flame consumed his bedsheet, along with his remains. Finally, the fire burnt the room. They would be ashes in the morning. No one would suspect her of anything.

When walking closer to the window, my eyes were locked in hers.

***

She took off to hover a little further away from me. She landed once I landed on one of the roofs.

We were at a safe distance. Close enough to see each other clearly. Far enough to keep her safe. To me she was too far out. To my Sword, she was close enough for one throw of a Blade.

Down on my knees, there was a need for her comfort to cool down the fire inside of me. The fire from the molester's house behind me brightened up the space between us. Her tears were already pooling in her nurturing eyes.

She placed both of her hands on her chest. When I stood, stepping forward, she took a couple of steps backwards.

"*STOP! Restrain yourself, Samael! You can't hurt her. Not her.*"

She pulled one of her hands from her chest. Her open palm stretched towards me. She let me feel her love even from a distance. Her touch would mean so much at this point in my lifetime.

After sheathing my Light behind my spine, I bowed to her. Her feelings for me had been speaking loudly to my heart since the time of origin. Through time, I felt her genuine respect in a way I could not yet understand.

Before she flew away, Lilith gave me a curtsy in the way I always loved. It might be her way of respecting me, and she looked enchanting when doing it.

27

Alliance

Last night was obviously different from other nights of Watching. There were layers of emotions involved.

Since the time of origin, I had always felt something from fulfilling my Duties. But I had never felt anything similar to last night. It was even different from the time of Eve's punishment.

There was such helplessness. It was as if there was nothing I could do to prevent it. The bad still happened to the innocent one under my Watch.

Although the young lady was already grown up, it was not because of her age. The youngling was no more since the first time it happened to her. Surely she was reborn into someone else when her innocence was murdered. The molester had murdered someone inside of the youngling.

Even after her rebirth, I still had no clue how to behave myself. Had I given her any Justice she needed when I gave him a painful pass? I did not feel like I had. To me, it felt like it was the usual Angel of Death fulfilling his Duty.

Lilith was different. Her naïveté remained, for she never had any Fruit of the Tree of Knowledge. If she ever gained any knowledge, it was from her experience.

She knew what it took to ease my fire. She knew how to fuel my fire. Those comprehensions were beyond the seeds that had been buried in the Blissful Garden. She got that understanding by herself, without me giving it to her. That way, she made me feel beyond proud.

My mind was so wicked to wonder if her face would show any naïveté when she knelt in front of me. Some part of me wanted her to be the Lilith in their tale when she fucked me. The other part of me wickedly wanted her naïveté to remain on her face when she became my amusing plaything.

***

"Okay, brother, what did she cook for you this time? Your smile's getting more and more obvious lately. Especially today, an entire day of smiling. It's rather annoying."

"Minced meat and vegetables, wrapped in leaves. Though I never knew she was good at cooking."

"Ooo, Nabu! The celebration meal was out already."

"Did she steal your shirt yet?"

"Hey, who told Nabu that I lost a shirt? Or it was you who stole it?"

"Well, I might be younger than you. But as Shulmanu said, I've got more experience with women than you," Nabu said with his know-it-all voice.

"You two are *definitely* getting into something here. Shirt stealing is happening, brothers! Samael has lost a shirt already."

"No worries. I got your back as the most notorious wedding planner in the town. You let us know when and where the weekend supper will be! We'll all be attending your wedding... with this mystery woman of yours." Obviously, he had not forgotten about the wedding plan.

"How did I miss a covenant of alliance forming behind my back? I thought Shulmanu alone was already bad. With you two together, it's far worse."

"Not behind. Right in front of you. Haha."

Shulmanu laughed, agreeing with what Nabu said. "What are you making, brother? A knife? For her?"

"No. This one's for a young lady in the neighbourhood. She usually comes home from work alone at night. This might be quite handy if she needs it. Though I wish she didn't even need any in the first place. It isn't right for any woman living a cautious life."

"Let me see the size... I can make the sheath for it. With a strap, yes? Easy for her to carry."

"So she can hide it well. Yes, that will be convenient."

"Hey, we don't ask for payment for this one. It's for her safety."

"Never knew you had a conscience in your mind. I appreciate it, brother."

***

Near sunset, I came to the young lady's house. A much older lady who looked like her answered the door. It was not fully open, but I understood her concerns.

"Please forgive my visit being this late. You can call me Samael. I believe you have a young lady living here."

"Tanith, do you know this man?"

She looked anxious when she saw me. "Yes, Mother. He walked me home last night."

"We made this knife at the smithy. The gift isn't much, but we hope it will help if you need it."

"We appreciate the gift. You can call me Tanith."

"I need to excuse myself now. Please send my regards to the man of the house."

Her mother stopped me from leaving. "My husband died last year, leaving me and my daughter alone. What is it that you do, young man? If I may."

"Looking after my men at the smithy."

"I don't mean to be rude. My daughter hasn't married yet. It isn't right for Tanith to continue to provide for me. Or to work until late at night to make ends meet."

Tanith immediately looked at her feet in silence. Her cheeks were blushing like blooming red petals. She reminded me of my Lilith at the time of origin.

"In a few moon cycles, she'll be twenty years old."

"I shall ask one of the blacksmiths about your daughter. I believe they're good men. As for myself, I belong to a woman."

"Please send our gratitude to the men at the smithy. I won't forget to carry this everywhere I go."

"Tanith, please be safe at night. I believe your mother cares for your safety."

28

Metalcraft

Everyone who came with no experience or skills started as an apprentice at the smithy. Some of these men came because of the need to survive but refused to be beggars on the street. Others were blacksmiths who came to learn our craft.

Hadad came out of passion. His parents wanted him to continue their work and become a merchant. He had started to work with them when he was fifteen. Apparently, it was not fulfilling to him.

It was metalwork that he wanted. Although he had been progressing with his skills, he was not too hesitant to get his hands on the bigger work. Meticulously working on bettering his skills, he treated his craft like it was an artisanal work.

"Samael, do you remember Tanith? You told me about her a few weeks ago."

"Of course, I remember her. How are she and her mother? Have you seen them lately?"

"I've been seeing her, you know. She's a kind woman."

"Good to hear that, Hadad. Are you serious about being with her? As you said, she's a kind woman. You can't fool around with a kind one, can you?"

"We're getting married right after the new moon. Will you come to our wedding, Samael? You introduced us."

"I'm delighted to hear it. I shan't miss your wedding. Will it be at her house?"

"Yes, it will. And then I'll move in there after the wedding. We don't think it's right to leave her mother behind. Besides, I don't want her to be alone while I'm here."

"That's very kind of you both. And how about your parents?"

"Thanks to you, Samael, my mother won't bother me again about arranging a marriage with the chatty, noisy neighbour's daughter."

"Ah, yes, that one I didn't forget."

"Also, Tanith can help my parents with the merchandise. She won't need to work at night anymore."

"That will be an even better decision for both of you and your family. Don't you think so?"

"For sure. You know, she still carries her knife everywhere she goes. The one you gave her."

"Shulmanu made the sheath, so it wasn't me alone. We thought it was best to protect her. Even from you, if some wicked thoughts come into your mind. You can't wrong the kind one, youngling."

"She calls you her Guardian. She told me about the night you walked her home. About the old neighbour of hers. And how it started way back then. I could tell that she was hesitant to tell me at first. I'm glad she did."

With relief, I smiled at him. Even though I was not his parent to take pride, I was indeed proud of him. "And yet, you keep going with the wedding. I know you can be a good man one day."

"I'm not even halfway there. Anyway, about the knife, she showed it to me. It's balanced and fits the grip of her hand. Functional but also beautiful. How did you make that kind of carving? It's beautiful, just like her."

"Sometimes, it only takes some sort of thought. Inspirations, if you want to call it that way. If it's Tanith in your mind, then make one for her. Make it about her."

"Can you teach me, though, to make one of those? The beautiful ones, well, if you aren't busy."

"Way back when my old friend Maamoun was still around, I made them from scraps. I couldn't make two of the same thing. It depended on what scraps I had that day. I just smelted and reforged everything. Then he sold those pieces to the rich.

He made some good money for his family. The rich saw them as one of a kind."

"Ah, yes, that made sense. Where do I start then?"

"This youngling can start by collecting those scraps."

"I'm pretty sure that *this* is your way of telling me to clean them up. You know precisely how everyone is lazy enough to do it. You saw an opportunity and you seized it, didn't you?"

"Indeed. Start with the bad ones if you want to reforge them into stronger ones. Besides, they're waste already. Also cheaper to practise with."

"Got it. The bad ones only. We don't want to make Shulmanu yell about wasting the good ones. I can't give him more reasons to yell at me."

"Ah, this youngling's learnt something, hasn't he?"

***

The following new moon, we attended Hadad's wedding to Tanith. It was pleasing to see the blacksmiths outside of work, especially in a celebration of love.

I had never known that Hadad came from a family of wealth. But it was also nice to know someone who had a work ethic. He had worked himself up from the bottom of his apprenticeship. It made me believe that when something went wrong, Hadad would have the capability to start over.

This also gave me hope and trust in humankind, particularly in the young ones. Living among them was also meant to witness their eagerness and persistence. The young ones might lack experience, but they were not all bad.

"Hadad, congratulations! I'm genuinely glad to see you full of joy."

"Thank you, Samael, though we're still looking forward to your weekend supper. The wedding of you with the mystery woman. Why didn't you bring her here?"

"I haven't seen her for a while now. She has things to do on her own. Besides, I can't pull her too close, too fast."

"Now, I'm concerned if this woman you've been helplessly in love with is a tale."

"She *is* sort of a tale. Enough about me. You need to enjoy your day."

"Thank you for coming, Samael. It means a lot to us that you're here to Bless our marriage. I heard from Hadad that you rarely go out."

"Young lady, you better not trust your husband *that* easily. He could be saying something untrue about me. Enjoy your day, you two."

Tanith's mother looked relieved to have someone taking care of her daughter. To make sure that she would not need to walk home alone at night from her work. We gave Hadad some time to enjoy his time with Tanith after the wedding.

There it was, my first matchmaking duty. Not necessarily assigned, but more for my own fulfilment. To experience love, even if it was not mine to begin with. That was enough fulfilment in my chest to witness their love. Even if my life was still empty without Lilith, my love, it was enough in the meantime.

***

Surprisingly, Hadad returned to work less than a moon cycle after the ceremony.

He continued to learn to reforge, perfecting his metalcraft. If only he understood that perfection was never meant to be on earth. It was not even meant to be inside of me as an Angel of Death.

It was quite interesting to see that he was passionate about his craft. We might need some beauty rather than relying only on functionality in our metalwork. Shulmanu agreed that we set Hadad up with another apprentice to work on designs. The younger ones sometimes had better taste for the craft.

About a few moon cycles after their marriage, Shulmanu made an agreement with Hadad's parents. We were ready to sell his collectible creations.

We, the blacksmiths, were mostly covered in sweat and dirt. We might not be presentable when bargaining with the rich. His parents had broad connections. They looked presentable enough to bargain on our behalf. It could be beneficial for both sides.

There was excitement about new opportunities. There was genuine happiness for them. Witnessing them also sent me into a limbo of loneliness. To desire a marriage. To live a family life with Lilith. For the time being, gratitude felt right.

Once in a while, I wondered if there was a way to meet her in the middle. The grey area between the light and the dark still remained a mystery to be solved.

29

The Lake of Blood and Tears

It had been too many moon cycles since Lilith's last visit. Her presence had already been missed, but what could I say?

Keeping myself occupied at the smithy until late was helpful. To avoid the silent void in my house. The dark hole could be consuming my sound mind.

All the blacksmiths and apprentices had gone home this evening. After the many orders we got this week, the men deserved to come home early to their wives.

Tools and supplies were securely kept inside. When I was closing the front door, my hand felt a piece of Lilith's fabric. It was tied to the door handle.

The door was now locked. There was no one around to see me, but the sun was not fully set yet. Regardless, I took off to look for her.

There she was, hovering in the northern sky. She looked different than the last time I saw her. She opened her right hand in front of her, towards me.

Slowly, she rotated her body. How round her belly was. My Lilith was pregnant.

She looked at her swollen belly. Her caring hands touched and rubbed it. She already looked so nurturing before, but now she looked so motherly.

My heart beat faster, pounding my chest harder. A smile was the only thing I could give her from afar. It was not appropriate to give her the least. I should have given her the most of everything good.

My hands should have caressed her pregnant belly. My voice should have told the tales to our unborn. Our baby should have kicked from within her womb. To tell me how amusing my tales would have been. That was how much I wanted to have children with her. She and I should have been raising our children together.

Following her, I flew, heading northwest. We were a bit slower than my usual speed, but our flights were to be understood. It was not easy to fly with more than one body to carry. As much as I wanted to carry her so she could rest, we were to maintain our distance.

We had been flying for a while now. My concern was whether she needed to take some rest. I never wanted anything bad to happen to her or the baby. There must be a way to ask her to fly easily. She should not push herself beyond her capabilities. We continued our flights, regardless.

***

We maintained the high level of the sky until she descended. She looked over her shoulder, ensuring that I was still with her. If only I could tell her that I would always be with her and for her.

After landing near the lake, she walked around. From time to time, she seemed to get the contractions. Her comfort was important to me. Their wellbeing needed to be my duty.

As her contractions became more frequent, she lifted the bottom of her dress. Her walking into the lake alone was not right. It should have been me with her.

Sitting there, she was waiting for the baby to come. She started pushing. After catching her breath, she pushed again. The crying sound told the earth that a newborn was here to live.

Joy filled my soul so much that I could not hold back my tears. I was so proud of my Lilith for giving birth on her own. Unless it was not over yet.

She gave another push. The second baby was born with a louder cry than the first one. There was so much love for them in my heart. I was supposed to sit behind her, being a pillar. She was supposed to lean against my chest, resting in my care.

She looked at me, smiling with her motherly eyes. Both of the babies looked healthy. That was all that mattered for me and Lilith. I did not care whose babies they were. Both of them were mine, as they already had my heart. All three of them had my heart.

The babies stopped crying when she started breastfeeding them. In the past, I thought that her breasts were beautiful. Now they were beyond what beauty meant. They were brimming with milk that flowed out of her nipples. She kissed them one by one while feeding them with her love.

All four of us, in silence and peace. Praising the beauty of her motherhood. Beautiful. Peaceful. Until peace was no more. Lilith started crying. Her weeping got louder and louder. She held our babies closer to her. Eventually, she screamed.

I did not understand what was happening there in the lake. She ripped off their cords from her before letting go of our babies from her arms. Even though she still could not properly walk yet, she stood, trying to walk.

She carried her dress, which kept slipping down her body. Her breasts were exposed. Both of them were still providing a livelihood. Her fast let-downs continued.

She tried to take off but only to stall. On the ground, my little bird crash-landed. Her tears started running down her mourning face once again. Then she turned her face towards me. I knew she could see how broken my heart was over the loss.

How powerful she was was unknown to me until I saw her smile while looking at me. After wiping her tears away, she fixed her dress and stood back on her feet. Once again, she walked. She took off and stalled several times before she was finally airborne.

Landing on the lake, I rushedly reached for our babies. *"How come they were bleeding, then rotten all of a sudden? They looked healthy when they were born. How is this possible?"*

Then the memory of the Red Sea came. It was what she was created for. When I turned my face towards her, she replied with a nod. She kept her hands on her chest. Somehow, I knew that she was crying harder on the inside than she was on the outside.

Out of the lake, I carried them. It was not me who took the lives out of them. Their vulnerable bodies were for me to properly bury. Into the soil of the earth, their lifelessness was returned.

She gave a curtsy in the air before flying away. She was not only beautiful but also *that* powerful. It was she who lifted herself again after the horrifying event happened only a few moments ago. Beside their graves, I wept out my grief.

Into the lake, I dragged my feet. To look for the remnants of her womb. To find her inner parts that had blanketed our babies for moon cycles before they were born.

Falling apart. Screaming my lungs out. The air inside my chest evaporated as my tears once again fell. Some of the water evaporated into the air as my frustration boiled the lake.

The living beings inside of it were no longer alive. In the morning, they would be found by those men. And those men would feed their families who lived around here.

A family life for Lilith and me was not a foolish wish. Even if I could not get close to her, I would have been taking care of our children. They were not sinners to be punished.

It could have been my duty to raise them. Even without any clue of how to be a father, I would have tried. For them. For her. For us, I would have tried.

Her motherhood was wasted, just like that. For reasons that I could not even understand. My heart was crumbling into pieces. It felt like the remaining devotion to the Most High was burning down to ashes.

But falling apart could not be a decision I made now. She would be in need of me at this moment. For her, I needed to be stronger than ever. Catching her whenever she fell became a solid decision of mine. It was not only solid but whole. My devotion was now to her.

30

The Smithy

If only I had not put my Sword that far away last night, I would not even have to come back to Dimashq this morning. If only I were not that foolish, I would know where she was.

Right after the morning light came up, I arrived at the smithy. Other things that I brought were only to conceal the Light. Terrifying anyone more than they already had was never my intention.

Against the wall, I laid my belongings on the table. Shulmanu and Nabu came into the corner near the kiln, answering my call. The three of us needed to talk secluded from the others.

"Tell me, Nabu. Do you have good intentions about this woman you're seeing?"

"I asked her parents for their blessing. We'll have our wedding the day after the new moon."

"Then I leave you with my house. It isn't much, but consider it a wedding gift from me. Build a home with her. Start a family with her in it."

"And where will you sleep then if we live in your house?"

"I need to find the woman I love."

His face now was full of concerns, as if we had switched roles, with me being the youngling. "All right, Samael. What did you do this time that made her leave you again? Hmm?"

"She was pregnant."

"Well, congratulations! I didn't know that you'd been busy." Nabu seemed delightfully surprised until he started to accuse me. "Don't tell me you were foolish enough to ask her if it's yours. Did you? Tell me you didn't."

It was supposed to be my Duty as the Accuser in the Heavenly Court. Although it was not his duty here on earth, I felt like deserving the accusation. "No, I didn't."

"What troubled your mind, brother?" Shulmanu shared his concern; I could see it in him.

"Nabu, I've never touched her, not even once." Their stares stabbed me to bleed out my truth. It was true that I had never touched her. She touched me in the time of origin, but I had not.

"And, Shulmanu, I didn't care whose babies they were. I genuinely didn't care at all. She gave birth to them herself. I was there last night. The moment they were born, there was this joy I felt. You know,

I've always wanted to build a family with her. But none of the babies survived. Now that she's away, I don't know where she went."

He placed his hand on my shoulder. That way, I could feel his sympathy for me. Shulmanu did not say a word yet. I knew he was waiting for me to talk first. But it was not me who spelt out the first words.

"You'd better go and get to her as soon as possible. *This* is the time that she'll need you the most. Be with her as much as you can, Samael. No matter how sad or angry she gets, well, she probably throws things at you, too. But you better stay with her. She might not be feeling like herself right now."

Nabu, for once, said something much more mature than his age. His confidence grew to match my towering height. Possibly taller than mine.

He then hugged me farewell. He placed his hands on the sides of my arms while saying, "I'll tell stories of how good of a man you are to my future wife and children. And also how desperately in love you've been with this woman. Well, I can't skip the hilarious part of the story, can I?"

Shulmanu gave Nabu the gesture to leave the two of us alone. "May I see it?" He had been a blacksmith long enough to recognise the shape of hidden blades.

We moved closer to the table together. Our bodies covered it from anyone behind us. To show him what it looked like, I pulled the sheath to the side. The blade was as shiny as the white Light of a luminaire.

"Never seen one like this in my entire life. I believe we haven't found this kind of material to forge yet."

"None of you will be able to forge this kind of material."

"What is it made of, brother?"

"Light," I said while sheathing it safely.

His face turned towards me with a sharp stare. "Are you made of the same thing?"

"No, Shulmanu." This time, I concealed my Light thoroughly so no one could recognise its shape.

As I leaned my back against the wall near the table, he took a closer look at me. With the kiln on my left and his facial expression, I knew that my eyes were already starting to flame with desperation. "It's made of Light, but I'm of fire."

"I would have said that it was an honour to know a good *man* like you. But that wouldn't be the right thing to say, would it?"

"No, it wouldn't."

He pulled my shoulders to hug me farewell. "It'll be my honour to meet you again at the end of my time. And I'm looking forward to it, Brother."

"I leave you with my smithy, Shulmanu. Take care of our men. They're your trouble now. Make sure to tell your successor that I shall be back here one day."

"After you find her, yes?"

"One day... after finding her."

He frowned, thinking. "You know what, Brother? I'm not willing to take ownership of this smithy."

"No one knows this smithy better than you do. Trustworthy is what you are."

"My *words* can also be trusted. You're not of sound mind to make such an important decision. Not at this moment, at least. I'll continue working here. I'll get paid the same way. You pay me enough to support my family, but my time has an end in this life. You'll need the ownership more than I do. You have a long path to live."

"If there's a man to trust this smithy with, it will be you. Shulmanu, my brother, I trust you with the truth of my existence."

Before I left, I looked at other blacksmiths one by one. They replied by nodding. Some of them then gave me a farewell tap on my side.

There were unspoken symbols among them. Somehow, these men acknowledged my struggles without saying a single word. Even in silence, their movement of respect was loud. At the smithy that we knew, I left my men behind. To wander along the unknown paths.

***

To the pink lake in Burgas, I returned. Even when I knew Lilith was no longer there, that was the first place I traced. She might be hurting somewhere at the moment.

She should not feel alone or abandoned at a time like this. She should feel safe with me. To caress her was my pure intention, even when I had no clue how to do it yet.

"Where would she rest her tired, hurting body?"

31

A Pledge to the Divine Council

The Time of Jared

I had not taken any rest for... obviously, I had lost count of time. Days roasted into nights. And nights smelted into moon cycles. Then moon cycles forged into solid years.

Cycles of their lifetimes had passed during my endless cycle. I had witnessed both their endings and their beginnings. The spin of time refined some lines in this blacksmith's lifetime. Those timelines smithed the Being I was at the present time.

Had I transmuted into a different Being? Others might think I had, contrary to my awareness. The core essence of my Being had not. Never had I ever stopped the quest to find her.

When it was time for humankind to be awake, I searched for her on foot. To wander around like a fool. Probably, I was a fool who was foolishly in love with my free little bird.

When the night came, airspace after airspace, I flew. To fly over like a night butterfly. Even humankind in some places called those harlots as such. Probably, I was a harlot, enslaving myself for her presence.

These routines caged me into an endless loop. The ownership of my ventures endlessly brought more belongings to me. Even without me involved daily, they kept piling up. They were hidden under the soil, concealed from the thieves.

The hills that my belongings made had become mountains. Those of mine helped me throughout my quest. They open passages for me towards new people, new inhabitations, and beyond.

When it came to Lilith, the weather around me felt like it was never built to be in my favour. Whenever I felt like getting close to finding her, the sky over the passage seemed to become overcast.

All parts of my Being could always sense her presence. Her warmth felt so close, within my reach, as if it were ready to melt my frozen loneliness. But then the bluish-grey clouds began to build. Thickening in the middle of the earthly sky. Darkening, to welcome the occluded front. Lowering down into sheets of fog on the mountain.

Without her torch of flame to brighten my path, I was forcibly withdrawn back into my loop. A sound mind might no longer remain inside of my head.

She was a wonderful being. Motherhood was not supposed to be a curse, especially for her. She wanted to be a mother; I knew it from the way she grieved in the pink lake. Why could she not have children of her own? What was it all about? I wanted children as well. With her.

Living among humankind for long enough time had made me envious of what they had. Family life, to call her my home. A place where I belonged, not simply a house as one of my belongings.

There was nothing I gained from those belongings that I had mined from the earth. Soulless houses were what I built, not a home full of life. A forfeited life was what I had been living.

Why could we not have a fulfilling life as they did? The only way to get the answer was to Ascend. To ask the Most High for answers to these Wicked thoughts felt right. Here I was, taking off to the place where I Resided.

***

When I arrived, Michael was already there. He got in my way towards the Divine Throne.

"Step aside, Michael!"

He went from grabbing my shoulder to pulling my arm. "I'm not letting you do something foolish."

"Yeah, Michael, foolish enough for not knowing *why* the Creator created a woman with a womb...

to bear children... only to give sickness to babies, including her own!"

"Samael, I know you care for her."

"Well, *that* is one hell of an understatement. Is that what you think? That I *care* for Lilith? Look who's the foolish one now. For Heaven's sake, Michael, I *love* that woman."

Other Angels started to Assemble. Hundreds of them were curious about the argument we were having. None of them dared to talk me through. It was only Michael who did, as he was the Defender in the Heavenly Court.

"My Brother, keep yourself solid. You are our Great Prince in Heaven. They've been looking up to you for a long time. Even Watching the Fiery One lives amongst humankind."

"So you know how long it's been." One by one, I looked at the Assembly straight in their eyes. Some of them either immediately lower their gazes or look away.

"You all know how much it takes to keep my distance from her. But no, I shan't draw my Sword out towards her if that's what the Divine Council has been asking. I do my part as a Tasker. And if that isn't enough, I don't know what is. All of you have no clue how it felt to bring an end to those whom I knew."

"But this isn't the way we do things." Michael kept on persuading me to calm down.

"Yes, it is, baby Brother." There was a calm breeze, Breathing into my chest. Even with the high density of Wisdom, She felt Lively. Merciful.

"I oppose your Wicked thought."

"Aren't you becoming Hasatan in the Divine Council? Isn't love the highest of the three? It's already within me. She only nourished how I should do things with it. Of course, everything I do is to deserve her love."

"Neither am I Hasatan nor opposing the highest one of three."

"The Most High will test if I'm of a sound mind; everyone may find it as Wicked as I was Firstcreated. When the Most High dissects everyone's guts, there may be different things inside yours and theirs. But the Most High is only going to find Lilith inside mine. *This* is my Pledge to the Divine Council. It shall be sealed as a Treaty by this Heavenly Court."

32

The Flight of the Fallens

He seemed to nearly give up on arguing with me. "Envy might have found you. From spending a long time amongst humankind—"

"Precisely! I've spent enough time with them. I know how good they can be. And I know how beautiful their daughters become when they're grown up. Yeah, those beautiful, grown daughters of men. Oof, begging to be fucked in the most senseless way possible."

The Assembly looked at each other. Not knowing which Angels of ourselves were in favour of which side—Michael's or mine. No longer sure where to put Lilith in this Heavenly Court—as a sinner or a victim. Not even sure in which place the Most High stood—as the Judge or the One to be Judged.

"What now...?! Getting twisted in the head yet, all of you? How do you think Cain got his star-like skin? All the descendants of Cain have the same skin as I do, yes?" Shocks hit their faces, including Michael's.

I moved closer to him with my fiery eyes locked into his. "Guess what Eve said. When I asked her if I should continue fucking her drenched cunt, she. said. yes! You hear me? *Eve* asked me for *more!* Like a filthy one."

"We can see that you aren't of sound mind. Samael, if this is about you, don't bring them to Fall with you."

With a grin, I asked, "What's that, Michael? Oh, I saw it cross your mind. If I Fall, you'll be the new Great Prince, won't you? Is it my baby Brother who wants my Title?" The unnecessary provocation felt necessary at the moment. Michael was known to be a devoted and fulfilling Tasker. He was always persistent with what he was doing.

"Careful, Brother. Don't get too close to the point where there'll be no return."

"Then, Falling, I am! And you're Falling with me, Michael." Grabbing him by the wings. Dragging him down with me.

He tried to get off of me as we were spiral diving. He did not stop throwing punches at me, as I knew what kind of Angel he was for the battle. Michael could be messy when needed. The Defender could be on offence in necessity.

While clinging to his foot, I spun my body. My legs strangled his waist. As my upper body curled around his neck, I grasped his arm. He was not to be an escapee.

His elbow hit me in the face. My balance was lost. It became a struggle to keep him with me. As his body worked better with air than mine, he was able to slip away. Only some of his ripped-off feathers were caught in my fist.

There, I saw the Creator Watching my luminaire Being. One day, as the Divine Self walked the earth, He would retell the Flight of the Fallens. The saga from a Higher perspective for humankind to listen to.

***

Entering the spin and out of the Heavenly cycle of time. Striking the earthly sky just like lightning.

Here, Fell the Great Prince from Heaven. Falling for my Lilith. Here, I Fell into the realm of her love.

On the last third of this night, the Morning Star Fell. The Light-Bearer of Salbatanu set as the dawn of the earth rose.

Here, we Fell from our Grace into the dark of our Wicked minds. From one Dimention to another. From one to the other ones.

One third; Heaven lost that many Watchers from our Falling Flight. The two hundred and I were like meteors, all streaking lights at the same time.

Some might call us wish-granting stars, while others might call us disastrous. It depended on how one saw us Falling. We could even be Wickedly both.

It was probably true that the words of this Accuser were venomous enough to lead the two hundred of us to lose the Seats in the Council. One third of vacancies in the Divine Assembly were now overtaken. Regions that once had become the domains of the Seats were now Patronised by the Creator.

The one who slipped away became the new Great Prince in Heaven. Let my Brother have my old Title. Maybe it was for the better of him. It might be even better, for Heavens' sake.

33

The Change of Plan

To some point, Michael was right that I could not keep a sound mind after losing track of Lilith. Then I Fell in the middle of my path of searching for answers.

Most of the Fallens were quite young in mind, even to talk to. Not to mention, they were getting busy fucking those cunts. It was challenging for me to find someone I trusted to clear my mind. Someone to talk with about the next path to choose.

Shulmanu was even right back then, saying that I was not of sound mind to make any important decisions. Even now, it felt like I still was not of it. A sound mind might even be further away from me now than in the past.

"Ah, finally, my Brother pays me a visit. I was worried you didn't miss me that much," he greeted me with his infamous, hideous smile.

"Certainly, I didn't miss your matchmaking plan." Letting out a sigh, I took my seat next to him.

"Seem to be more troubled than the day you left. You know, you never mentioned her name to me. Have you found her yet?"

"No, Shulmanu, I haven't found Lilith yet."

He was startled. "Lilith? As Lilitu? Lamia? The one in Nabu's story?"

"She and I have many names. Different people from different places call us by different names. They tell different stories about us, too."

"Oh, let's pretend that you ever cared what anyone thought about you. A bit too late for that, don't you think?"

"Something has never changed. Something has."

"Well, I've changed. Look at my hair now! Can you see them? Neither can I. My head is all scalp now. But look at you. You haven't even aged for a day. Same old Samael. Oh wait, did you mention ancient back in the day?"

His dark humour was something that I missed quite a lot. There was something in his every word that made sense. "So, what *has* changed for you so far?"

"I have..." Fixing the wood in the fireplace in front of us, I paused, not knowing how to begin this conversation. "I've Fallen from Grace, Shulmanu."

"Haven't you fallen all this time? You've helplessly fallen in love with Lilith."

Shrugging my shoulders was the best answer I could give him. No matter how hard I tried to elaborate on it, probably none of it made sense. To him or anyone else in particular, this might not be something humankind could comprehend.

"So, it's *that* bad, huh? How bad are we talking about?"

"Two hundred Angels have Fallen with me. I don't know where to go from here," I said, leaning back on my seat.

"Yeah, you've been searching for Lilith by yourself. It didn't seem to work out. Not that we didn't want to help you, but we simply weren't born with wings." He moved his body towards me in the same way he did when we discussed something at the smithy. "Now you can form a Legion with two hundred of your Kind. That's a *huge* help you've had so far. Maybe you can divide them to search in different places, just like you did at the smithy. You know, each blacksmith for each work."

Chuckling at his words was my spontaneous reaction. His words showed how clueless he was about my Kind. "Oh, Shulmanu, they aren't the same Being as those men we had at the smithy.

"Well, I could only imagine having to look after two hundred Beings with wings. Wait, are your feathers falling like us men getting hair fall?" Rubbing his scalp, he asked one innocent question like a curious youngling.

As far as I can remember, no one ever asked me that sort of question. It was not something I ever thought about, either. "More or less. Sometimes, not always. Some have a pair; some have more, as I do. You might even have met another Tasker unknowingly."

"Is that so? Are they all the same as you? Made of fire, bringing a Sword made of Light?"

"No, we're different from one another. We also look differently, depending on what Duty we have to fulfil."

"What's your Duty, again?"

"Death, punishing sinners, and destroying them. Lilith was one of them. She grew her wings after calling the Creator's name. It was forbidden. That was the reason I couldn't be too close to her in the past. Now that I've Fallen," taking a deep breath. "There's a chance that I can finally be with her."

"If you falling in love with Lilith is a sin, and if Falling from Grace because of it is also a sin, then I don't know what the word 'sin' truly means. I'm only an old man. I don't know what Falling precisely looked like. But not once have you ever let any blacksmith down. I might never see your wings, but you've always caught us every time we fell into trouble."

"I can tell your words have gained some wisdom, brother."

"Well, it was my privilege to learn it firsthand. You have this Wicked way with words, but not like those thinkers. They wouldn't spend even a day working at the smithy. You have *this* different way of talking. Even better at asking questions. No less than handing us a bucket of water to see ourselves clearly."

"I am to question everything... To Challenge, even to Accuse."

He seemed hesitant to continue his words. "If I may ask, were you sent to us on purpose, or did you come on your own?"

"All I can say is a little bit of both. It's been a great time with you. You treat me no differently than other men."

"Of course, I treat you differently. I had to give you some special treatments so I didn't lose my job." His laughter filled the room in his house. "I can say you're a good owner. Might not be the best one, but you're all right. You took care of us enough, even if we were only troublemaking younglings in grown men's bodies."

"Speaking of which, how is it?"

"I trusted Nabu to run it as I've got weaker. I believed he would continue my special treatment of our very special owner. He surely would enjoy making more fun of you."

"Glad that you have joy in life, brother, even if it's quite irritating for me." My immediate thought was that he trained Nabu well in a darker sense of humour while I was away.

"Shulmanu, I've always trusted your judgement for work. But why Nabu?"

"My mother never saw me as a wicked child. I was her favourite. Then I became everyone's favourite."

"Was that a problem, becoming everyone's favourite?"

"Not really. Not unless it became the need to do everything in everyone's favour. Well, I told Nabu that you'd come back. Just like this Accuser, he accuses me of lying. There are some parts of you that I saw in him."

"Ah, I see you didn't miss me that much."

"More joyful with him, if you ask me. I couldn't yell at an Angel, could I? Haha."

"Who said no one ever yelled at me? I've been blamed for many things already. All of those just never bother me."

"That's my point. You two don't have the need to favour anyone. He has fallen into trouble many times, perhaps not in the same way as you have. But both of you know how to learn from those falls. Sometimes the ones who have fallen learn more than the ones who haven't. You learn different things or even learn in different ways."

What he said never crossed my mind, even though I had paid close attention to how humankind rose after their falls. Their adaptation could win the evolution. Certainly, I had never noticed it in myself. How I had been changing was never something that I traced.

"Where did you go, Samael? I saw you doing it from time to time. Your head flew elsewhere."

"My Kind is supposed to Watch humankind, not to be watched. And yet, you did." I took my shirt off for Shulmanu to see me.

"Oh, it turns out you have many wings. You know, I was planning to say, 'Hey, Angel, I *knew someone like you. His name is Samael.*' Now that you've Fallen, I've changed my plan."

"Why is that?"

"What if they ask me about you? Not once in my life have I ever unveiled anything about you. What if they torture me to reveal your secrets?"

"You aren't to be afraid, brother."

"It's been an honour to entertain an Angel in my lifetime. You might have Fallen, but all I see is the same Being whom I call my Brother." He gave me a warm smile this time. "Remember, Samael, a Fallen Angel remains an Angel. When I meet the Creator, I'll ask Him to go easy on my miserable Brother."

"It's been my privilege to know a good man like you." I kissed Shulmanu on the forehead. "Farewell, my brother."

34

Our Legion of Watchers

The Fallens had spread to different regions of the earth. To find wives or companions for themselves. They gave themselves to those grown daughters of men. They were to bear their wicked ones.

Not once did I look at any of those women the same way as I looked at Lilith. Not once did I desire any of the grown daughters of men for myself. Not once had I given myself to any of them.

From time to time, I visited the Fallens. Not only to ask how they were. With humility, I asked them for favours. To spread the word about Lilith. To help me align with my twin.

Shulmanu might be right; there were more regions to look into at the same time. It might be a more practical way to search for her than my way in the past.

One thing that never crossed my mind was how eager they were for a quest. Another challenge besides chasing pleasures from their wives and companions.

The First Five of the Fallens and I gathered one night to form a Legion of Watchers. Twenty of them became Leaders of ten each. To Lead the Twenty was never my consideration. My hand was not the upper hand for this quest.

Yequon, the first one who Fell, went with three other Leaders. Forty of the Fallens were to Watch from Thrace and Haemus and to the north beyond.

Asbeel the Deserter, the second one who Fell, went together with four other Leaders. Fifty of the Fallens were to Watch the far southeast of the earth.

Gadreel the Wall, the third one who Fell, went with three other Leaders. Forty of the Fallens were to Watch the border from Palermo in the south, the Alpes—from Chur to Como, Roses in the west, and the northwest beyond.

Penemue the Insider, the fourth one who Fell, went with three other Leaders. Forty of the Fallens were to Watch from Anatolia to the east beyond.

Tamiel the Perfectionist, the fifth one who Fell, went with two other Leaders. Thirty of the Fallens were to Watch from the Levant to Kemet and beyond Alkebulan.

We all had the regions divided. They flew outbound towards their designated bases. We planned to gather as much information as needed.

We needed to spread any news about each region among each other.

Once we knew the circumstances, we would have an easier time making plans. Further contingency plans were needed. We acted accordingly after that. From there, we worked our way forward as a Legion.

No region should be overlooked under our Watch. No being on earth would hide from us. Nobody fled out of our Watch. They should not, because they would not be able to.

Lilith should not have flown away from me in Burgas. And I should not have let her go. But if my little bird wanted a seek-and-find quest, I would play with my prey.

This was the start of my hunting. Let this hunter play with the food. I could try to satisfy myself with my plaything. I would try, but the outcome was never a promise.

She would always come undone. Her face when she came was always my favourite. Her pleasure rushing in her body simply made me want to watch more. Hunting her releases would become my new cycling quests.

She might not know yet that one cycle of quests would not be satisfying to me. Another cycle would start after the previous one finished. She would only be done being my plaything when I was done playing. That was if I wanted my playtime to be done.

35

Strategies

The Time of Bronze

Aktiki was a flourishing city full of thinkers with their idealism and merchants with their capitalism. Everything in between laid out opportunities for anyone to seize.

This city had a lot to offer. Someone needed to be aware of what one was capable of. Potentials had wicked twins, called temptations. There was a lot to handle with those. Someone needed to be able to control the wickedness within. The wicked twins worked well with what was within.

The myths and tales were being told as a part of the control of their society. There was the tale of Lamia among people in Ellada. According to them, she was a half-humankind and half-serpent creature. The night creature was known to visit their little ones.

Lilith and I had lost our newborns. It made sense that she would want to be around their little ones. It was important for me that her heart would heal.

Their concern was about an unknown being approaching their babies. From there, they spread the tale of the newborn eater. The newborn part of the tale was understandable. The other part of it was quite untrue. What was it about the half-serpent?

How untrue the tale was. Lilith had smooth skin, and her legs were beautiful. For only thinking of how appealing they were to touch, my cock was already caught in trouble.

What was in between her beautiful ones controlled my mind. My body reacted to it in alignment. It was easy for me to imagine how delicious she would taste. When my mouth was in between her legs, her thighs would make my ears deaf from what they said about me.

When I was with my Lilith one day, we would not need to care about what they thought about the both of us together. They could call her my Hetaira. She would worship me as I did her. It was in Aktiki that I took another chance at finding her.

"What do we owe for the pleasure of this visit?" His embrace welcomed me into his place.

"Yequon, my Brother! It's a pleasure to see you again."

"Come in, our Great Prince. We're about to have a feast tonight." My appreciation should go to his efforts in Ellada, especially since he was the first one who Fell after me. He believed in me since the very beginning.

"Batariel said he would come. And Turiel and Chazaqiel, are they here yet?"

"I didn't know they were coming. More play with more of us then." Turning his face to his helper, he said, "Three other Watchers are joining tonight."

"We'll prepare for more meals," the helper said before leaving us.

What they served would not satisfy me. Not those of humankind's meals. Nor their Hetairas' flesh. Her pussy should be my feast. The outburst of her release should intoxicate me. My release should shower her beautiful face right after.

***

Later in the evening, the other Three joined our table for supper. These Watchers mostly waited for me to start any conversation. That was riveting to me because it was not moved out of fear.

Never had I ever asked to be their Great Prince since the time of origin. I did not even ask them to follow my every plan after our Falling Flight. They could be flying towards their paths on their own.

"How is Thrace doing, Yequon? I saw them build those cities quite well."

"That's something I've been wondering about. Why did you tell us to start by being worms to humankind? They have a fast-growing society here, Many opportunities we could have seized by now."

"But humankind have limitations in their lifetimes. We don't grow old the way they do, do we?" It was easy to think about it from a short-term perspective. "One friend of mine, Shulmanu, taught me to think for the far, long path ahead."

"So what would you suggest for us to live by?"

"We're called the Watchers, aren't we? Then we shall Watch. Watch from afar and closely at the same time. Then we Watch what lies in between, Batariel. We shall work out those opportunities accordingly. Not too fast, neither too late."

"Do you always work like this? I thought that you were a predator. It turns out that you're a hunter. You're fond of playing with your food."

"You can't blame me, though. My first job among humankind was for food. I pushed the carriage for an honest merchant. Maamoun was kind to me. His wife's cooking had this special ingredient called love. You might see it as low. What I've learnt from him and his wife was countless. Priceless as well. We can't purchase those lessons."

"All right, then. Anyway, our vault in Odessos is almost ready. But I need to ask about the gold. Why are we stocking gold? I thought gold was cheaper than metals nowadays," said Turiel.

"I've learnt that from Maamoun as well. At the moment, they're still doing things for functions. But my old friend sold my creations to the rich. They saw those as one-of-a-kind pieces. They were never the same thing, depending on the scraps I had for the day. When their livelihood improves, they'll see things differently. They'll be wanting more, let's say, in different ways. We need gold after all."

"Ah, that makes sense. We need to learn a lot more from you, Great Prince. As you said many times, we're still younglings."

"We still have so much to do. You see, if we want them to see things differently, they might need our help here and there. They aren't there yet."

Chazaqiel, in a pessimistic tone, said, "So you want us to help them to help us in the long term? What makes you think they would benefit us later on?"

"Wasn't that why we were built? To Watch how they would react when given more or when given less. It'll come around to us. I've been living long enough among them to learn about it. You'll see what humankind is capable of," I said to him with a wink.

"They're different, though. One is given more and becomes better. The other becomes better because they were given less." Chazaqiel touched his beard, thinking deeply. "What should we do on the daily with them? We can't just Watch the entire day, can we?"

"Look after the grown ones, even the older ones. But for the younger ones, we need to nurture their minds first. They had the speed and power to do things. But for them to endure the long path, we need to get into their heads."

"How do you mean by that? Testing them out? Like a long sport?" Chazaqiel's Wicked scenarios amused me from time to time.

"Firstly, we Watch them to see where they are now and what they need. Then we help and spark them with clues and thoughts. Teach them to make things, signs, and symbols. They'll work it out. It'll benefit us eventually."

Turiel slapped his palm on his forehead. "You know what? You're pretty terrifying sometimes. You see things that we didn't. Probably because you were Residing higher than most of us to see a more vast view." He paused. "But that also meant you Fell from a higher place than where we were. You took a harder hit than us. And yet, you have this grand plan with the mind trick. Obviously, getting us, younglings, lost most of the time."

"First, they called me Wicked. And now you call me terrifying. What's next, Turiel?" It was rather enjoyable to have some laughter once in a while. Then we had a more serious conversation. "Now, about the vault in Odessos. I believe you've already divided one section for my belongings.

"We have, indeed."

"Is it possible to divide my vault into two? Half of it is for mine, and the other half is for Lilith's. She left the Bliss long before me. It makes sense if she has belongings."

"But... you have to find her first, Samael. Then share a bed with her, maybe. After that, you may share your vault. Does it make sense for you to take the time?" Turiel laughed to find some amusement in my life story. He might be thinking about how foolishly in love I had been. "No worries; we shall get the vault ready as you wish."

"Have you found a new site for another vault yet?"

"We found a site in Kemet, but we'll build them in a more tricky way. Once we complete it, you'll understand why we need gold. You see, Kemet is more for routines, while Odessos is more for contingencies. There's another one that I actually want to build. Beyond the wall, Batariel, on the other side of this earth."

"Oh, Samael, can you please stop thinking too far too fast? We know that we don't grow old the way they do. It's keeping up with your mind that's challenging sometimes. We're still learning to walk while you're already running fast," said Chazaqiel.

Understandably. Not every being could understand how Wicked my thoughts were when speeding up. With more wings on me, I flew higher; I saw broader than them. As could my mind go much faster than theirs. That was all right for me if they did not understand me at the very moment. They would eventually comprehend one day, in their own time.

"Was I not Created to challenge everyone? And isn't that what younglings do? Stumbling when learning to walk?"

He continued, "We haven't even understood the cave you're building in Chur yet. What's that all about? And those tunnels underneath?"

"I wish all of you could see what I see inside of my mind. Nonetheless, I appreciate your belief in me."

Chazaqiel remained in confusion. He turned his face towards the other Three. "Can anyone who understands care to explain to me?"

With his hilarious whining face, I could no longer contain my laughter.

Batariel shook his head. "Obviously, beyond me."

"We're building a bunk cave in the Alpes. It should have enough space for all of us. Just because we have wings, we can't solely rely on flying. We need to land from time to time. In case something happens during our resting time, we shall have a safe place to recover before striking back. Those tunnels will be our way to move freely without being seen from above."

"I have no clue what's on your mind, Samael. Is that why you trust Gadreel to make those? What do we call it, then? Safety measurements?"

"Let's say that I trust Gadreel the Wall to Guard the perimeter. In Palermo, Como, and Roses, we shall be Guarded. Would be giving us some recovery time in the bunk, Yequon. Well, in case something concerning comes up, those undergrounds would give us shelter from many things. We also need to keep the soil of Chur and around it neutral for as long as possible."

"Neutral from what, precisely?"

"From any conflicting sides. You haven't seen how they fight, have you? Actually, I was wondering if we can build another contingency place in the far south of the earth."

Yequon sighed before speaking to his helper. "We might need a stronger drink than this one."

36

Remedies

After the supper, a hot bath was necessary. Not only to clean myself but to clear my mind as well.

There were two hundred of us and me in the Legion, but we had not found Lilith so far. Either we were fooling around in this quest, or Lilith was that sleek at veiling herself in the crowd.

"How can this Legion be the preparation for Lilith to come home? Can I be the home she needs?"

The delusion I had in mind was so profound. It got me to think about being her protector. Why would she need me to protect her? She had been protecting herself all along.

Why would she need me to be her home in between her struggles? She had been strong all these times on her own. I was delusional enough to even think about referring to myself as her home. Would I even be fit to call myself that way?

It was I who needed her in my life. It was I who needed her to be my home. To keep me solid from crumbling apart. How could I be so selfish towards her?

I might not only be delusional but also foolish. I might be The Fool among all of the archetypes. I took the leap with only my faith in her. Faithful towards her, I had been since then.

Feeling exhausted for too long was not even close to what I felt. A bed to rest my noisy mind for a while could be useful. The mind was lacking sleep. My bed was still lacking her.

After taking a relaxing bath, I returned to the hall, half asleep. However, that sleep would not be happening soon. Six young women became the sacred companions of the Four. All of them were already giving themselves to one another.

"These younglings! I can't leave them even for a moment, can I?"

"Samael, please forgive us for starting ahead of you. Young ladies, meet Samael, our Great Prince. Samael, meet Evangelia," said Yequon while having her sit on his lap.

She was stroking his cock with one hand. Her other hand circled her own clit.

Turiel praised his companion's drenched pussy. "This is Diamantina. She likes her diamond to be polished well." She was laying down with her head dangling at the edge of the table. She had his cock filling her mouth and his fingers stretching her tunnel.

"Stamatia here looks so delightful. Don't you think? Look at her serving cunt on the table," said Batariel before continuing to suck her nipple. His fingers ran along in between her legs before sliding inside of her.

"This one, Melina, oof, I wonder how her throat would feel. Must feel good," said Chazaqiel, gripping her hair with his fist. She got down on her knees, swallowing his cock so willingly.

All of the young women looked so willing to surrender themselves to the Fallens. Each Hetaira volunteered. They came from different places. Only the finest ones from their origin land were chosen.

They saw themselves as offerings for the Watchers to Watch their families and regions. Their people proudly celebrated every pregnancy that came from the sacred companionship. After giving birth to the Nephilims, they came back to their people.

From what I heard, the Hetairas could no longer find satisfaction from men. There must be a slight taste of Heaven when mating with Heavenly Beings. The taste they would miss when coming back to their men. From longing for the Fallens, a slight taste of hell might grow inside of them.

"No worries, Samael, I brought you Chara and Nomiki. Please help yourself with my hospitality." Yequon tapped their naked arses, ordering them to come to me.

"Pleasure to meet you, Chara, Nomiki. I'd prefer to be left alone tonight."

Nomiki's hand moved to my chest from behind. Chara's breasts were now facing my mouth. Moving them away by their wrists, I denied them.

"As I said, I'd prefer to be alone. Now go back to your Mates."

"Well, thanks to you, Samael, now we have more cunts to fill," said Batariel, embracing Chara.

"Come here, Nomiki. Evangelia's craving your lips."

She kissed Evangelia, while Yequon welcomed her with a spank. He then rubbed Nomiki's pussy, finding out if she was already being needy.

I did not mind watching them fuck. It was a way to learn how to touch my Lilith when the time came. It was my duty to please her during our intimate time.

My imagination went to Lilith once more. She might gag once or twice when she had my entire length. Her emerald eyes must have looked more beautiful with tears pooling in them.

37

Their Hetairas

Melina got her first slap while her throat was held still in his other hand. Chazaqiel seemed more aroused when he saw her tears pooling in her eyes.

"Prepare your cunt for my cock." She started to rub her clit as commanded. She slid the fingers of her other hand into her cunt. Massaging her own walls. Shedding more tears.

Turiel opened Diamantina's hood with two fingers from his left hand. The fingers of his right one rubbed her little hill vigorously. After slapping her clit, his fingers thrust into her cunt. His girth kept filling her mouth. Her dangling head at the edge of the table was his free path to gag her.

Yequon put Evangelia down. He then moved his chair, facing me. "Lie on the floor, Evangelia. Head between my feet. Show Samael your swollen little hill. Let him watch how good you fingerfuck your cunt." He pulled Nomiki to face me. "Now, Nomiki, give your wet cunt to Evangelia's mouth. Sit on her face while you swallow my cock."

"I agree with Yequon. You need to give Samael a show to enjoy. Show him how needy your cunt is, Stamatia." Batariel dragged her around by her hair, placing her cunt towards me. "Chara, lie down beside her. She'll prepare your cunt for me."

Stamatia rolled her body onto her side. She started rubbing Chara's clit. Both of the young women kissed each other, locking their tongues. Chara started to put her fingers inside Stamatia. Side by side, they kissed while fingerfucking each other.

Chazaqiel continued to hold Melina's hair. Down to her throat, his cock was ramming. "Touch yourself. Make sure your cunt is as wet as a lake for me." He slapped her every time she gagged. His cock must have felt everything her choking throat was giving.

It was Damantina's aroused breasts that became Turiel's plaything now. He tapped Damantina's cunt twice, saying, "Swallow everything I give you. And keep pumping my cock with your pretty hands."

She complied and was eager. Both of her hands caressed him. He slapped her cunt before feeding his balls to her mouth. Onto the table, he placed his knees beside each shoulder of hers.

His arsehole was for Diamantina to eat. The rubbing of his hand became more brutal towards her cunt. She let go of herself while begging him to not stop.

"Spread open your cunt. Be wild with your little hill, Evangelia." She moaned louder as she fingerfucked herself faster than before, as Yequon commanded. Nomiki continued to massage his balls. His entire length was swallowed deep in her throat.

"My nasty Nomiki, let her tongue fuck you deeper." Her fingers opened her cunt wider for Evangelia. Yequon stood to thrust her throat harder. Evangelia spread her legs wider. She rubbed herself wilder. Her fingers reached her cunt deeper. Squirting her release.

"It seems like both of you don't even need me here." Stamatia broke the kiss with Chara. Both of them looked upwards at Batariel's cock.

"There you are, craving for my cock, I can see." They licked his length from head to root in turns. He pulled their hair with his fists, making sure that his command was heard clearly. "Now you make each other come."

He thrust one of them until she gagged and turned to the other until the other gagged. They both waited patiently with their tongues out, as if they were dogs waiting for their meat.

Waking them up, he slapped them both at the same time. "Use both of your hands, young ladies. One for her little hill, one for her insides. Don't you dare be gentle!" Making them cry. Making them rougher towards the other woman than before.

Both of them eagerly awaited their turn to have Batariel thrust into their throats. "Harder! Faster! Both of your cunts need to be ready for my cock!"

They fucked one another vigorously, as if it were a race for their release. They whimpered and moaned loudly when they released themselves.

Melina was dragged by the hair. Chazaqiel laid her down on the table. Her pussy was drenching for him. "Now your cunt is ready to be used." He held her throat with his controlling hand. With him feasting on her breast, it only made her beg even more.

"Let me feel how good your cunt is." He slid two fingers inside of her while rubbing her clit with his thumb. "Oh, I thought that you were tight. It turns out that you're smooth. So smooth... and my cock likes the smooth one."

He set her neck free. Only for his slap to land on her breasts one by one. Chazaqiel's fingers kept thrusting. Even getting wilder. "Beg for my cock first. Come hard, you filthy one."

Nomiki gagged herself when Evangelia slid two fingers inside. "Evangelia, what a show you've given Samael! Now, make Nomiki come onto your mouth. Use your wild fingers," said Yequon.

His cock filled her throat so deeply, with her tongue out. He stayed still for a while, pinching Nomiki's nose to choke her. Gagging while having Evangelia's fingers and mouth. Until she squirted out her release.

"Oh, such a release, Nomiki. Now rub all of it on Evangelia's face. Let her beautiful face smell and taste like you. With your cunt, don't rub her with your hand."

Diamantina whimpered when she came. With her undone voice, she begged Turiel to rip her cunt apart. He slid halfway inside of her. He slapped her face before his entire length rammed deep into her hilt.

She screamed and whimpered, begging for more. And that was precisely what he did. Granting her wish, he did not stop ramming her cunt.

He held her in place by the throat. Slapping her face and breasts in turns. His come now filled her cunt. If only she knew that he would not stop there. The come leaking out of her was only for him to use it against her swollen clit. He chased another of her releases.

Having Melina's release in his hands only sent Chazaqiel craving more. He turned her over. She was on her stomach with her legs dangling from the edge of the table.

With her release, he covered his thumb. Once all his length was inside her, he slid his wet thumb into her arsehole. "Dance, Melina! Fuck my cock and thumb."

Chazaqiel's other hand slapped her arsecheeks one by one. She screamed loudly each time his hand landed hard. Her tears were in between pain and a craving for more pleasure. He kept slapping her arse in turns, harder than before, until he came.

Yequon moved around to fill his length deep to Evangelia's hilt, while Nomiki smeared her release on Evangelia's face. "Crawl back here, Nomiki. I need both your cunts close together."

Nomiki, on top of Evangelia, was waiting for her turn to be fucked. She screamed when his hand landed hard on her arse. "Clean up your mess from Evangelia's face! Clean her with your tongue." He kept thrusting Evangelia's cunt roughly.

"Aaah... So much release for Samael's eyes to watch." Batariel slapped them. He spat on both of his women's faces after they came. "Lick your faces clean, both of you."

He turned to the other side of the table. His hands landed hard on their arses. Stamatia and Chara could only scream. "You did well making each other come, but not quite right. Let me show you the proper way."

Placing one leg of each woman on his shoulders, he pulled their hips closer to the edge of the table. "Your cunts aren't ready for my cock yet. They need to be stretched first. You're not going to like it."

He slid two fingers each into their cunts, rubbing their walls harshly. He continued stretching their holes by adding another finger to each hole. And then another one to each hole after that.

"Spread open her cunt for me. Evangelia, it's her turn to get fucked now." Yequon landed another slap harder than before, this time on her other arse.

Evangelia started by fingering Nomiki from behind. She squeezed Nomiki's arsecheeks. He spread open Nomiki's cunt while Yequon still fucking her own cunt.

"Oh, poor Nomiki... denied by Samael. He didn't want you, did he? Be grateful that Evangelia even bothers."

Pulling a fistful of Nomiki's hair, he said, "Now turn her favour, Nomiki. Please her clit. Make her come again."

Yequon pulled his cock from Nomiki. His cock slid into Evangelia. His fingers fucked Nomiki. "You want me to come inside you? You want my baby in your womb? Hmm?"

Nomiki begged him to impregnate her. Evangelina begged him, too. Both of them wished for the same from him. "Enough seed for everyone. If any of you don't get pregnant, I'll fuck you more."

He fucked Evangelia harder but gave the first pump of his release to Nomiki's cunt. Then he gave his second pump inside Evangelia's cunt.

Once his cock was hardened once more, Turiel used his come to easily slide into her arsehole. Diamantina kept begging him not to stop. His cock fucked her arsehole. His fingers fucked her cunt. Everyone heard her screaming his name when she came. When Turiel was close to coming, he walked to the other edge of the table. Her face was now covered in her tears and his release.

Both Chara and Stamatia faced each other with four of Batariel's fingers in each of their cunts. "You think you might like it, but you won't."

Chara held Stamatia's neck when she had his entire hand inside of her. "Oh, you're helping me so much with her neck. Slap her, Chara! Let her feel your pain."

His thick cock kept fucking her cunt until he sent Stamatia into seeing stars.

"Now it's Stamatia's turn to get hurt, Chara." He thrust Chara's cunt roughly while his hand started to fist Stamatia.

Batariel fucked and fisted their cunts in turn. Both of them were crying. Both of them begged him not to stop. Both of them wished to get pregnant. He filled a pump of his release into each cunt when he finished.

***

All of them were catching their breaths after such intense fucks. I brought some water for the young women for refreshment.

From the back, I brought a bucket of water and a piece of cloth. I wiped their faces of tears and sweat with the damp cloth. That was the least I could do for them.

Chazaqiel asked with a curious face, "Oh, Samael, your self-restraint is truly the Great One. How are you not hardening even for a bit while watching us here?"

"I've spent time with people longer than any of you. I've learnt how to behave myself. Maybe you can learn from one of the thinkers. They teach about retaining self-control. Still in their beginning, of course."

"You mean the endurance-for-pain kind of teaching?" Chazaqiel asked.

"Yes, that one. It's quite practical, though, at least for me. Controlling myself from unnecessary thoughts. Now that all of you need to behave yourselves, give them a good bath. Clean up these young women nicely. Take good care of them after what's been done. That's how you do it, younglings."

These Hetairas were to bear the Fallens' descendants. They were to return to their people. These were the future mothers of the Nephilims.

For now, these young women were in waiting. The Fallens did exactly as I said. To give the young women the care that they deserved.

Crashing my body on the bed, I was feeling so much heavier than ever. My thoughts felt as if they were being smelted. My head felt like it was being forged.

It would be lovely to have Lilith in my bed every night, especially tonight. Only Lilith and no one else. My mind needed to rest in a flow of thoughts and dreams about her. Flowing... until it was flown away into the night.

38

Allegiance with the Fallens

It was exciting to see their society here. They had a better city plan in Aktiki than anywhere else in Ellada.

Early in the morning, the merchant area was already awake. Their trade part of the city was separated. Their living areas did not connect with others with different functions.

Different people came to Aktiki from different origins. They were moved by different reasons. Different dreams pushed them to reach the realities they had in their minds.

Here was a melting bowl of their different societies. They could look similar to one another. It was how they sounded differently that revealed their origins. They could also look different from one another. Their behaviour mostly could tell me that they lived in the same household.

"I cannot believe my own eyes. Never thought I'd see you again!" Hadad had not aged much since I left him at the smithy. He looked even younger than he did in the past.

"Pardon me, do I know you by any chance?" The young man looked confused.

"Ah, forgive me for interrupting. I thought you were someone I knew."

"I believe you know his father, Hadad, my husband." Tanith aged gracefully. Her voice was familiar in my ears. This strong woman had been through hell on earth. Her strong will and hopes kept her going. "It happens that my Guardian Angel hasn't changed a bit. Always Watching over us."

"My young lady, I'm glad to see you again."

"Samael, look at me. I'm no longer a young lady. This is my son, Ashur," she said, introducing her grown son. "You better go to your father. Tell him that his old friend is here."

"I can see you and Hadad are expanding. How has he been doing?"

"We've been trying our fortune here in Ellada. Since his parents passed, we continued their work. Hadad sometimes spends his time alone. Working on his creations. So far, our son's helping us with the customers. Come by if you have spare time. We sell on Mitseon Street."

"You don't see me as Wicked as anyone else—"

"That you haven't even aged a day after all these years? I've sort of known about you. Since the first night we met, actually."

"And what have you *sort of known* precisely, if I may?"

"That whom I called Samael is clearly my Guardian Angel. The night you walked me home, you thought that nobody saw you. There was always someone watching. At least *I was* watching that night."

I placed her hand to hold my arm. Through the crowd of people, we walked. "How do you mean by that, Tanith?"

"Through the window, I saw you jump from the ground so high. And then vanished into the air. I couldn't sleep that night. I wondered if what I saw was real. It could simply be my imagination. My tired eyes might have seen something unreal."

"It was possible that your eyes were tired. You were working until late at night. It was also possible that I was being reckless."

"But I never heard anything about the horrible person again. He lived in the northern town. It wasn't possible for a person to reach that far that fast. So it must be a Guardian Angel looking after me."

"And so the Watcher had been watched." My face turned towards her. "You didn't say anything when I came the next day."

"You brought me a knife as a gift. After that, you brought me another gift, a husband, although he was clueless. And that husband has been showering me with gifts. The metal crafts that you taught him. Our children... well, you didn't teach Hadad about making those, I assume."

"Of course I didn't. Have you ever told Hadad about any of this?"

"Before our marriage, I told him only about how we met. Simple things, like you walking me home to protect me. Then giving me the knife to protect me further. Briefly, nothing in detail. A few years after you left the smithy, he had so many questions about you. At the time, I tried to explain things that his mind could agree with. Years later, I told him the entire story about you. What I saw that night sort of made him find the missing clue."

"And how was his reaction to it?"

"He believed the same way as I did. You truly Watch over us. He watched you looking after your men at the smithy. We believe the same way to this day."

"That was one of the reasons we found the courage. They called us wicked for expanding to the unknown new places. You taught us things that didn't make sense to any of us at the time. But it made sense that you knew things that none of us could reach."

He embraced me with the warmth I had not felt for a while. An embrace of welcoming home a long-lost brother. "We believe our Guardian Angel will always watch over us. And here you are, still Watching over us. You won't let us fall."

"This time, I was the one who Fell, brother. An entire Legion had Fallen with me. That was on my behalf."

"That's not new. As far as I remember, you've been falling for this mystery woman. We've never been introduced to her. Now I'm concerned if she is actually a tale."

"Haven't I told you that she *is* a tale?"

"What's her name, Samael? Maybe I can ask around among the women here. We have gatherings with them every other week."

"They might be terrified for being asked about her, Tanith. Here in Ellada, they know her as Lamia. Back in Dimashq, we call her by—"

"Lilitu... Lilu? Was she the one in Nabu's story?"

"Yeah, that's my Lilith. The reason I've been flying around at night. I've always been searching for her. Including the very night that I walked you home.

Tanith, I don't think I ever deserve to be called a Guardian."

"Then what exactly is your Duty precisely, my Angel?"

"Punishment for sinners. And death. It wasn't always easy, especially when it came to someone I knew."

"Ah, now I understand. What you did to the molester was your Duty. To protect us from sinners who did harmful things."

"Exactly the reason I couldn't get too close to Lilith in the past. I could be hurting her. I care about her enough to keep my distance from her."

"My Angel Brother, the word 'care' is an understatement. You can fool others, but not Tanith or me. The entire time I've known you, not once have you ever looked the other way. Any other woman didn't catch your eye."

"Not even when my mother told you that I was unmarried at the time. You sent me straight into Hadad's life. That must be love that you have for her."

"Tell me, does she still look the way Nabu told us? Long black hair, green eyes, and the same skin as you?"

"The same night sky hair. The same emerald eyes. I believe her appearance hasn't changed that much.

We don't change the same way as humankind does. I hope her feelings haven't changed about me." My shoulders shrugged. *"I've been known to be that desperate when it comes to Lilith. I know."*

"What I'm thinking is the practicality. Search for her with the help of both worlds. You know, with your Legion in the sky. Your brother and sister search on foot at the same time. Tanith and I can search from the ground, while your Kind search from above."

"We'll ask around. You brought us together from the beginning. We would never be able to repay you for the Blessing. We built our family with your help. Have hope for Lilith the same way we have hope for you, Samael. You *will* find her again." She said it with a hopeful gaze towards me. Her hands held mine with confidence while she nodded.

"Anyway, Samael, have you heard that Shulmanu passed away? Nabu continues to run the smithy now."

"Yes, I know. I was there. I've told you it wasn't always easy for me."

"He must be glad that it was you who came at the end of his time. I'm sure of it. He always saw you as his Brother."

"That was precisely what he told me. But it was never meant to be less heavy for me."

"Samael, if it isn't too troubling for you... um, would you mind visiting me at the end of my time? I always believe that you're my Guardian Angel. You've always looked out for us. I can trust you with my life. And it's only right for you to be my Angel of Death."

"Oh, Tanith, my young lady... How can you see everything in a bright, sunny way?" There was so much heaviness in my chest when I delivered those words. Cupping her face, I said, "I wish I could see everything through your hopeful eyes."

"That was because I witnessed something that not everyone did. I have hopes for the both of you together. Maybe you can bring Lilith and introduce her to us."

"Well, I agree with Tanith. I want to meet her, too. I'll tell the story of how her beauty could make my Brother here so helpless. Even desperate all these times. I need to tell her that the tale is true. The Lilith only comes to a man who's been alone for too long. So you keep yourself to yourself for so long. Only to wait for her to come to you. I'm sure she'll come back to you."

"Hadad, my love, don't be ridiculous. Of course, she's beautiful and smart. And strong as well. Imagine all these years without Samael being her Guardian."

"You're right, Tanith. She's a strong one, though I don't think that she needs me to Guard her. I'm sure that it's me who needs her."

"Even more reason to start asking around about her. My Angel, have hope for her."

I meant it when I said it to her. Truly, I wished I could see everything through her eyes. There were times that I felt like losing hope in finding Lilith.

The gaze in Tanith's eyes was different than the gaze in Lilith's. My young lady might have been able to see the brightness of the Blissful Garden even when she was still on earth.

39

Catching Her Fall

His people were spread throughout the mountains and hills of Haemus. That included the regions of Illyria and Moesia.

Turiel built his homebase in Serdika, although he spent most of his time at the peak of Tangra. He was known as the Mountain of the Divine, Watching from the highest point of the Haemus. He was to see better and to guard solidly.

Those who were on the ground relayed a message. As soon as it landed in my ears, I made an immediate takeoff to his place. One of the Fallens under his leadership had crossed her path. If there were any clues about Lilith, I would follow them.

"Ah, my Great Prince has received the message."

"How far is she?"

"She's probably at the end of her pregnancy." He paused. With a pensive face, he was trying to read me. "Then what, Samael? What grand plan do you have in mind? Marrying her and settling down? Raising her children as your own?"

"Precisely, Turiel! Any problem with my grand plan?"

Turiel smirked at me, but more in a pitiful way. "And so the Great Prince has spoken. We shall follow you even then. We follow as we always do."

"Where was the last time any of you saw her? When?"

"Outbound of Kendrisiya. She was heading east a few nights ago. With her pregnancy being that late, you can still catch her flight in time."

"And anything else you want to say? Is there anything useful that makes any sense?"

"Actually, yes, before you go chasing her. I believe you might find yourself disappointed about your grand plan."

"And why is that, Turiel? If you'd care to share your concerns, now is the time."

"You didn't realise how powerful she was, did you? After all this time, you didn't? She was created to cause illness in newborns. Even her babies wouldn't stand a chance against her power."

"Not sure if I'm following the lead of this talk. Get to the point, will you? Don't waste such time."

"It was said that a hundred of her children would die every day. Those Ellenes even believe that Lamia eats their babies. You might find her, though

I don't think the Daddy thing is going to happen for you."

"Oh, you think the Daddy thing hasn't happened all these times? It isn't easy dealing with you, Watchers. Just like younglings running around, doing whatever have you, isn't it?"

When I was about to leave, I saw a pile of fabric for bedding and curtains. Pointing to the corner of his common room, I asked, "Can I steal those of yours?"

"Help yourself, Samael. Now, off you go. Pursue her. Now is the time she'd need you the most."

And so I left Turiel. Burgas was my best prediction. There was so much hope that I still had time to catch her flight. I could not miss her this time. I could not lose her again.

As fast as I could increase the speed of my flight, to her, I was heading. Homing. Inbound.

***

It was her scream that I heard while approaching the Atanasovsko Lake. Lilith was there, holding our newborns. Her waist and legs were under the water. She saw me coming for her.

The blanket landed on the dry ground. Circling to land in front of her, I kept her in sight. She crawled towards my landing path, crying. A celebration was what I wished to welcome me home. Instead, it was her devastation that greeted me.

"Oh, my Angel of Death, I surrender myself to you. Only to you, I submit. Take away this pain. I can't keep falling apart. Please, my Great Prince!"

"I'll catch you when you fall, my love."

Just in time, she fainted in my arms. She was still bleeding after giving birth in the water. Her beauty looked whole in my arms. So strong yet so delicate. My gentle care at a time like this was needed. "Oh, my Lilith."

I ripped off the cords that connected her to our babies. Her dress was soaked when I carried her out of the lake. Gently, I took it off with no permission. She was to be kept dry and warm. With the blanket, I wrapped her naked body.

While resting wearily in my arms, she sobbed unconsciously in between her breaths. My Lilith had submitted to me at her most vulnerable time.

"Rest, my love. I'm here with you, for you," I whispered in her ear. It did not matter whether she could hear me or not. She could feel me; I could feel her breathing a little easier now. So I laid her on the ground to rest after another tragedy.

No one would tell the difference between her blood and the pink colour of the lake. I kissed each one of our babies before laying them down.

I buried our three newborns near their sibling's graves. Their remains were to be kept close to one another.

After burying our babies, I sat still. That was when I felt something in my chest. Something that I could not explain. My tears could no longer be contained. Near the graves of all five I had buried, I took my moment to grieve.

"Oh, Our Most High, they deserve their place in Heaven. Not for their mother, not even for me, but for these pure souls. I've never known them, but they had my heart. They were all my children. All five of them were mine. And now they become your children in Heaven. Please give them their special place. Let these trustworthy words of mine be true."

Here, this Tasker wept. The tears of the Fallen One fell. From here, this Angel's prayer Ascended. Watching the sky, this Watcher hoped for the evaporated words to reach Heaven.

Outbound of Atanasovsko, just the two of us in the silent sky of the Earth. I kept our flight out as smoothly as possible. She deserved to rest in my arms. And I deserved to have her resting in my arms. She had claimed my heart since the time of origin. It had been a long time of waiting, only to have her here.

There were seven hills. We landed on the highest one. No one could possibly find us here. I simply wanted her to be safe. I wanted her to feel safe with me.

She needed her peaceful rest for a while. It had been too long for her to be alone. She had carried the weight of her burdens on her own. My Lilith was always capable of it.

40

The First Ray of Light

In my entire lifetime, I had always been able to survive being alone.

Each of us, on our own, was always sovereign. We were adept at relying on ourselves. Each of our sovereignties had built us to be self-sufficient. It was necessary.

Now we were to carry our weights together. Our weights and other weights we were carrying. Lilith and I would carry all of those together. Last night was our loss.

Getting lost was what had happened since I Fell without her beside me. This time, it was she who fell without me guarding.

She would not fall when I stood. As I would not fall when she stood.

Even if she fell, we would not fall when I stood. As we would not fall when she stood, even if I fell.

It was better for the two of us to be together. We would only have fallen if neither of us had stood. There was 'us' from now on.

The Old Man had his own Algol star in his large constellation. Lilith and I dancing in the sky would be our own Algol star in the here and now.

We kept orbiting each other. The two of us eclipsing would create a massive force. Let us build our own force within the work of our hands.

The Legion would revolve around Lilith and me. The allegiance would follow the lead of the Legion with its own revolution. Alliances on their own orbit would synchronise with the allegiance.

***

Watching Lilith sleep in for the entire night was fulfilling. It gave me the best feeling I had ever felt.

Her hair glowed beautifully when our first morning sunbeam hit it. She snuggled deeper into me before slowly opening her eyes.

"Good morning, Lilith. How was your sleep, my love?" My voice startled her.

"Samael? How—how is it possible? I'm too sinful to reach Heaven, my Great Prince." She paused, thinking. Her gentle hand touched my face to seek the truth in this reality. "You're one of the Fallens, aren't you?"

"Haven't I been falling for you since the time of origin? I'd do it again with no hesitation. And I'd be pleased to punish my sinner. This one is only mine to punish." My hand cupped hers on my cheek. My kiss landed on her palm.

Never had I imagined that the tragic moment would be my first time of touching her. To give her proof that she was not dreaming, I continued to caress her hand. From her hand to her forearm.

Her skin looked smooth in my eyes from afar. It turned out that I had been right all these times. Her skin was indeed as smooth as the silk that people in the far east made.

"I can't believe you're here with me." She hugged me tighter. She poured kisses anywhere that her lips could reach. Kissing me again and again.

Chuckling, I said, "You didn't tickle me in the past, but now you are. I don't mind, my love; that one never changes." I held her head and placed her ear close to my heart. "I'm here. My heart's been beating faster since I finally held you in my arms."

She put her hand on my chest, feeling me breathing. Every breath I took was for her. All the air in my lungs was hers. None of her words came out of her lips, but it was all right. Already, I knew what she wanted to say.

"My Lilith is so strong after all of this happened. If I may ask, my love, who took care of you all these times?"

Tears started to pool in the nurturing emerald eyes. It was not because she was weak that she cried. I could only imagine how exhausting it was for her to keep herself strong. All by herself for so long.

"Oh, my little bird, let me take care of you. You claimed me a long time ago. It's all right to rest your wings, for I'm here with you. Take a rest now."

We stayed here for a while without saying anything. It was more than enough explanation for me. Not a word of hers was needed to travel the speed of sound.

She was already small, like a precious stone in my hand. With her being vulnerable like this under the wrap, I just wanted to keep her safe.

Smoothly, I swung my body back and forth to get her to sleep. Her eyes were closing in relief as her breathing eased once more. My fingers kept brushing her hair until she fell into deep sleep.

Others might see me treating her like a newborn. Their thoughts were not mine to care about. This Lilith was indeed my bundle of happiness that I cared about the most.

***

Around noon, I woke her up gently. She needed to rest well, undoubtedly. But she also needed to know that I was not going to abandon her. "Lilith, my love, I need to go find some food and clothes for you."

Pouring my care on her, I kissed every part of her face. I wanted her to feel taken care of. She hugged me tightly in return.

"Please don't leave me. You only found me a while ago. Stay, please."

I felt her longing as much as I had been longing for her. "I shan't be long. I need you to heal. We're high enough on the hill for anyone not to find us."

She nodded and cupped my face with her small hand. And I made sure to kiss every part of her face one more time before I took off.

41

Gathering Our Council

"Have you got anything she can wear? I ripped off her dress. It was soaked with the water of her womb."

"Can you get a couple of women's clothes? Pack them with some food as well," said Turiel to his helper.

He turned towards me. His concerns were shown clearly on his face. "Is Lilith all right? Where is she now?"

"On the top of the seven hills. I appreciate your help."

He paused and hesitantly asked, "Are you all right, Samael?"

"*Why did he ask me that?*" No response from me; it was rather an unnecessary question. "Get all the Leading Watchers here on the day after tomorrow."

"Please be sensible this once. None of us can reach the far southeast that fast. We don't have as many wings as you do to fly higher to get there faster. Flying here is different than up above."

"Are you suggesting that I leave her alone so soon? It's you who needs to be sensible now. You don't necessarily have to go that far. Not if you kept practising to communicate from afar as being told."

"All right. All right, I get it. It's useful when it's needed. This time it is needed."

"That's what I've been saying all along. Have these younglings ever listened?"

"Why don't you bring her here tomorrow? We can prepare the guest room for her. I'll tell my helpers to assist her during her stay. Then you can get the Leaders in the far southeast."

It was nonsensical to leave her so soon. To be away again after finding her made me anxious. But his offer made sense. It was better than leaving her alone on the hill.

"All right then. But I don't want anyone touching her while she's here. Prepare a closed place for her bath. Three meals and as many small bites as she wants. I shall pay for your hospitality."

His smirk became so hideous that it almost made me punch him in the face. "I don't think I've seen this version of our Great Prince."

"Have you seen the version of me ripping your balls off and shoving them down your throat? I don't think choking to death that way would be majestic."

"She will be cared for in the way you told me. But please, you owe me nothing, Samael. I'd be pleased to Watch more of *this* version of you."

His helper handed me clothes and some food for us. "We weren't sure about her size, so my wife prepared two different ones. There's food for the both of you, our Great Prince. You need to be good as well."

"I appreciate your concern. When I bring her here, would you mind helping her with her meals?"

"I can only help so much. Perhaps it's better if my wife and daughter care for her. They can help with bathing and pampering, you know, to soothe her. So she can heal."

"That's very thoughtful of you. Send my regards to your wife and daughter."

"You see, amongst all of us, the Fallens, we see you as the only one who hasn't *actually* Fallen."

"Elaborate!"

"If there are times you've ever fallen, that would be for her. There's a reason why we, Fallens, look up to you even before our Fall. We have strong reasons to keep following you after that."

"I'd fall over and over again for her. You can trust my words, for sure. I'm not sure why you, Fallens, are foolish enough to keep following me."

"We fuck those grown daughters of men, yes. But I doubt any of us have ever fallen in love with any of them. Well, at least not the way you do with Lilith." Turiel tapped my shoulder and nodded. "There's a reason you've been called the Great Prince."

"You see, *that* got me confused. I've never asked to be called that way. Not after the Falling flight, not even in the time of origin."

"You've always had hope to be with her. Those who didn't understand might call you delusional." He chuckled in between his sentences. "But we, the Watchers, understood. We've Watched how you didn't stop. So we've put our Faith in you. We didn't just Watch your love for her. We Witness the kind of love."

"And the greatest one is love? Is that why? Huh, I never thought that you, younglings, were melodramatic."

"The greatest is Divine, Samael."

"Eve bore Cain from me. That was my betrayal. Therefore, I shan't be the Most High Holy Great One."

And so I left his place to go home to Lilith. She had always been my home. We spent the rest of the day and our first night on the hill. Only the two of us together.

42

Finding Sanctuary

The next morning, her gentle kiss woke me up. "Good morning, my Angel. How was your sleep?"

"Perfect, my love." In silence, I celebrated waking up to her beauty. As much as it soothed her, brushing her smooth hair kept me in a peaceful place. There was peace within the morning haze.

Her hand rested on my chest, then her chin rested on the back of it. Paying full attention, she asked me, "What do you think? About our first night?"

"It was perfect."

"Is there any other word that you can say besides 'perfect,' my love?"

"I love making love to you, Lilith. You made me whole."

"Oh, that was what you call making love?"

Undoubtedly, concerns must have filled my face. Although I could not see my own reflection, I could imagine my own face. "Was I that bad last night? You need to tell me if I did you wrong. It isn't about me alone."

"Last night was perfect. Though I wouldn't call it making love. It was a perfect fuck. So yes, you were *that bad*," she said, in a very bad way. Only the thought of it made me want to fuck her again. "We should do it more often."

"As much as I wanted a fuck, I was concerned. Well, you know, after giving birth. Without a womb, I wouldn't know what you've been through. I thought you might need some time to heal."

"I don't mind a bit of hurting. You might see me as small and fragile. Maybe because you have a bigger body than me. But I'm pretty sure that I'm all right." She continued with her teasing, "Besides, it's your Duty to punish sinners, isn't it?"

"Oh, I like my sinner to be bad. I'm keen on punishing this one." It still felt surreal that she was finally with me. "Lilith, I've never done this before. I might need to learn how to do it right."

"And what haven't you done precisely?"

I never thought about how calming her hand felt on my chest. She must know how intimidating it was to be with her. My Lilith was *the* Lilith. The one they had been spreading tales about.

"Sharing my life with someone other than myself. I've watched humankind with their wives. But doing it with you might be different. You're important to me. I need to keep you in my life."

Her smile was heartwarming to me. "And you still aren't a mind reader, are you?"

"No, that hasn't changed, as my feelings for you haven't. Even if my feelings have, they've grown bigger and rooted deeper. Would you mind sharing your thoughts if I don't do it right?"

"I wouldn't mind. I'll share my thoughts to be listened to. And some other times, I'll share my thoughts to ask for your help. I get myself into trouble sometimes. I shall let you know which one is which."

She kissed every part of my face again. "I might be annoying my Angel, too. I might not be able to stop sharing my thoughts. Would you mind if I shared my life with you as well?"

"I'd love to be a part of your life. I've been waiting for it." I kissed her lips gently while my hand started to trace her back. My hands now sat on her arse, following a command of their own. Squeezing her arse, I asked, "Are you still sore, my love?"

"A little bit. But you know, our bodies heal much faster than theirs, humankind's."

"Didn't I say I like my sinner bad?" My first spank landed on her arse. The first of many spanks ahead.

"Mmm... hmm," she hummed, nodding.

My fingers started to reach her pussy. "Oh, my Lilith... You're already drenched down there. Let me kiss and lick you better. Then I can start fucking my sheath real bad again."

Rubbing the crown of her pussy, I heard her saying, "It's my Master's sheath. Your cunt. Always remember that."

I rolled her over. It was the perfect breakfast that she served me. It was my time to devour her. It was the tasteful nectar that made me crave her even more. "So delicious, Lilith."

She slipped out a moan when I slid my fingers into her. The smooth inner walls of hers deserved to be woken up. She was sensitive to my touch. Her body easily answered my mating call.

My fingers inside of her felt her muscles clenching tightly. Everything she served was not to be wasted. Feasting on her crown until her rhythmic moan told me how near her release was.

"May I come now, Master? Please—" Her words could not keep up with her release.

"What did I tell you about coming without my permission?" Kissing her lips roughly, I let her taste the nectar of her release. I did not even give her time to reply. "That's bad, Lilith. You've been bad."

"Please forgive me."

My cock slid into her gently. "Call my name if I start to hurt you. You tell me to stop, then I shall."

"Yes, my Angel," with her tamed voice, she answered.

Trying to make love to her, I kept holding myself back as much as I could. Feeling her inside smoothness became my personal heaven. "You were made for me. My sheath. Mine, Lilith."

"Yes... Yours. Always yours to take." When she started moaning this way, holding back was no longer possible for me. It led me to start a rough fuck.

Her moan kept fuelling me to give this sinner the punishment she deserved. It might have been way too long of me fulfilling my Duty to punish those sinners. But I could not help myself; holding back on my desire for her was impossible.

Those moans and whimpers of hers were songs to my ears. It was her pleasure that I craved. It was rewarding for me to punish my own sinner with pleasure. More pleasures than she could handle. Pleasure was to be her reward for being bad.

"Do you want me to stop fucking you badly?"

"No, please don't stop. I disrespected my Master. Coming without your permission. Punishment is what you were created for. You were created for me. Punish me to please yourself, my Angel."

"And you were created to fit me. Only for me. Oh, you feel so good, Lilith... You think you deserve every drop of me?"

"I need every part of you inside of me. Please..."

Here she was, drowning me with her second release. Her tears dropped when I came inside of her. Seeing her cry like this was only fulfilling my primary duty. Knowing that it was not sad crying. It was something that needed to be cherished.

"But was I really that bad in her thoughts? Was I doing her right, though?"

43

A Nurturing Home

Kendrisiya was the first city for us to reside in. Right at the beginning of our marriage, we made plans. To build our home together in different places.

To move frequently around Haemus for the first couple of years was our earliest decision. Lilith had spent a couple of years living in this city prior to our reunion.

She opened the door of her house for me to live in. Somehow, I felt like a stray beast whom she let into her home. She provided shelter for this stray.

Here, my long-lost shirt reunited with me. Never had it ever been stolen from my house in Dimashq. She kept it safe on the bed as her blanket.

There was plenty to cherish in Kendrisiya. The city had so much potential. We had our morning walk every day. She let me know where she went and wandered.

She showed me her way of living. Her work was a way to bury herself to fill the void from loneliness. Her way was similar to mine in murdering the endless lifetime. Only during her pregnancy did she take time off from the place she used to work.

She introduced me, as her husband, to the neighbours. Of course, people asked further questions. We were to tell them the truth about us. We told them how we had lived far away from each other. That I was a blacksmith working with the miners.

We told them the truth about our babies not surviving. It was the truth that, right after the tragedy, I decided to follow her. It was the truth that my wife had become the most important thing in my life. Truthfully, I hoped that everything else would follow.

Freeing myself from work for a year was an effortless decision for me to make. There were enough of my belongings to provide for us. My decision was to follow her during the year or even beyond. Others might not be as fortunate as I was as a husband.

As much as I wanted to keep her for myself, I knew my limitations. Only until a certain point that I could soothe my wife. To be her perfect someone was never meant for me. I was Created whole, but perfection was never built within me.

On the outside, our bodies could heal fast. But for her healing on the inside, I was grateful for the women in this city. They had been so generous in soothing my wife beyond what I was capable of.

Lilith and I made another agreement after we got married. She was to be trusted in the kitchen. Her cooking was always fulfilling to me. She would trust me with the plants. She told me that she could not keep any of the plants alive.

She had quite a portion of land at the back of our house. Here I spent my day when she was not with me. There were more varieties of flowers grown for her. She deserved to wake up smelling the scent of the blooming ones.

For her cooking, we had herbs, leaves, stalks, tuber crops, root crops, and some fruits. To the neighbours or anyone knocking on our door in need of food, we shared some of our harvest.

"Ah, you're in time. I'm about to finish cooking for supper."

"Excuse me, lady? Uh, I'm Gundahar. A miner, uh, I'm here to see a blacksmith. I mean, the one be called Samael."

"Oh, you know my husband. Why didn't you say so? He's in the garden. Come in, then. You can call me Lilith."

"You're so beautiful, Milady. I—I'm sorry, it isn't appropriate."

"Of course, it isn't appropriate. You aren't stealing my wife, are you?" Embracing him, I said, "Still stutter when talking to a woman; I can tell."

"I still don't have your look, Samael. Of course, I stuttered. You're lucky I didn't pee on myself. It makes sense that you kept yourself to yourself for a long, miserable time. Those women didn't have your wife's look. Anyway, the little one is Gunther."

I lowered myself to him. "You can call me Samael. Let's pick some fruits for you, youngling. We grow plenty of them in the back. You'll see." I gave him a wink.

The little Gunther looked upward at his father. Once the father nodded, the little one held my hand to follow my lead.

***

Gundahar and I watched him run around the garden. Compared to his small body, it was massive. "Is he not one little curious wanderer, just like his father?"

"Haha, he is. I'm not sure how he keeps moving without getting tired."

"If you let him loose in this city, he might be wandering around the seven hills. With his small body, he might also dig caves under the hills. Just like his father did."

"Ugh, we better not let this little human loose. People might mistake him for a dwarf and catch him. He isn't yet talking, so he won't be able to explain himself. Haven't you got any children, Samael?"

"Do you see those plants in the far back?"

"The ones inside the fence?"

"Those Silphiums aren't for everyone. We had five, Gundahar. They didn't survive the sickness. I said goodbye when I buried them myself. Those plants are for her. I don't need to put my wife in such trouble again."

"It's hard to bury our loved ones, isn't it? My wife, his mother."

"How did she pass, if I may? The innocent ones aren't always mine to take."

"Gunther is actually our third one. We lost two unborn. Some of the neighbours talked and blamed my wife. People said that we were fools to try for the third. But we did. He was born healthy. My wife passed away not too long after. She was bleeding too much."

"My respect to you, brother. And how about work?"

"I made a promise before she passed. I missed the mining quests, though. I work on anything that allows me to bring Gunther. Not much of a choice. It's necessary so I can raise him myself."

"You've been missing her."

"I don't think I miss her that much for her to rise from her grave. Can't you see I'm becoming you in the past? Not seeing any other woman while raising my youngling. Are you familiar with the story?"

"I am, indeed. Haha."

"Because I've seen you live that alone life, I know I can do it, too. Only this time, I'm with Gunther. Care to share anything before you forget about your lonely life?"

"Seems that you forgot about my story with the woman after her."

"No, I didn't forget it. Didn't mean I'd stop asking for a clue."

"At the time, I hadn't Fallen from Grace. Neither had I any discipline to deny rage within me."

"It was an everyday battle, was it? To be faithful to her."

"One thousand years here is only a day in Heaven."

"So it isn't that long for my wife."

"You can focus starting with that thought. The impulse within is only another thing to deny."

"Does she know?"

"I confessed. But she had already known about it. If only my confession had come to her first." Both of us took our deep breaths almost at the same time. Some things we had not let go of yet.

"Goran started to bring Ognyan when he was around fourteen. Once Gunther's old enough, maybe you should work in our smithy. So you can continue spreading whatever myth you told them about me."

He covered his mouth with his palm, flabbergasted. "You heard about that?"

"As I said a long time ago, different people said different things about me. What you told them about me was rather kind. You know, compared to the other ones."

"I agree to spread the myth even further. From where I come from, they call you the hermit in the mountain. They need to start calling you the hammering man, though. You aren't only a miner but also a blacksmith."

"Why hermit?"

"Well, mostly you're clothed like us for the day. Other times, you wore your dark-hooded cloak like a hermit. You helped the good miners. But you enjoyed giving trouble to the bad ones. A lot of troubles. I could see you enjoyed it."

Hearing his story gave me delightful laughter. "Couldn't help myself when those younglings couldn't help themselves. Them being disrespectful in the copper womb tickled my nerves."

There was a gratitude for every word that came out of his mouth, even if it was another myth about me. Gundahar did not talk much. It was not right for him to keep everything to himself, especially when raising his son alone.

"Still need to be careful with your poisonous words. Have you ever heard me talk this much to anyone?"

I shook my head, giving him an answer.

"Precisely!" With Gundahar, eliciting worked the best for me. His defence crumbled before my questions reached him.

"I say you two should spend a few days here. Lilith must be glad to have a little one in our house. And I shall keep you telling more tales."

"We'd appreciate it, Samael. We can spend the night, but we're actually on our way to Aibunar. I've heard that Goran has been sick."

"He's been sick for a while now but stubborn enough to keep working. What can we say? That's typical of Goran."

"But if we stay longer here, I'm not sure if—"

"Oh, I know it isn't his time yet."

"Ah, yes, I forgot *that* one little detail about you."

"You shouldn't worry about it. We shall be there in time. Besides, we need to see the youngling's face when being carried to fly."

He gasped. "What? Fly?"

44

Heirlooms

A few days later, the four of us headed to Aibunar. Gunther, as predicted, was amazed throughout our flight. His innocent eyes were filled with wonder when Lilith carried him flying.

His father, however, vomited once we landed. So had Goran been in the past. Goran's first flight had also been my first time carrying anyone. Apparently, my skill at carrying humankind had not improved since then.

Lilith never had any problem with me carrying her. She was a being of the sky. Our flight time was always freeing. There was freedom for us within the air.

One day in the future, humankind would try to gain freedom in the sky. Obviously, not in the same way we did. Regardless, they would make things to carry them flying. Until then, the Watchers were only to Watch. Let them learn from the birds.

We stayed with Goran and his unmarried daughter, Kelila. The particular humankind kept being stubborn even after we arrived. As always, he was known to be persistent with his work. Undoubtedly, a loyal one.

He showed us what the smithy had become. There were plenty of tales he told little Gunther. The plot of how the mining process went allured the youngling.

The storytelling uneased Gundahar. He wondered whether one day his son would be a miner as he had been one. The father knew how perilous the work could be.

Ognyan did not help with the concerns that much since he only added the sparks to his father's tales. It took my wife to tell the little one that his bedtime was calling.

***

Goran understood the reason I came this time. One night, he gathered his children.

The night was time for Goran to share the story of the origin of his son's name. Ognyan Goranov did not believe it at first. As he recalled the many moments of his childhood, it all made sense to him.

It was Goran's last wish for himself, Gundahar, and me to start the fire once more. We made heirlooms for his children. From good materials this time, not from scraps.

One heirloom for his daughter, Kelila Goranova, to be passed down to her daughter. A diadem decorated with precious stones. This time, the art piece was not made with Lilith entirely in my mind. This time, the inspiration came from the Crown of the Most High.

The Stone of Heaven sat at the centre of it. So that the woman who wore it had a mind as vast as the sky. Azurite represented the eye colour of its maker, the one who planted the Tree of Knowledge. She would know how to separate the good from the evil.

A carnelian stone sat on the left of it. On its right, there was an emerald. Both stones represented Lilith's changing eye colours. One stone became the opposite of the other. One another, they balanced each other.

My Lilith was whole, as was this diadem. A grown descendant would wear this diadem upon giving birth. It was to proclaim the sovereignty of a mother. She was to be the ark of her descendants.

One heirloom for Ognyan to be passed down to his son. A flame-bladed sword with riverflow patterns. The heir would raise this flammard sword towards the sky when his elder passed away.

The sword was to separate the cloud, giving a path of ascension. There would be an open path towards Heaven by the order of the Angel of Death. The

Beings in Heaven would recognise who the sword maker was.

***

We all could tell that our brother's passing was not easy for Ognyan.

There were many questions as to why I, as someone he and his father trusted, should be the one who came at the end of Goran's time. Those questions remained unanswered in his mind. At least for the time being.

After the passing of Goran Goranov, Azazel came. He helped us to teach the miners and blacksmiths. It was important to make a smooth transition during this grieving time.

The four of us then flew back to Kendrisiya. Little Gunther fell asleep in the middle of our journey. The second time of flying was easier for Gundahar. He did not vomit once we landed.

Once again, the place of his origin became heavy in Gundahar's heart. Lilith and I asked him to stay a bit longer. We let him see if the city would suit Gunther's upbringing. We let his sound mind decide.

45

Rooted Home

"Milady Lilith, I apologise. We didn't mean to cause you two so much trouble. I feel awful about it."

"That. is. nonsense! We love having this little man around the house. Why don't you give him to me? I know you haven't slept all night." Lilith offered some help with Gunther.

"Follow me, Gundahar." Bringing a basket and a pot, we went to the garden. "These leaves go to the pot, as do these roots and those stalks."

"How much?"

"For his small body, a handful of each will be enough."

I moved to the other part of our garden. "The herbs are different. We can't use them if they're too young or too mature. Pay attention to their stalks. That's how we can tell how much they have aged."

Gundahar was always a quick learner. "Like this one?"

"Yes, that'll do. They go to the basket. We make some tonic from them. Ah, before I forget." I took some of the flowers before we returned inside.

"These white flowers can be made into a hot drink. He can't be lacking in drink. They add fragrance so it'll smell nicer."

Once we were in the kitchen, I started the fire. Together we prepared remedies for Gunther. "We boil the leaves, roots, and stalks for his bath. He inhaled the aroma to clear his breath."

He placed the pot on the fire. "What do I do with the pestle and mortar?"

"We make the tonic for him. He needs it three times a day. We make it fresh every day."

"Do I only crush them or make it like a paste?"

"Crush. Make sure you clean the herbs thoroughly. Check their roots and stalks before crushing them."

***

Lilith and I agreed that a decade might be the longest to reside in one place. Unless there was a particular reason to prolong it.

We could not let them realise that we had not changed through the years. When we had nothing new to learn, then it was our time to move to another place.

Gunther was getting better a few days later. We told Gundahar about the time of our stay. Lilith decided to leave her house for him. A new neighbourhood might be good to raise his son. And of course, we left the garden for Gunther to explore further.

It was fascinating that Gundahar turned out to be better at talking back. He persuaded me and Lilith to prolong our stay. He agreed that there might not be anything new for us to learn. But he argued that there were still things to teach in Kendrisiya.

He witnessed how the plants worked well with Gunther. From there, he was eager to learn about each one in the garden. He wanted to know how to use them to help others.

We introduced Gundahar and Gunther to our neighbours. At the same time, we asked for their favours in the garden. One of their sons and two of their daughters came to our house every day.

It was supposed to be for the following couple of moon cycles. Then moon cycles were prolonged into a year. More sons and daughters of men came to learn about our plants. They were keen to learn to make remedies.

We had opened our smithy for apprentices to train. We worked on what had been dredged from the mines. Now we were once again to open our door. This time, we welcomed the apprentices into our garden. We worked on the plants that the soil had nurtured.

Lilith became quite busy cooking for all of us. She insisted on cooking three meals and two light meals. Gunther mostly helped her make a mess in the kitchen. That way, I witnessed how motherly Lilith could be.

She taught him to speak the language of their origin, even though they speak a different language here. Lilith insisted that he should not forget where he and Gundahar came from. That question I had missed asking.

If it were not for this father and son, I would not know that Lilith had been among the Volcae. She had lived around Hercynia Silva. And then among the Boii she had lived.

I had been right about my wife. Without me, her curiosity had led her to wander the earth. Now she had me with her. She was to be kept interested. I could not rely solely on our mating time.

46

Transitions

The Beginning Time of Dimashq Steel

"Gundahar, this is Armaros, another of my Kind."

"I've heard so much about you, Gundahar."

"Oddly, I've never heard anything about you. What do you do as a Tasker? The same with Samael?"

"No, my Task is different from his. But my task here is to show you how to neutralise what he makes with you."

"Neutralise as if what? Samael, I'm lost."

"Hasn't this youngling been lost and kept wandering around?" The sight of his confused face was amusing in itself.

"What we make can be healing, but you know that already. What you didn't know is that those can be as venomous as deadly. If you don't make them the right way, you need to know how to nullify them."

"Ah, I get it. So you called him because he knows how to resolve the wrong remedies."

"You were right about this one, Samael. He learns quickly."

"One moment, please. I need to digest it. You really told them about me?"

"My Kind needs to know where the myths came from. So they can Watch you closely."

Gundahar clearly could not see himself as an important being. At least in Kendrisiya, he was indeed important. His myth about me made him an important source of knowledge in the foreign land.

"Even my name tells how I could be ' the Most High's Venom.' In another meaning, it's 'the Medicine of the Most High.' There are always the two sides of me."

"I didn't know that. Another myth I need to spread around."

"The meanings behind my name weren't relevant back then. Nothing more than that. In this very moment, they are."

"Makes me wonder how much of what you know hasn't been told to us."

"One thing I haven't told my wife yet. One day she will hear it, but not yet now." A day of reminiscence about Heaven might feel like one thousand years on earth. "There were those seeds I buried in the Blissful Garden. Lilith saw it as me planting them, so she cared for them."

"What kind of plant?"

"The kind of Knowledge of Good and Evil. From those seeds, it became a Tree. For our Kind to distinguish between the two. Do you remember the woman after Lilith left the Bliss?"

He nodded without any words.

"She picked one of the Fruit. She ate it first and shared it with her husband."

"Clearly, I'm captivated by this Saga. Go on, tell me more."

"The short version of the Saga these younglings need to know is to measure. You need to know how much those plants become medicines. Also, you have to understand how much of them will become venoms."

He became the old-time Gundahar who struggled to elaborate his thoughts. "Are both to be used?"

"Both are useful for different purposes. As this Tasker is useful as a Medicine and a Venom for the different Tasks at the given time."

"If I may, Samael... Uh, how many of us blame you?"

"Haha. Highly misunderstood since the time of origin. I simply gave up convincing anyone." I turned my face away from the troubled humankind. "Armaros, these younglings are your trouble now. Show them how to make it right if they mess up."

Lilith and I gave the warmest farewell to Gunther. We shall meet him again one day in his lifetime. Probably later in his life, we would be like a family again. He would be another youngling in our house.

***

The day after I took Lilith as my wife, I promised a year of following her. But I ended up teaching the sons and daughters of men.

When I apologised to Lilith, she did not accept it. She said that having Gunther helped her heal on the inside. As much as he helped her, she nurtured his rooted memories of home.

Although she said that she did not need me to apologise, that did not make me any less wrong in my mind. This time it was not her or them blaming me.

Another year of following my wife was needed to keep my promise to her. This was my path of making amends. Other Watchers understood when I sent the words.

From Kendrisiya, we moved to Aibunar. Having Azazel work with Ognyan surely helped him gain comprehension. It took quite some time for Ognyan to realise that his father's passing was another cycle in life.

He eventually understood that death could come one way or another. His father had given me his loyalty a long time ago. It only felt right for me to release him from it.

The loyalty his father had given me was never meant to be passed down. None of his descendants were under the obligation. It was important for Ognyan and Kelila to understand it.

We spent a couple of moon cycles helping Ognyan make some adjustments to running the smithy. Although the men in the smithy were helpful, they were eager to know about the new thing that started to catch many ears.

As we heard, the blacksmiths had become more famous for their metalwork. The Dimashq Steel was only starting. Azazel and I agreed that it was not right to put my hands on it too soon.

We did not think it was right for us to interfere with their process. We needed to Watch how they were doing a bit longer. Let them fall and learn from it on their own paths.

Lilith and I decided to return to Dimashq. But first, we needed to make a stop in Aktiki. Our next path was to fulfil a request from my long-time allies.

47

Their Hell on Earth

"Still looking over your shoulder, I can see. Having a hard time sleeping, young lady?"

"Oh, my Guardian Angel is here. Hadad, wake up, my love. Look who's coming!"

"Great to see you again, old friend. I've never seen so many wings. Oh, wait, I've never seen any pair of wings in my entire life. Except for the birds, of course.

Lilith was waiting at the door until I invited her inside. "Tanith, Hadad, this is my wife, Lilith."

She lowered herself beside Tanith. "I heard that you're such a strong woman."

"Well, not as strong as you are, my lady angel."

"I'm not an angel, Tanith. Was never created as one."

"That's nonsense. Come sit next to me, Milady Lilith."

She gave Lilith space in her bed. My wife held Tanith's hands. Both of them were the strong ones, forged in hell on the face of the earth.

"Well, your husband here has been Guarding my wife. And looked after us, his younglings, at the smithy. If you didn't know that he has younglings, I'm telling you, he has many of us."

His laughter stopped. "Milady kept him in hope for so long. If that wasn't the work of an angel, then we don't know what an Angel truly means."

"A Tasker. The word simply means 'Tasker.' Angels need to fulfil the Tasks," I explained.

"And I've heard that you two are good at keeping things to yourselves. That helped my husband in some way. As you know, he fulfils his Duty at night."

"That's at least what we could do to repay the Blessing." Her attention moved towards the black wings. Tanith asked, "Are they strong, Milady?"

"They're strong enough to carry me flying. You can touch them."

The ageing hands of my young lady gently touched the feathers. Those years in her lifetime had given her grey hair as a crown. Wrinkles on her skin had built storylines. Each line would be the force for her in climbing the ladder towards Heaven. In my eyes, she would remain a young lady for the rest of eternity.

"Your wings suit you, as black as your shiny hair."

"No wonder that your husband here never looked at any other woman. He kept himself alone all the time, only for you. We made quite a lot of fun of him sometimes."

"And by sometimes, you meant most of the time. You couldn't leave me alone even for a bit, could you?"

"We couldn't help it. Oh, especially when Milady cooked supper for him. He got more creative reforging those scraps. More beautiful things he made."

Tanith reached for something under the edge of her bed. She gave her knife to Lilith. "Speaking of which, my Guardian Angel made me this beautiful piece. I carried it everywhere I went, even keeping it under my bed every night."

Lilith turned towards me. "This is beautiful, my love."

"It was necessary at the time. I wish no woman ever needed to carry one of those."

"Since I won't need it in the place where I'm going, it'd be right for Milady to keep it. It's as beautiful as you are."

"That's very kind of you. I promise to carry it everywhere I go. And I shall always remember how strong and hopeful you are." Cupping Tanith's face, Lilith said, "One day, when your son marries someone, this will go to his wife. And then his daughter, or his son's wife. And so on."

"I always thought that you were a tale, Milady Lilith. What an honour to finally meet you! I wish only the best for both of you. And, my old friend, thank you for everything you taught me. To think differently about creating something beautiful. To make something valuable from what anyone thought were scraps. And for finding me a wife. She's the best thing that ever happened in my life."

"And I cherish every moment of our time, Hadad."

"We leave you our house here if you need to settle for a while. Our son, Ashur, returned to Dimashq. He's at your smithy. If only he could learn under your Guidance, Samael. He's young and still has so much to learn."

"Hadad, there are many good blacksmiths for him to learn from."

"I believe you've heard about Dimashq Steel. It'll need knowledge from your Kind to forge it right. My time has passed, but his time has only begun."

"There's nothing for you to worry about from now on."

My kiss landed on Hadad's forehead while Lilith was hugging Tanith tightly. Her black wings covered my young lady's eyes from seeing.

"Farewell, old friend." Then I laid Hadad's cold remains to rest.

Tanith kissed her husband on the cheek. "I'll see you soon, my love."

I was now sitting where Lilith had sat, beside Tanith. I lifted her body and placed her on my lap. And then I hugged her tightly in my arms. "You no longer need to look over your shoulders. You'll always be my young lady, full of hope. That's your grace, Tanith."

"I'm glad that it's my Guardian Angel who put me to rest. Thank you for keeping me safe all these times."

Cupping Tanith's face, I kissed her lips gently.

Releasing her was to keep my promise to her.

She kissed me back until she did not.

Tears flowed down my cheeks. Eventually they fell onto her cold remains.

"Oh, my young lady, there's no more hell for you on earth. There's only Heaven from now on."

From fire, I was Created to Guard the raging fire of the North in the Third Heaven.

But this young lady had walked through the burning hell on earth.

She walked through her hell strongly because hope had always been lwithin her.

The Watchers saw the hope within me. It had always been Tanith's voice that resounded in my ears.

While I ran my fingers through her grey hair, I felt that her hope lived. It surpassed the young lady's lifetime.

A Task was fulfilled. With her lifeless flesh in my arms, this Tasker mourned.

Lilith's gentle hand woke me up. "Come, my love. Let's lay them under to rest."

48

The Abyss

They had been inseparable since I introduced them. We should not separate them in burial. Their remains were laid next to each other because they deserved to rest in peace together.

Only until a certain point could I hold my emotions. Near their graves, I sat with a quiet mind. Quiet... until it was completely silent.

My state of mind went into a trance.

Descension was here and now.

It landed me in the abyss.

The dark place was void.

It was filled with nothingness.

The void was where my lifetime paused.

The pressure in the air was different at this depth.

My eyes did not blink even once.

Tears started glazing them until they fell.

Like a waterfall stream, they burst silently.

Snot ran down from my nose.

The flesh of my Being remained in stillness.

My ears heard the ringing sound.

Ringing into roaring, and then into buzzing.

The silence of the abyss whispered in my ears.

The reflecting darkness of it was already revealing its charms.

All of its hidden potentials were alluring me in.

The dark void was in stillness, waiting for my shadow side to take over.

This Alchemist was tempted.

Transmutation was so close. Too close.

The unalignment of my mind and my Being almost imprisoned me in the boundless depth.

"Come home to me, my Angel." It was the sound I recognised.

The hair on the back of my head always rose when expecting her arrival.

Her words flew straight to my heart, shattering the medium-less space and time.

Her voice, softly and calmingly, woke up my mind.

The gentle voice of hers became louder in my head.

"Come back to me, my love. I know my Angel can hear me. Just follow my voice to the here and now."

Her fire ignited a torch for me to realign with my twin.

She was the beacon to help me navigate.

My consciousness was now in its course, homing towards her.

Ascending I was, out of the abyss to the here and now on earth.

She stood our ground. The gate she built for us was powerful. Her defence did not let the boundless depth trespass our boundaries.

"It's time for us to go. Why don't we take a walk? Then you can have me however you need."

It was her voice that brought me back home. Her touch settled me down at home. Lilith shielded me in her embrace, keeping me from breaking into pieces. She poured kisses onto me.

"And thereafter, you should rest in my arms. Let me caress you this time."

She washed my hands, gently rubbing the dirt off them. Lilith was always meticulous. She wiped them dry with a piece of cloth. The way she took care of me was always thoughtful. That was what I loved about her.

Begging for her mercy, I looked into her nurturing eyes. "Would you trust me, my love?"

Her soft, caring hand held my face gently. "For the rest of eternity, I would, my Angel."

49

The Lingering Essence of Her

We took off to the higher ground with me carrying her. And on the highest ground, we landed.

Tanith's lingering essence might have remained within me. Once her pain sank in, it could have been infecting me further in my lifetime.

She had been a strong woman. It had to be a much stronger one to wash Tanith out of me. "Kiss me, Lilith. Kiss me until I can no longer taste her pain."

As ordered, she kissed and lapped my lips. "Every part of me will be the only thing my Master taste. Only mine and no one else's." Tilting her head, she led me to her neck. My tongue tasted the scent of her flesh from neck to ear.

I wanted her taste to fill me. I needed her scent to be all over me. "Lilith, my love, I know myself better than you do. It's all right if you refuse. There's only rage inside my head. I don't think that I can be gentle this time."

"Haven't I told you that you can have me however you need? I meant it when I said it. I trust you." She paused for a kiss. Those permissive words sounded as if they were a challenge. "Besides, since when has my Master ever made love to me?"

She continued to rub my hardening cock. She was only a few layers of fabric away from having me. She let me kiss her roughly, taking every breath out of her.

One hand of hers wiped away my tears while the other one slid to reach what was hers. The way she held my cock and stroked it put me in my place. She then kept me still, demanding to be listened to.

"Do it for me. You let me feel your love. Now let me feel your rage. Finish what you started." Her words not only fuelled me but also combusted me. Hers burnt me up while burning everything else down.

Roughly, I ripped off her dress. There was no time to wait for her to do it by herself. Otherwise, we could have been too late.

Moving down to her breasts. Nibbling her lactating nipples one by one. Sucking her breast milk as I needed to be full of her. Sucking them empty was always the right way.

It was the only way to make her live within me for the rest of eternity. Her fire purified the hell that Tanith had walked through. Her milk cleansed me of any remaining taste.

The lively liquid was Lilith's way to cool my head down. My unsound mind was exploding in rage. All the tension from fulfilling my Duty was now relaxed. There was calm now. Then calm became hunger.

She squirmed when I licked her stomach. It might tickle her a bit, but I simply did not care. It was my time to be selfish since she surrendered herself to me in Burgas.

As I kept moving down, I sought refuge in her underworld. Spreading her legs apart, I found her already drenched for me. From her hood, then I kept moving to her inner thigh. All of hers deserved to be praised.

She had smooth legs, although I know that they had endured a long path in life. Strong enough to keep her standing by herself when we were apart. Kissing her knees one by one. They only knelt and crawled towards me.

Her body knew how starving I was. Her swollen glans served only for my mouth to consume. Her pulsating tunnel knew how thirsty I was, so it welcomed my tongue home.

The nectar of her arousal was the only drink in the universe that could fulfil my thirst. I squeezed the providing breasts, as if they were the only thing I could hold onto. As if my life depended on them.

Her moans became the best song my ears had ever heard. Her whimpers ignited the flame inside of me. "Fill me with your rage, Master. Let me feel what hell really feels like from the inside. Please... purge me inside out." She should not have asked for it, because that was what I was giving her.

Ramming my cock inside her. Sheathing my entire sword. Her wrists were restrained in my grip above her head. Her tears started running down while I sought redemption.

How beautiful it was to have her whimpering and moaning. Surrendering and craving at the same time. "Do you want me to stop, Lilith? You tell me to stop, and then I shall stop for you."

"Please, don't. Be free with me. Let me serve my Master." She knew I would never get enough of her. However she served me, I always craved more. "Have me as your feast the way you want. No matter how hard I cry, you don't need to think about me. I shall call your name if I can no longer take you. Every part of me is yours to have."

My hand moved to hold her neck gently. Those emerald eyes were glazed when I held her in her place. When her pussy clenched tighter, her moans started to get louder.

"Come for me, my night butterfly, like a filthy one. Sheath my sword tight when you come."

"Yes. Mmh..."

"Yes, what, Lilith?"

"Yes, Master."

Licking the tears off her cheeks. Thrusting her pussy wilder. The wilder I fucked her, the tighter she held me inside of her. I held myself back from slapping her face when she came.

"That's my filthy night butterfly. You feel so good when you come. You make me feel so proud. It isn't easy to take me rough." I tapped her cheek twice, rewarding her for coming for me.

"You don't need to hold yourself back. I know that you are. Trust me, Master, I can take you."

It felt like Lilith knew me better than I did after all these times. So I rolled her over. She was on her stomach waiting for me to return home once again. With my hands squeezing her arse upward, my cock slid freely into her. She needed to be ridden well and badly this time.

I pulled a fistful of her hair and whispered to her, "You were right, Lilith. I was holding back, but I'll no longer be this time. Do you still want this?"

"Yes, mmh... Please don't stop."

My other hand was to caress her smooth back. If only I could scratch her back and leave red scars on it. Taming this beautiful night creature. Taming myself from the rage.

"Now I'm not sure if I should treat you like my good little bird or use you like a filthy night butterfly."

I slid her hands under her stomach. "Touch yourself, Lilith. Just like you did when you fucked those sinners. You gave me a show in the past, watching you play with your little hill. Now make yourself come again. Let me feel how well you please what's mine. Tell me, is it still my sheath?"

"It'll always be the sheath for my Master's sword."

Every beating pulse inside of her pussy was for me. Burying my entire existence, only to live in her underworld.

"Don't be shy, Lilith. My little hill needs to be fucked roughly." Both of my hands sought balance on her shoulder. To fuck her rougher than before.

She widened her hood and rubbed her crown wilder. "That's more likely, Lilith. Do you like pleasing my sheath like this?"

"Yes, Master."

My sheath was close to coming. Once again, I could feel it. "Then don't hold yourself back. Be rough with my belongings."

Her pussy clenched tighter. More of her tears ran down. Her small body shook when she released herself. Her come melted my last guard of gentleness. Her release gave me the fuel to fuck her even harder.

From her shoulders, my hands slid under her chest. My arms held her entire body from behind; she was not to move away from me. My legs locked hers together. "You're the filthy one, aren't you? You want this body to be used selfishly?"

"Indeed, Master."

My cock was to thrust into her deepest realm. Until I could no longer hold my hell from breaking loose. Holding her body tighter, I buried my rage in her underworld.

Her flood of release purged me. "Thank you, my Angel," she said once I came inside of her.

With Eve, my rage lived. It remained inside of her as my seed grew inside of her womb. It was completely different with my wife.

Inside of Lilith, I gave my rage the death it deserved. She gave me a rebirth when the rage was no more.

50

The Scent of Home

Here I was, on top of her back. Tamed. While catching my breath, I inhaled the scent of her flesh. She brought me back home from the abyss.

Heaven was never perfect, but whole. There was only heaven on earth with her. Neither Lilith nor I was created as perfect.

"You've been good, little bird."

My chest was never unlatched from her back as I rolled our bodies. We watched the morning sky together. My red star was up there along with the others. It was the morning star for me to Rule, but my home was here and now with her.

"I think I need to learn how to make love to you. To be gentle with you."

"Hmm..." She turned towards me without saying anything else. Simply smiling while she played with my beard. She took a closer look at my face.

My hands continued to cherish her silky skin. "But I'm still not a mind reader, Lilith."

"My Angel, you're always gentle with me. In everything you do for me, I can feel your care. Even when you're mating me roughly, you caress me right after. Just like this very moment."

"Undoubtedly I care about you. But to hurt you hurts me, too. Sometimes I forget that you're small compared to me. And you're soft and—"

"And you know that I'm not soft or fragile. I've been leading my way alone for so long. But I'd love to follow your lead. Giving me the peace of mind that I can trust someone other than myself. Now kiss me, my love."

"Ah... My little bird can be demanding, as I can see. Do you want a kiss or a hug?"

"Both, my love. I want both. Lots of them."

"Well, I was wrong then. My Lilith isn't only demanding but greedy as well."

She fell asleep in my arms easily. I carried her flying to Hadad's house. Letting her rest her wings once in a while might be good for her. It was good for me on the inside.

After laying her down in bed, I kept running my fingers through her hair. "Lilith, I need to go for a moment. I shall return as soon as I can."

"Please don't leave me for too long. I need you here with me."

"Only for a while." I kissed her as much as I could without being ticklish. "You have claimed me, Lilith."

She nodded, half asleep. Before leaving, I looked around to see what we might need for the day. I had never cooked for Lilith since the time of origin. It felt right to let her rest from cooking in the kitchen today.

They sold me some ingredients at the market. As promised, I returned immediately without making another stop. I did not want her to wake up without me around.

***

Around noon, I woke her up, bringing the lunch to bed. "Lilith, it's time to eat. I made you something."

She woke up with pouting lips. "You shouldn't have to. I'm the one who should be cooking for you."

"Oh, Lilith... You've been cooking for me every day. Can I have at least one day to cook something for you?" Kissing her temple gently, I then scooped up her meal. "Here, have some. You need to eat, my love."

She closed her eyes as she breathed in her first bite. How lovely she looked when I fed her. Her hands sought comfort on my chest.

Her emerald eyes were looking at mine. The face she gave me was as if I had returned home from winning a battle. She knew how to show me how proud she was of me.

"Thank you. Have some for yourself. You need to eat, too."

After having a bite, I almost choked on the food. "All right, now I know it isn't as pleasant as your cooking. I'm not that good in the kitchen, you see."

"I shall have anything you give me. I appreciate the way you take care of me. You're important to me."

Feeding her the next bite and the next one until she finished her lunch. Our time like this was something to enjoy and cherish.

My little bird should have been fed more frequently. Not because I wanted to make her dependent on me. But because of that gaze during her feeding time. Because of the soul that I saw through her emerald eyes.

She made me feel appreciated. That she was appreciating everything I provided for her. Appreciating my effort. Appreciating me being with her.

***

It was fulfilling to see Lilith enjoy her time. She met new people here in Aktiki.

She was important to me. She became my priority. As I always believed, everything else would follow.

I wanted her to be the most important part of my life. I wanted to be a part of her life as well. I was still on my path to deserve her.

We stayed in the house for an entire year before returning to Dimashq. I could not wait to show Lilith about the smithy and what we had been working on so far.

51

A Fallen Youngling

The Time of Dimashq Steel

The house that had witnessed so much compassion. It had become a home for the wealthiest ones. Those who had become wealthy from the abundance they had built.

Here was the place that we were familiar with. The place where loneliness had been my companion without her. It was the house that had witnessed the void in our hearts.

At the two-thirds mark of the night, Lilith followed me into the house. We paid a visit to an old friend of mine. He had become one of my men. Near the fireplace, he fell asleep on his seat.

Placing my hand on his shoulder, I woke him up. "How is this youngling doing?"

"It turns out my eyes weren't wrong at all. Your skin truly glows like stars near the fire, Samael."

Turning my face towards Lilith, I asked her to come closer to us. "I believe you met my wife, Lilith, a long time ago."

"Not once in my entire long life have I seen him with any other woman. This one can testify if needed. He kept himself only for you, my fair Lady."

Their eyes met when she lowered herself. "I'm glad that someone finally found the love of his life. He was desperate, Milady. That one, I can also testify." He glanced at me.

"Nabu, what I did to you in the past wasn't right. Your forgiveness is something I can only hope for."

"It was Samael with Shulmanu. They actually warned me a lot of times. I started a lot younger than others back then. A foolish teenager who was full of flaws... mostly ignored anyone's warning. You were only waking me up. I should thank you for that."

"If it wasn't for you, my husband could never have heard of me returning to this city. That one I'm always grateful for."

"I was only trying to have his back, warning him. Even talked bad things about you. The same way Samael here always had our backs whenever we got into trouble."

He smiled, remembering the way he had been in the past. And the kinds of foolishness he had done. "Mostly me. He took care of us at the smithy. You've got yourself a Great One for a husband. And you're as beautiful as the first time we met."

While pausing, he watched Lilith closer. "No, wrong. You're far more beautiful than in the past. Your skin is still lighter than ours here. But it's no longer pale. There's glow now."

What he said made my wife smile. "Ah, see that, Samael? Her face is blushing. Must be you doing her right. This old youngling knows women. Haha."

"I still don't feel like deserving *this* Angel."

"You two become foolish younglings now? Both of you deserve each other. Too bad that the wedding planner missed the weekend supper. Tell me, how was the wedding going without me? Tell me nobody came."

She giggled, "He and I did. He made sure the other Angels were there to witness us. And then he branded me."

"Those I didn't foresee. The wedding planner isn't that notorious after all."

Lilith gave Nabu a kiss on his forehead. She then took a seat in front of him.

"So, I heard about the metalwork. It's quite famous out there in foreign lands."

"Samael, it all started with the work of your hands. Playing around with copper, tin, and then bronze. And even gold. Let's not forget about that. Who thought about gold at the time?"

"We just happened to have known since the time of origin."

"That one thing I forgot. Haha... Ancient, indeed. You might forget, but you taught us not to be afraid to mix one with the other."

"No, I don't forget easily." It was my turn to have a seat beside him. "But how to forge them wasn't always known to me before coming here."

"We made lots of useful things back then. So I guess we learnt a lot together, too. It was different how you trained us to dance with the fire."

"Different how?"

"Different from other experienced blacksmiths who teach others."

"I'm of fire, Nabu. I feel like myself when working near the fire."

"Ah... no wonder. When you worked late at night, your eyes seemed to change colour like the fire. I wasn't sure if it was only a reflection from the kiln or because your eyes were actually flaming. Or I was the one imagining things."

"It helped a lot to work at night. My head could be full of noises sometimes. My chest got some heavy things for quite some time at that time. You know the reason behind it." My eyes glanced at my wife. His eyes followed.

"Was that how you taught Hadad? Making things about her?"

"Don't our women keep inspiring us to better our skills?"

"You know, I taught them everything I've learnt from you and Shulmanu. Our metalwork could only come this far. With the new kind of iron, it'll need your craftsmanship to go beyond."

"There are still a lot of Blacksmiths out there with better skills than mine."

"But none of us came from the fire. They'll need your Guidance, Samael." His eyes moved to the Light. "May I see your Swords? I can tell it wasn't made here. We don't have the skill to make something like it yet."

"None of you will have the skill to make one like this." I showed the Light for Nabu to see.

"Well, if my Lady Lilith wants to make Dimashq her home this time, there's not much of a difference. The smithy is still in the place as it has always been. Shulmanu trusted me to run the smithy before he passed away."

"He told me about it. And kindly, he shared the reason behind it. The day I left, he asked me to come at the end of his time."

"I was concerned about him becoming delusional as he aged. He didn't stop believing that you'd return to the smithy." He started reminiscing. "Before handing it over to me, he even said that I wouldn't get the smithy. It'd be payment for the work but not the ownership. He had always known the truth about you, yes?"

"And for everything he had known about me, he always treated me as his Brother."

"Now it's time for those blacksmiths to learn some new lessons from you. At least teach them one thing. They're your trouble once again."

"They are, as every blacksmith has always been since I claimed ownership of the place."

"Samael, I understand now. I still remember the time when I found myself a wife. You left me this house to make a home with her. She had filled this house with her love for me and our children. My younglings are now grown. I can only take care of the house so much since my wife passed away."

All I saw in his face was a reflection of myself when I had lost track of Lilith in the past. Shulmanu had been right about seeing a part of me in Nabu.

"I've lived a long life, even longer than everyone you knew at the smithy. Samael, I've been missing my wife dearly. I had no clue how you made it through without Milady Lilith. For how long? Only you two who knew. But I'm not you. Surely, I'm ready to be with my wife again."

"Consider that lesson of longing as the last one you've learnt from me. I apologise that it has to be me in the end, Nabu."

"After all the lessons you've given this youngling, how could you say that? I'm glad it's *this* Angel of Death himself at the end of my time."

"As I said, I don't easily forget. I've seen plenty of myself within this youngling. As had Shulmanu seen me in you."

I took off my shirt. My wings expanded for him to see. Lilith stood from her seat, expanding her set of wings.

A kiss of farewell from me on his forehead. "Reunite with the woman you loved, youngling. You're deserving of her love."

***

Seeds of different flowers were planted around him.

For the first forty mornings after Nabu's passing, my wife faithfully came to his grave to water them. This time, the plants survived, surpassing Nabu's lifetime.

In the afternoon, Lilith came again to tell the story of her day. Those that he had not had any chance to hear in his lifetime. Most likely, he would have turned them into something amusing afterward.

That way was her path in grief. During the first forty nights, I did not touch Lilith in bed. To honour the memory of him in this house. To respect my wife's grieving time.

Usually, I would prefer listening to her than talking. But during this period, I was the one giving her the bedtime stories. Never had I ever thought she would enjoy listening to my stories.

Nabu had told me how closely she had listened to him the first time they met. Lilith probably had seen it long before Shulmanu had seen it. That both of them had seen some part of me in Nabu had to be the truth.

Watching her become sleepy under my care became my lullaby. She looked peaceful because there was trust she gave me. In my arms, the night creature surrendered herself to the night.

Here I was, easing my little bird from spreading her wings. Letting her fall asleep in my arms soothed me. There was relief in knowing that my duty as her husband was fulfilled for the day.

52

The Dimashq Steel Artisans

Lilith had settled comfortably in Dimashq. We decided to make this city our home for the next decade because of this metal, iron. We had not decided beyond that yet. We tried to cherish every moment given to us together.

There was grace in her femininity. Her cycle began when the full moon rose. Sunrise would be the beginning of my cycle. Early in the morning, we would walk. My wife came first in my day.

Her pale skin immediately blushed when the morning light warmed it up. Hers was as feminine as pale-looking metal reflecting the light. Her emerald eyes look more vibrant that way.

In the market, we purchased things we could not grow. When we first moved here, her concerns about her planting skills resurfaced. More concerns had grown in her mind about the nature of the soil. She found it much different than the soil in Aktiki.

Nothing I would change about her. Not even the skills that she had been concerned about. Nabu happened to be on my side this time. The flowers that bloomed around his grave proved her concerns were not the reality on earth.

Since the second new moon following our arrival, our garden had been growing. I would grow every portion of land I found to be her garden. Only for her. Then she would cook for us using everything the land and I provided.

As the sun rose higher in the earthly sky, I left my wife for work. There was comfort in seeing a familiar face at the smithy. The son of Hadad and Tanith was indeed a silhouette of my artisan brother.

Ashur had started his apprenticeship before Lilith and I returned to Dimashq. He was willing to learn more about his passion, regardless of the family he came from. Like a father, like a son. "Samael, can I speak with you?"

"What trouble are you in now?"

"No, not trouble. I heard that when Nabu passed, he left you with the smithy. Well, I figured he knew you well."

"Nabu told me that he met a beautiful woman one day. Let's say... he shared his concern about me being alone for too long. Though he wouldn't leave me alone with his matchmaking mission. He was right. That woman is undoubtedly beautiful. And I'm fortunate enough to have her as my wife."

"Never thought it was his doing. Good for you that you got yourself a wife."

"Indeed, youngling."

"Why did my mother call you her Guardian Angel? You remember when we met in Aktiki? I can't ask her any more."

"I didn't realise you remembered that. It was a long time ago. I was waiting for my soon-to-be wife one night. Your mother was walking alone; Hadad wasn't with her. So, I walked her home."

"That was very kind of you. She always carried a knife everywhere she went. She even placed it under the bed when sleeping."

"And I'm grateful that your mother gave it to my wife before she passed. It might be handy when Lilith walks alone. You know, I could be working here. Though I believe no woman should need any knife to defend herself in the first place," I said, reminiscing about the last memory of Tanith.

"My mother said that the blacksmiths here made it for her."

"It was forged here, yes."

"And since now you're the owner, I need to ask. Can I learn to make one of those? I grew up seeing it every day. It's beautiful."

"Of course, youngling. I'd be glad to teach you." I could recall the time when his father asked me to learn reforging metal crafts. Hadad was still an apprentice full of curiosity. So was Ashur this time.

"You know what? Maybe we can learn to mix them with iron. We shall learn more about this new kind. Let's see how far we can go with it."

"Yeah, sure, it'll be great. I'd appreciate it. I won't disappoint you for saying yes."

"Start by collecting the scrap we have. We can't waste the full raw ones."

"Haha... Or you can simply tell me to clean up those scraps. Clearly, no one wants to do it besides new apprentices, who *clearly* don't have a choice but to clean them."

"Huh, apparently this youngling has learnt something. Glad to know that."

"Yeah, yeah. It's cheaper with the scraps than the raw ones."

"And stronger as well."

Being surprised, he asked, "Really?"

My nod should be enough to satisfy his curiosity for now. The more people heard about our craft, the more orders came. It made sense how many scraps we had.

He seemed to be overwhelmed once he gathered the scraps from the previous week. We were only beginning our second day of this week. It was not that I became ungrateful for the growing venture we had, but there was a particular way in which Shulmanu ran this place.

Dagon came to us as I called for more hands. Teaching them together might save more time. The thought simply came to me. These two young men might have more ideas for creations beyond the necessity of life.

***

It was here that Shulmanu and I had begun mixing copper with gold and other elements. Now, I taught them things that I knew about iron. Not all at once, of course.

Nabu was right; it would take more craftsmanship to work with these different types of iron. That youngling had gained some wisdom from his experience. That way, he became a humankind with so much humility.

At the end of his time, his wish had not been for himself. The smithy was indeed one of my belongings, but these blacksmiths had been under Nabu's care. The wish I was granting was for his men.

People started to call us alchemists. It was all right for me. How the others thought of being called this way was something I was unsure about.

All of us were eager to see how far we could go with Dimashq Steel. Goran and I had built a stronger kiln in Aibunar. The fire there undoubtedly burnt hotter than the one here.

It was not merely the building to go further towards the future. These highly skilled blacksmiths became the most vital element for transmutation. The blacksmiths ourselves were another one in the mix.

Around sunset, I came home to my wife. As Shulmanu said about someone to go home to after work. My time in the kitchen in the past was only a necessity. It was her cooking that filled my soul. Now I understood what this house had witnessed during the time of Maamoun and Nabu.

Unless she started telling me her story, I did not feel the need to ask her about her time alone during the day. The spirit of my little bird was full of freedom. And I loved that about her. Besides, I loved listening to her.

She had her way in storytelling. Curiosity remained in Lilith when we had been on our own in the past. She never lost it, even when she was with me. She kept learning from anything outside of us to build her realm. My wife kept me curious about what would happen next.

There was always a saga within her story. When she spoke, her hands and body moved. Mimicking the storyline, she completed it with such fascinating facial expressions. It was right to say that she added more flavour.

Although there was a part of me that wondered if she had ever been a storyteller, I adored her that way. As she finished the tale-telling, I felt like tucking her under my shirt. Keeping her small body hidden until the next storytelling time.

She was mine to keep safe from anyone or anything outside of us. Keeping her away from her guilt and regret was still something I needed to learn.

My home was rooted so deeply in me. Every house we lived in simply became a place in our path. Wherever I was with her on earth or in the sky, the time and place became my home.

53

Our Partnership

We were only finishing to clean after supper. She asked to have a bath in the quietest part of the river. Off we went, to be on our own, away from anyone else.

"Do you enjoy your time alone during the day?"

"I do enjoy my own time. Mostly I walk. It's pleasant to talk to women and their children here. Sometimes, time and place simply passed by. And then I find myself walking a long way to the new part of the city. I don't quite know what to do before cooking for supper."

"Oh, my Lilith."

"It's the first time you've ever asked where I've been. Is everything all right, my love?"

"Sometimes I wonder if you ever feel abandoned or get bored. But I'd prefer you telling stories than me asking about it."

"I don't look for any other men, if that's what you're asking. We both know what I did in the past. It wasn't right; I know that already." Then there was her silence. Her guilt passed through her shield for me to sense it.

"It isn't what I'm asking. Come here. Sit on my lap. Let me pour some kisses." There was this way my little bird squirmed whenever being tickled. Exactly the reason I loved doing it to her.

Not once had I ever questioned her loyalty or blamed her for what happened in the past. I, too, had mated with someone else. Out of rage, I had fallen from keeping myself only for her.

"I did you wrongly in the past, too. We both are flawed. My little bird always comes home to her nest. Here and now with me is our nest. Your loyalty to me is unquestionable."

She kissed me gently. "Then what's troubling my Angel this time?"

"I don't think I'm good at everything. Before our Fall, I was alone. Those belongings I got from working are still buried. Now we have the Watchers to guard those vaults. From humankind, not from you."

"All my belongings are still buried, too. I don't know what to do with them. You provide me with more than I need. And I'm grateful for everything you've been giving me."

"So I was right about you then. You never needed me. You could support yourself. But I'm grateful that you chose to be with me."

Her washing her body meticulously was enchanting, tempting even. She prepared herself to be a delicacy for me to feast on. She kept me starving while I watched her. She knew how to make me salivate and drool. She always had this way of getting my sword ready to be sheathed.

"And I'd choose you again and again, my Angel. I appreciate that you chose me as well. This sinner is much filthier than other harlots."

Whenever I held her by the hair, her eyes locked into mine. Giving full attention, she waited for my next command. My other hand started to explore her freshly washed body.

"You see, we built vaults in Odessos for us, the Watchers. The site is done. We had another site in Kemet, almost done by now." From her neck, my fingers moved down to her breasts.

"They gave me some space for my belongings. So I asked them to divide it into two. One half for mine and the other half for yours."

"You did? That's very thoughtful of you." Her face was filled with surprise. She reached for my hand and kissed my palm. "I'm one of your belongings.

Would you keep me in there, too? So no one can steal me from you."

"Another vault sounds intriguing. You're giving me a clue to build it with a dungeon. Should I chain my filthy sinner inside of it? I'd fuck the only prisoner in it. I'll give her the punishment she deserves."

"I see you have no trouble planning. How my husband's fulfilling his duty." Her body hair rose when my fingers continued caressing her skin. "So how can I help you with your trouble? I'd like to help if I can. I tend to miss you during the day."

"In the past, I had Shulmanu. I enjoy doing metal crafts, but I'm not that good at running the place. Figuring out how much of the sale comes from the raw materials we spend." My kisses landed on her neck. "How much is needed to retain the labour. Will you help me with those?"

"But I could be tough when working. I worked more with men than women in the past. So I know how their reaction would be towards me."

"Oh, my little Lilith, let's pretend that I've never seen you handling men before." Whispering in her ear, "Some interesting time, that time. You know how to make them surrender to you. But you surrender only to me."

"Gladly you enjoyed my performance. Will I get paid for working with you, Master?"

"You'll get paid for your work during the day. I'll make sure you get rewards at night as well." My fingers tended to have a mind of their own. Once reaching her pussy, they slid inside of her. It was her smoothness that they craved to feel. "Would you like to work with me at the smithy?"

"Mmmh... my love, haven't I told you that you are my Master? I shall work with you during the day at the smithy." She closed her eyes as my thumb rubbed the crown of her pussy. "And I shall work for your pleasure at night."

"Then you'll work *with me* during the day as my partner to run the smithy. And you'll work *for me*, giving me pleasure at night... as my filthy harlot. You shouldn't get confused between the two."

To feel her release nearing was a pleasure in itself. I held myself back as I held the back of her head. I kissed her lips smoothly, torturing her with softness.

"Yes, Master has made it clear to me. But what if I made some mistake at work during the day?" That was my Lilith; she was enslaving herself for my roughness tonight.

"Then I shall punish you more in my pleasure time." It always ruined my guard when she moaned. I kissed her hungrily, sucking the air from her mouth. I slid another finger inside of her, to hear more whimpers coming out of her parted lips.

"Come hard in this river, Lilith. This river will become a part of you."

"Yes, Master. Mmh... Can I have your sword inside of me?" Her hand reached for my cock. "Please, I need you."

As she asked, I turned her around. Her back rested against my chest. "See what you've done to me, Lilith. I no longer have any control over my body."

Kissing her neck from behind, I slid my hardening cock inside her. "Let me feel how good my little bird sheaths my sword. Give me every drop of your squirt. Let me share your release with others who benefit from the water. They'll know how good my harlot tastes."

She kept pumping my cock deep inside of her. She tried to kiss my lips but could not contain her moan. Her pussy was hugging me tighter. "That's my harlot, getting so close. Show me how obedient you are to me."

I circled her crown generously while my other hand squeezed her breasts one by one. Her tears ran down her cheeks as she moaned louder. Her pulse was beating when she came.

My fingers moved from the crown of her pussy to her neck. My grip rested around her neck to keep her in her place. "That's my good little bird being obedient. I need to give you some rewards for that. You want that, Lilith? Hmm?"

"Yes, please. I've been good."

I thrust my sword up to her hilt until my release filled her. That became her first reward for the night.

While she was resting her body on my chest, I washed her clean from all of her sweat. She seemed to always love being pampered with hugs and kisses after I had her.

Giving her one reward was not my plan for tonight. Especially not after the past forty nights of not using her body as my plaything.

***

We returned to the house after finishing our bath. Carrying her straight to our bed. Laying her down for another fuck. The aroma of her clean hair filled my nose.

"Maamoun said a long time ago that I shouldn't be alone for too long. Otherwise, Lilith would come at night." I started showering her with a regiment of kisses. "I've been alone and waiting for you long enough. But you've never treated me the way you treated those men. Never, as far as I can remember."

"I submit only to one. I don't know if I can do those things to you, my love. But if Master demands it, I shall try to obey."

Carrying her, I sat against the wall behind our bed. She tied my wrists to each of the pillars. She started kissing me as if she had been craving me.

"Am I allowed to take off my clothes now?"

"Yes, Lilith. You'll become my feast for tonight."

"Only for tonight?"

"More of... starting tonight, my love."

She was on her knees in front of me, feeding me with her breasts. The warmth of her milk always calmed me down as she held my head. In her arms, she fed me with her essence. At the same time, she made me thirsty for hers even more.

"Would you like to have more, Master?" Either she did not quite understand how this worked or she had completely submitted herself to me. By handing over her control to me, leading our way seemed unnatural for her.

"I want all of you, Lilith." It seemed to me that Lilith chose not to be in charge of me. She fully trusted me with all of hers, was all I could think. Underneath that independence and self-reliance of hers, she remained submissive towards me.

I did not think she understood what I saw while sitting underneath her. She rose in front of me with her majestic wings expanded. Serving me her wet pussy and swollen glans. Feeding my mouth.

When releasing into my mouth, she let her guards down for me. She let down the remaining taste of my come mixed with hers. It was the taste of us together.

"Untie me, Lilith." There was this wicked feeling when she was sitting on my lap. It burst while her head rested on my shoulder. She was being vulnerable, only to receive my care.

I rolled my spent wife over. She was on her stomach while my chest latched on to her back. Grabbing her hair, I whispered, "I told you to lead the way, Lilith. That was another act of disobedience."

She was consumed with her own pleasure. "Please forgive me, Master. It felt wicked for me to lead." Her legs were spread underneath me. She let me thrust into her once again.

"Now you've been bad, Lilith. And I said I wanted all of you. How many times do I have to tell you? More, Lilith." Pulling her hair tighter. It felt *that good* to fuck her this way. She sheathed my sword tighter with each stroke. Tighter, until she surrendered herself to me once again.

Without giving her the time to recover, I kept fucking her hard until I was spent. Softened by releasing myself inside of her smoothness. I told her that I was punishing her. The truth was the opposite. I was only rewarding her with all of me.

54

The Starlike Metal

At first, the men needed time to adjust to a woman being around them. She was the first woman to ever work here.

Since we were to make more blades lately, I started carrying my Sword to the smithy. Besides, Lilith was mostly here working with me. She came before or around noon, bringing our lunch. This very smithy had become an extension of our house by now.

Lilith insisted on preparing our meal, saying that she wanted to cook for me and the men. She said that the new apprentices would no longer be ashamed of themselves for not having any food. Others would have more for their families to keep.

She convinced me that it was a good thing to take good care of our men. She wanted to nurture their loyalty, starting from their stomach. But I had known my wife long enough. It was her nature to desire a family to nurture.

Her thoughtfulness on this was something I agreed upon. The days of her red moon cycle were the exception. The feminine body needed to heal while her womb bled. Pushing hers was nothing I was fond of.

She listened to her husband. She trusted my judgement when she was not able to make one with a sound mind. My wife understood the difference between when to work for me and when to work with me.

We had been receiving more orders from Ashur's family. His sister and brother-in-law had been running their merchant work in other parts of Levant and Ellada. But we still had people in the city who came to our smithy to make their orders.

"How can I help you with, young man? Is it the first time you came to this city?"

"I'm only looking around. I'm looking for a blacksmith who Guarded the North." He paused. "Wait, how did you know that I'm new here?"

"Firstly, my husband and I aren't originally from here. In a way, we can tell. Secondly, you know about his Duty. I shall call my husband. May I know your name, young man?"

"So here you are, the infamous demonic Lilith who made him Fall from Grace. I'm Tubal-Cain, but he wouldn't know who I am. He wouldn't even bother to search for his bloodline."

The moment I heard his insult, I pulled him by the collar. While pinning him to the table, I pointed my Sword straight at his heart. "Then you should know that every drop of my bloodline needs to respect my wife more than all of you respect me."

"So that's what the Divine's Sword of Light looks like. Seems light but balanced. It fits your grip, though. Nice to see it in person. Oh, hey, nice to see you, too, great great great great grandfather. Not sure how many times *great* I should repeat."

All the blacksmiths paused their work, staring at us. They were startled to see my flaming eyes. It was not every day that I let out the aggression. It was necessary, especially in a moment like this. I was to defend the one that I cared about the most.

"My love, please. He's only just arrived in the city. And he's young. Still has a long path to live. It can't be his time yet."

"My wife just saved you from my Sword. Remember that, offspring!" I released his neck and withdrew my Sword away from him.

Lilith handed me the sheath, looking straight into my eyes. Her hand on my chest soothed my soul. Her smile always calmed my nerves. I never knew how she did it to my Being. She did it effortlessly.

"Anyone, close the front door. Not a single word goes out of this place. Do you understand me?"

They nodded their understanding in silence. Some of them were still holding their tools, clenching them in their fists. My men were anticipating whether or not they needed to use those tools as weapons. Even so, they were anticipating more about which side they were in favour of defending.

I took a step in front of Lilith, crossing my arms. "Speak of what you want, offspring!"

"I heard about Dimashq being great at metal crafts. You made quite a name for your work."

"Never mean those crafts are mine. You see these blacksmiths here? They're good men. And they are *that good* at their crafts. You better skip the mumbling. We don't have all day to listen to your nonsense. What made you come here to insult my wife?"

"They call it the 'metal of the Great One' in the foreign land."

"In some regions, it's the 'Starlike Metal.' You can buy one and leave in an instant."

"Not sure if it's a coincidence that our skin is similar to what they call iron. How come you never visited, not even once? You know, asking how we're doing."

"And to do what precisely? Family assembly? You don't want me in your life. Besides, all of you won't do any good for my life. Too much drama, isn't it?"

"Not once have you ever looked for us. All we heard about you was that you were flying around, from side to side, looking for *this* Lilith. And now you're saying that we're not good enough for you? And your mythical demon wife is?"

Throwing a punch straight in his face, I did not even think twice. "That mythical demon wife of mine was the one who nurtured the seeds of the Tree."

Throwing another punch at him. "So that pathetic thief could steal the Fruit from it. That One belongs to my wife!" Throwing my next punch.

"She fed herself and her pathetic husband—" Another punch landed on him. "To get the Knowledge of Good and Evil." After throwing a couple more punches at him, I said, "My fair share was hatefucking Eve's cunt with all the fury I got. *That* was more than enough for trying to be like our Kind!"

"Stop. this. now! Please, my love." Lilith's chest was moving fast, trying to breathe. Confusion and sadness were covering her beautiful face.

Her breathing started to calm down after I pulled her waist closer to me. I held her face in my hand, giving her a kiss on the temple. Smelling her smooth hair.

"I heard Eve had a bite of the Apple from a Tree." She paused. "But I never knew that they got it from *our* Tree."

"It was indeed from our Tree."

"Was it beautiful?"

"It was, but not as beautiful as you are. Remember you nurtured it willingly without me even asking?" I gave her another kiss.

"But—" She paused. "It means that they got all the Knowledge from you. Just like that? You planted the seeds from—"

"Let them have that Knowledge, my love. But *you* have me here." I held her in my arms. "Let it go, Lilith. I'm right here with you. All of me is yours. Let them have it."

She turned her face to the blacksmiths one by one, then finally to Tubal-Cain. Right there, I could see her sorrow. "Well, young man, since you are my husband's descendant, our open door welcomes you. We consider you a family member. I think the blacksmiths here would agree that you can learn from them."

Releasing her body from mine, I said, "We have enough blacksmiths. Enough apprentices to take care of. We have a big family already. Don't think we need another one."

"And I think we should cherish any descendant you have since I cannot give you one."

As much as it hurt her to say that, it hurt me more to hear her say those words. "No, no, no, don't go that path. We aren't having this discussion. You're more than enough for me."

A mournful smile on her face before turning away from us. No word came out of her lips.

"Lilith, could you please not walk away from me?"

"I'm not walking away. The shipment from the southeast of here just arrived. They're in the back. I need to weigh and count them. Anyone, please don't disturb me in the back."

"Lilith..."

"Well, I can't lose count of any single one of them. It's hard enough to find raw material these days, let alone those Utsa." We all could see her eyes starting to glaze.

"Oh, Lilith, my love, can we not—"

"I said. I need. to weigh. and count!" All of us heard her squeaking voice. Tears nearly fell from her eyes. It was her pain that she needed to swallow. Almost choking on her words, she said, "I need to get back to work."

"Then do weigh, Lilith. We shall be here if you need any of us." She left us to go towards the back.

55

A Family of Alchemists

Silence filled our smithy right after Lilith walked out. I leaned my back against the wall, facing everyone in the room. My arms were crossed. None of them dared to even make a sound.

"Lilith and I would understand if any of you decided to leave. But no word is going to ever leave this smithy. Please mind my wife's heart. She had been through a lot more than you could imagine."

Shamash, with low confidence in his eyes, started by saying, "I'll stay if allowed. I haven't had much experience. And I have no chance of finding the Tree you were talking about. From what you said earlier, you planted the seeds. It'd be right for me to learn firsthand, without any Tree or Fruit in between."

He was one of those who started apprenticeships later in their lives. He and his wife had been married since after her parents had passed away. Once he had enough belongings, he started his time in this smithy.

"My intention was only to bury my heavy thoughts at the time. But Lilith saw it as I planted them. She took care of the seeds. She nurtured it. My wife has this way of seeing things differently, in a better way even."

"Yeah, my wife does that, too. Maybe not the same, but something like that."

Dagon followed, "Since I'm an orphan, I'll also stay. I know I'm new here. It's the only family that I could get, for sure. Besides, you feed me well. My Lady Lilith's cooking is great."

He looked around before continuing. "And since we're having a conversation about who you two truly are... uh, what do we call your wife now? Lady Angel? Or lady demon? And what about you?"

Smirking at him, I said, "She was created as a woman, not from the side of a man. Never was created as an Angel. She grew her wings on her own. They're beautiful, as black as her hair. And as strong as her will."

There was a sense of relief I felt, knowing some of them would stay. "You can call us the same way you called us this morning. Besides, it's nice for her to have you as one of our younglings. You see, she always wanted children. A family for us to build."

"Now I understand why my mother called you her Guardian Angel. She knew about you, didn't she?"

He paused to look around. "The owner of this smithy has always been you, yes? Did my father know about you while he was here?"

"No, not always been me. But the first smithy I worked for before claiming the ownership. It was in Shulmanu's time, the one before Nabu. And then I left for a while." The questions he asked confirmed how trustworthy his parents were.

"Your mother knew since the first time we met. I wasn't aware that Tanith saw me flying that night. She also walked through hell on earth. She was a strong woman. Probably the reason she was good at keeping things to herself. Your father knew about me. Your mother told him years after I left here. She knew the best time to speak. You see, she was smart."

Pausing, I recalled Tanith's last moment. "You know, Ashur, I couldn't use that Sword on your mother. I kissed her, and she kissed me back until she was gone."

Ashur raised his eyebrows, staring at me. It must be a wicked moment for him to hear what I said.

I licked my lips and touched them. "I could taste all of her pain and struggles. I could feel all of them rushing in at once. Those memories and feelings shook every part of my Being altogether. They lingered not only on my lips but also in my head.

I felt how heavy her battle was. Oof, my young lady fought her fights well. I might have more wings than most of the Angels, but not for flying with the kind of heaviness that Tanith and Lilith had."

"Wickedly, this is the best way someone confesses that he kissed my mother," he said, smiling at me. If he laughed at me, I would not be mad.

"By that, I also felt your mother's love for you, your sister, and Hadad. How proud she was of her children. And your father was a good man. Not every man was willing to walk alongside a strong woman. Let alone the one who has fought the battle of her own. He knew her struggles even before they were married. Yet he was with her until his last breath. That kindness I witnessed."

"I remember you calling her your 'young lady' in Aktiki. My mother didn't blush often. But she did when you called her that."

"Not by her age. She taught me about hope. That way she remains to be my young lady for the rest of eternity. Her hope lives in me, in you."

"My mother will be remembered as hopeful. I believe she trusted her Guardian Angel. No need to worry about me; I'm staying. I'll keep my mouth shut about you two. Just like my parents did." He placed his hand on his heart. In his words, I put my trust.

He continued hesitantly, "I know it's not my place to ask, but what did she mean by not being able to have any child? If you don't mind sharing, is she sick?"

The heaviness in my chest went out in a sigh. My hand rubbed the back of my neck. "Both Lilith and I are ancient. We've been around for so many generations of humankind. I've watched her lose our children enough times."

I picked up some of the mess from the floor. While putting them back on the table, I told them our losses. "They were healthy when they were born. Moments later, they got sick, bled, and turned rotten. Eventually, they died. Even now, whenever she hears a baby crying, her breast milk will start to leak. I don't believe that she's sick. She's perfectly all right to be a mother."

Ashur followed where his curiosity led him. "But what went wrong with the babies?"

Some of the men started helping me to clean up the workplace. "She was created to bring sickness to newborns. My Lilith is *that* powerful. None of the babies ever stood a chance to survive."

"Why was she created for that? She's a woman. She's able to be a mother, as you said. That didn't make any sense."

"Huh! That's the same question I've been asking since the time of origin. Haven't got any answer so far."

"Look, we might be fools with not so much knowledge compared to your Kind. But this is the time when your wife needs you the most. That one, I know for sure. No matter how upset she gets, just stay with her. We've been working here long enough to know the routine," said Yam.

"I agree to that. Make sure everything is secured inside. See if the fire is out before you close. Or maybe the seniors can take a turn."

"You can trust us with that, Samael." Yam goes silent for a few moments. "Then why are you still here talking to us? Uh, your wife, in the back... What are you waiting for?"

"Because I've known my wife longer than you have, younglings." I chuckled at their frowning faces. "If I immediately went to her, hell could have been here on earth. We're sort of mirroring each other, Lilith and I. Like a set of twins. Let her take a breath alone for a moment."

"Yeah, that makes sense. Is it what those women called twin flame?"

"You tell your women it isn't better than mates for your souls. Especially if you weren't built for it. Let's say we're for different purposes."

"You want us to tell our women that? You'd better explain why. Otherwise, we'd be in trouble."

"Are you ready to see the reflections that the river shows you in daylight? Without any distortion from the stream? Reflections in the calm water under the sun might show something you aren't ready for."

"That's pretty terrifying if you ask me."

What they did not know was how long Lilith and I had been separated before our reunion. One had been the escaping prey, and the other had been the hunter. The prey had escaped for being unaware that the hunter had always been falling for her.

"The twins' alignments are for the lessons. Not all alignment ends up in companionship."

"Now we're even more confused."

"Lilith and I had not always been ready to see the reflections of ours. We were separated for a very long time. There were those lessons in our lengthened lifetime. They had prepared us for what was coming. By the time we reunited, we were ready for our alignment. From there, we built our home together by learning from each other."

"You were searching for her when we first met. All makes sense now," Ashur responded. "Wait, you gave a kiss to my mother. How come your wife is still alive?"

"Have you ever seen any humankind with wings? She's one of a kind. The one and only."

"Did his great great great great great grandmother die when you... well, you know."

"Almost did. But I know self-restraint." Some might find me grinning as unsettling. "It's in my name—the Most High's Venom."

"Nobody here is planning to kiss you now. Haha. We're good with our wives," Shamash threw in a banter. "Then what do you want us to do with the offspring here?"

"No clue." Shrugging my shoulders, I turned my face towards Tubal-Cain's guilty face. "Hey, offspring, whose son are you?"

"Son of Lamech. I—"

I could not hold myself from laughing. "Pfft... So someone came here for redemption. Seven generations until Cain's sin is forgiven. Am I right?" Then I paused, remembering some details of their story. "Wait. Are you here for redemption or to learn to make more weapons? I assume you were born of Zillah. Were you from Adah or Zillah?"

"I'm from Zillah. How do you know about any of us? We've never seen you around."

"Right... Having wings gives us some advantages. And there are reasons why we're called Watchers. We're to Watch, even when humankind can't see us.

I know Lamech helped you with copper. You want to know how to make things out of iron now?"

"Yes, but I haven't got the skills you have here."

"Do you know how to use them?"

"Sort of yes, uh, the swords."

"Right, the swords." With my arms crossed, I walked closer to him. "Have you learnt how to sheath them?"

His frowning face showed his confusion. Tilting his head, he asked, "What do you mean by that?"

"Huh, I figure you haven't. My smithy, my rules! You start from the bottom, the same way as other new apprentices. You've met all these men. You respect them as much as you respect me. And as I said earlier, you respect my wife more than you respect me. Otherwise, I shall cut your balls off. I'll shove them down your throat until you're choked to death. For I'm the Angel of Death, aren't I?"

Tubal-Cain nodded. "Understood. I'll make sure to remember that."

56

Forging the Smiths

The moment I removed my shirt, their movements froze. Even some of the men lowered their gaze. This was obviously their first time seeing wings with their own eyes. Words were not necessary to elaborate on their gestures.

"Being afraid of me is unnecessary. You better not be. My Kind comes in different shapes and forms."

"People in the east from here... uh, they call you something else, yes? And they praise you as one of their gods?" Shamash paused. "I've heard of them because—"

"Because your name came from one of Them?" He shrugged his shoulders and smiled at me.

"They gave me plenty of names. As you all heard from the offspring here, I've Fallen already. But don't we all praise our wives as goddesses in our beds? They deserve to be worshipped that way, don't you think?"

They who were married nodded their agreement.

His next words stopped me from leaving. "So what's our plan here? What do you need from us?"

"The plan is to not let any word out of here. That's all. Why would we ask for anything from you? Lilith and I already have much more than we need. We've been living longer than all of you, piling those belongings."

Dagon stood straight from leaning his back against the wall. "All right, I'll change his questions." The men gave him a way to walk deeper into our circle. "Were you two Created with all that you know? Or because of the long life you've lived?"

"Both. Why?"

"One more thing. Is it our kind that learnt more from you? Or is it you who knows more things from living with us?"

Lilith surely learnt more than me from living among humankind longer than I had. My Lilith here and now was far more enhanced than what she had been in the Blissful Garden. I was the Firstcreated, but my wife's experience and wisdom surpassed my longer lifetime.

"Again, both. Though I've never weighed either of them."

"Ugh, not really getting clear answers here." He stepped backwards from us.

"You changed his questions. That was a marvellous start."

"Then forge us, Samael."

Frowning at Yam, I was not quite sure of what he was asking for. "How do you mean? To me, that fire is cold. Not freezing cold, but all right. Your flesh won't even survive the roasting in there. You'll turn to ashes before anyone finishes his meal."

"Cold? Did Samael just call it cold?" He looked around.

Not everything I could elaborate on adequately. Shrugging my shoulders sometimes gave them the unspoken answers needed for the time being. My wife was good at elaborating on things for others, including for me.

"No, not our flesh. Our insides. The thoughts. The guts. The instinct."

Shamash followed, "We've been called alchemists already. Why don't you smith us, too?"

"Azazel teaches our miners and blacksmiths in Aibunar. Armaros in Kendrisiya with medicine plants. They only followed me when I Fell from my Grace. I'm not saying they're less than me. But yes, they're still new when it comes to living amongst you."

"Then it's true that we got it firsthand. Straight from you. What is it, Samael? What's the obstacle for you to teach us more?"

"Oh, I'm the Firstcreated to give obstacles to others but not to myself."

Looking at my men one by one, I sought affirmations. My hesitance was probably an obstacle for me to go forward. At this very moment, I became my own Satan.

Some of them nodded. Their confirming gestures were loud within silence. It was for me to answer their call. "Utsa. Some call it Ukku. Some of you might have never heard of it before working here."

"For me, it's true," said one of the apprentices.

"They're unheard of because those smithies around Sindhu don't have what we have here."

Ashur chuckled. "Haha, no, they don't have you there."

"Wrong. They don't have the blacksmiths who we have here."

His smile reminded me of his father. "We'll take that as a compliment."

"Mind you, you'll only prove them right for calling you alchemists. By sharpening your skills, you'll be bound with the title. If you agree, you'll become one of those they're talking about. Those words won't always be the truth."

"We'll watch how you do it."

"It takes great carelessness. In the meantime, don't let them speak behind your back. Turn around. Face them with your head held high."

"We confront them? What do we say?"

"Nothing. Let them know that you're watching and listening. When you work, keep your heads down. Work in silence on what you're making. Let your work speak loudly when it's done."

Yam confirmed, "Then alchemists we shall become."

"Under one condition, I shall agree."

"We're listening."

"If we're to forge you, your metalcraft will stand the test of time. Earthquakes, volcanoes, and even floods aren't going to ruin it. What you'll gain from working on it needs to be passed down. Your descendants, your apprentices, will have your skills. Might even be better skills than yours."

"Right... anything else we should know? Seems that everyone already knows what we're in favour of. Ask us one by one if you need."

"I'm to bring the Light. This Sword is made of it. Even I was made of the Infernal Fire. If you feel the wind to be hot, that might be me doing my Task in a larger region. Bringing Light to those that are hidden in the shadows. So more of you see more reflections of yours."

As he was massaging his forehead, Ashur said, "You told us to not be afraid of you. Now we're terrified of ourselves. At least I am. Do we decide on bad things? Or is it you convincing us?"

"My Kind is whole, but not perfect. It is your discretion between the Good and the Evil. The Most High tests our minds. We shall forge our minds first."

Dagon asked further, "Who is 'we'? You said 'our.' Will others from your Kind come, too?"

"Not only do the apprentices need to be forged. The teachers' skills, too, need to ascend."

The Watchers were to Watch. We had been learning from what we Watched. Our Kind had been gaining more knowledge than humankind because we lived longer than they did.

Shamash walked towards me. While shaking my hand, he said, "A covenant it is, with the Fallen."

Nodding, I slung my Sword on my back. "You can be trusted with the smithy, yes? I need to be with Lilith."

"We've got your back, Samael. Just be there for her. You can trust us with the smithy, all right. Not sure if you can trust us with the offspring here," said Yam.

"Neither can I be trusted with the offspring," I said while walking out. Then I stopped. Towards them, I turned my body one last time.

"I know only a little about the matter of the heart. The sound mind makes the choice of whom to keep inside of the heart. When the Most High cuts you open, the part where the Merciful Spirit lives will be searched. Those hearts of yours we can't forge. Entering this house of alchemists is to enter a covenant. That way, we probably bond closer than bloodlines do."

Dagon replied, "Glad to know this orphan found the right house."

57

Breaking Away

Coming out of the back door, I saw her keeping her head down. She hid her face while wiping the tears away. "I'm still counting here—"

"And I'm still your husband, Lilith." I took off, carrying her to a higher sky. We needed to get far from here.

"Put me down, Samael," she said while squirming to free herself from me. Tears began to pool in her eyes once again.

After some time, she finally stopped moving. She hugged me tightly this time, sobbing.

"I'll catch you when you fall, my love." Kissing her forehead gently, I kept her close to me. "Why don't you have a rest for a while? I'll wake you up when we get there."

She nodded.

"You are important to me. More than enough for me. Remember that." We flew higher than usual for a smoother flight. For her to sleep in my arms peacefully.

Her breathing became calmer the further we flew. She was the little bird whom I branded as my wife. Her burden of motherhood should not be hers to carry alone. Even without any surviving babies, she remained motherly in my eyes.

***

After flying for a while, our destination was in sight.

Lilith was still asleep when we landed smoothly near Atanasovsko Lake. There was a dry spot for us to sit. Watching her sleep, I took a few moments before waking her up.

"Lilith, my love. How's your sleep?" Kissing her lips gently, I get myself ready before her storm came.

She stretched her body. She then hugged me, half awake still. "My sleep was all right. Are we here, my love?"

My fingers kept running through her hair. "Yes, we're here. It's all right; take your time. We aren't in a hurry. I'm here with you."

She opened her eyes. After kissing me, it took her a moment before she realised where we were. "Are we at the pink lake? Why are we here?"

She jumped off of my lap and looked around. She was walking around back and forth anxiously. "Why do we *need* to be here? For what, Samael? For me to mourn again? How could you do this to me?"

When she started to cry, I pulled her close to me. "Let it out, Lilith."

She pushed me away from her, but I tried to keep her close. "I'll catch you when you fall. Let it out, my love."

Pushing me away once again, she said, "Let *what* out precisely, Samael? What do you want from me?" She turned her back on me, crossing her arms.

Holding her from behind, I kissed her shoulder. "I'm not your Master tonight."

Her body turned around towards me. Here it was, her first slap across my face. There was something igniting in the way she slapped me. Pulling her close to me, I smelted my lips on hers.

She pushed me off and slapped my other cheek. Then she pulled me close, kissing me roughly. She took her clothes off, as my Lilith was ready to fuck me real hard tonight. Her emerald eyes turned carnelian once more when she climbed on me.

"I'm yours, my little bird. You can take me however you desire. Have a free flight with me."

She gave my mouth her nurturing breast. Her flowing life liquid was the fuel for the fire inside of me. Elements of hers ran through my body.

Whenever she gave me hers, it reminded me that I was of her. "You like it when I give you my milk?"

"Yes, Milady." On a giant rock beside the lake, I sat down.

She held my neck, demanding my full attention. "Then suck me empty. Don't waste my motherhood the way they did it to me."

She was commanding, which left me nothing but to obey. The more times I emptied both of her breasts, the more milk she provided for me. Her body always nurtured me. With her, my Being was fulfilled.

Once both of her breasts were drained, another slap landed on my face. "Get on the ground."

In her grace, she crawled up towards her throne. Her drenched pussy sat perfectly on my mouth. Feeding me with her nectar, she knew how much I craved her delicacy. She rode me as if I were only a camel in the desert to walk by her lead.

"Your cock ready to come home now?" She must feel me nodding. Her hands moved to her hips. Squeezing her arse cheeks, she widened her sheath for me. "But I know you're still craving me. No sheathing your sword yet."

She moaned when I slid my tongue inside of her. My hands were seeking comfort in her silky skin, constantly caressing. To give her the friction she needed for the sparks. They would not leave any part of her skin untouched. From sparks, she became the vessel for my fire. Let our flame combust.

"You want me to come into your mouth?"

"Yes, please, Milady."

"Let me see if your mouth deserves my come."

My fingers slid inside of her, diving into her underworld. Hunting the rewarding treasure from her. My fingers felt her clenching them. She was close to coming.

"No reward for you yet." She lifted herself from my mouth. She moved down to bare my entire body. Another slap was given.

Her tongue tortured my cock, licking the crown thoroughly. From the crown to the body and to the root. Finally, I was planted entirely in the deepest part of her throat.

"Milady, I shall be spent being tortured like this."

Her hand softly gripped my sac. She denied me, pulling the sac down. "No reward unless you're deserving."

She crawled on top of me. She licked the remaining taste of hers that lingered on my face. Now my sword was sheathed. She deserved to fuck herself using me.

Her hand locked my throat in silence, suffocating me with her lust. Her carnelian eyes enchanted me, keeping me obedient in my place.

"Lilith, I—"

"What do you want, Samael?" Slapping my face even harder than before, she expanded her wings powerfully. "Use your words. Otherwise, widen me open. Let me sheath you deeper!"

What I did was fulfilling her command. Squeezing her arse, I sheathed my sword deeper. The crown of mine ascended to the highest of her heavenly realm.

All these times, I was wrong about my wife. I had control over her because she let me. She had always been the one with power over me. The power of allowing what I could do or could not do was always hers.

Milady Lilith fucked me roughly until she judged me to deserve her. Slowly her head landed on my chest to catch her breath in between tears. Her body became calmer once she recovered from the wind of her pleasure.

She let me carry the burden she endured this way. I massaged her scalp, caressing her. "That's my little bird. You used me so badly tonight. Yet you feel so good."

She reached for my sheathed Sword and handed it to me. "You're great with blades. Do you mind cutting my hair? Below the shoulder, maybe around the middle of my back."

"Of course, my love." I sat myself up with her on top of me. My sword was still sheathed inside of her.

"How about this much? Not too short, not too long," I asked while pointing somewhere between her shoulder blades.

She nodded. "That would be fine."

I brushed her hair down. With a clean swing of my Sword, I cut it for her. "You look beautiful as always, my love. That never changes."

The twelve spans expanded, only to wrap her in comfort. My sword never left its sheath, even while I rolled us over together. Feathers of mine became her bedding. The roughness of the ground was never supposed to hurt the silkiness of her skin.

"Is it still my sheath, Lilith?"

"Always, my husband."

She deserved to be loved with care tonight. "Let me make love to you. I'm here for my little bird." Cupping her face, I wiped her tears away with my thumb. As my lips kissed hers gently, my sword sought peace inside of its sheath.

Battles on earth and in Heaven were no more when I was home in her underworld. Even if the battles on earth and in Heaven were endless, I could fight in each one of them when she was with me.

Either Lilith or I being alone was sovereign from others' domains. Together, neither of us would let the other fall. I would catch her when she fell, as she would catch me when I fell.

"I need every part of my Lilith to be with me. I always want every part of you. This little bird is mine. I want more of you, my love."

***

More of Lilith.
More time with her.
More of Lilith for all lifetimes.

58

Battles of Their Own

The Time of Full Iron

Copper, bronze, and iron had led the society of Dimashq to flourish in craft and trading. The city had become an essential region, especially since the arrival of the Aramaeans.

They had better records for their civilisation. That could be important for the future. To learn from their glory. Most importantly, to learn from their downfall.

The region had become vital for them to start the battle over power. They referred to the region as the Kingdom of Aram-Dimashq. Here began the battle between the Aramaeans and the Israelites. By that, I got excited to Watch how humankind fought with one another.

The Most High decided that I had power over other kingdoms across the world, except the kingdom of Israel. But of course, I would have power over their sinners on the Day of Atonement. It certainly piqued my curiosity about the reason behind it.

I would never forget about the house of Maamoun and Anat. Their lives had been full of love for each other. It had nourished their marriage, as well as their family.

Memories of Tanith would always keep me looking forward with hope, even if it felt hopeless for the time being. In Hadad, I learnt to love someone stronger than we ever could.

The memory of Nabu would forever remind Lilith to take a leap of faith and enjoy the paths, for we never knew where the path would lead us. Each path had intersections so that we could intercept each other's journeys to learn from them.

They said that we were to blame for teaching Divine Knowledge. But for quite some time, it was for the Watchers to learn many things from humankind. Humanity fascinated me. From them, I had been learning so much.

Lilith and I decided to return to Dimashq from time to time. Therefore, the city of Dimashq became a reminder of who I was and who I would become. It was a journey of constant learning.

One could always decide to answer the Call as needed. I remained a Tasker of the Most High. Ascending and descending to and from the Heavens and the earth. Even if that meant that I was to blame for humankind or other beings.

As a Tasker, I kept answering my Call to fulfil my Duties. Some of them happened to be wearing the title of *Satan*. Many thought that the title was Created as a solid being. The title of adversary was sometimes about a being in opposition. Towards others, or even towards oneself.

It could even be oneself challenging the mind not to be settled in one thought for too long; that lesson was from Goran, the mountain man. Some might call it 'obstacles'; others might call it 'deconstruction'. They might not have the adequate word to call it yet. I believed they would have it one day. And so we Watched.

And we Listened. Many would follow the line of Gundahar in telling the tale. The Saga would travel through the words of the storytellers. One would tell one version, while others would tell other versions.

Words were proto-origin. The Breath of Wisdom of the Merciful Spirit had swept the water off the abyss, but the Creator's Words had given us Light. The Light was for me to bear.

Bonus Chapters

Rada Lyubomirova's "The House of Alchemists" contains the following chapters.

The Leaders' Council
The Time of Bronze

Lilith

***

Constantly being watched—that was how it felt to me.

All of the Leading Watchers were summoned to this very hall. Fifteen of their Leaders had arrived, and they were waiting for my love to come with the other Five. How anxious I was about being the only being who was never created as an Angel.

Leading men of humankind was familiar to me. But they were not Beings of the Sky as these Leaders. Most of them who arrived were aware of my presence, but they did not say anything when their eyes met mine.

Turiel had a beautiful place here in Serdika. Even this hall felt majestic. These decorations were thoughtfully put together. An ensemble of art pieces. Each one of them was one of a kind. Impressive. Tasteful.

Although it was beautiful here, this city was too big for me alone in the past. I would prefer Kendrisiya, with more hills and warmer people. That was probably why I made more close connections in that city than everywhere else I had been.

"Have you had a good rest? The Great Prince gave specific guidance for your care. He wanted to make sure that you healed properly."

"I shall be all right. Your hospitality is as high as the sky. Those helpers of yours provide me with so much comfort."

"He simply wanted to take care of you, Lilith. He had searched for you for as long as I could remember. When he finally found you in Burgas, he found you in such a tragic event. Let's say... not in your best condition. I could understand his concerns."

Nodding, my answer was enough. Leading the conversation elsewhere, I asked him, "Where did you get the decorations, if I may? They're exquisite. I assume they weren't originally from here."

"And I assume you were unaware of the Great Prince's ventures. What he built while searching for you all these times was obviously unbeknownst to you." He gave me a warm smile. Unless they were close enough to know me, I rarely gave anyone any.

"Hmm..." Averting my attention towards another piece of art, I simply avoided being read further. "And this one too? I'm fond of this type of fabric. Delicate enough for the wall, but not too stubborn for the patterning."

"Most of what we have here was learnt from the Great Prince himself. He generously shared a lot of knowledge with us. I believe that he was thinking about you when making things."

Without showing too much curiosity or seeming too eager, I asked, "What does he do with his ventures, if you don't mind sharing?"

"No, I don't mind sharing. Regardless, it isn't my position to tell his tales."

Turning my face towards him, I looked at him straight in the eyes. I made sure Turiel saw the disapproval on my face. I never liked to be kept in the dark, even if I knew that they were higher Beings than me. *Especially* when I knew that they were higher Beings than me. I was never one of their harlots for them to look down on. I had no problem harloting myself into Samael's bed.

"All I can say is that he's been taking care of his men. Since the Falling Flight, he's been taking care of us, the Watchers. I can surely tell that he's been building a home for you. Please make yourself at home in my place. The helpers are to assist you." Turiel walked away to rejoin the table.

I could not say that I was *that* strong to stand up the entire time, but I would not know what to say if I sat there. Because of that, I kept moving slowly around the hall to admire each ornament here. To give attention that each of them deserved. To overhear what each Watchers said to each other.

My legs were still sore. After giving birth, of course they were. Yet I kept them spread widely since Samael found me. He fucked me badly. *That* badly, that he made sure that I was never feeling enough of him. He made me want him more.

Here he came, entering the hall. The One who was no longer the Great Prince in Heaven. He was now the Great Prince of the Fallens. Even after the Falling Flight, he remained my Great Prince in my own heaven.

With five Leading Watchers from the far southeast, he came home to me as he promised. The five Leaders greeted the others, embracing them with warm hugs and smiles. Samael went straight to Turiel to talk.

He smiled at me when he saw where I stood. With a curtsy, I welcomed him. He always replied by bowing to me. There was a concern on his face this time. He glanced at me a few times in between his conversations. He signalled for Turiel to close the entrance door.

"Is there something wrong? Is it me? Did I do something wrong? What did I do?"

Turiel ordered his helpers to leave and close all the doors behind them. Then he took his seat at the table alongside the others. All of their Twenty were here now.

Samael turned to see all the Leading Watchers. All of them remained in silence. No one was speaking in the hall. They were waiting for him to let out the first word.

"Are they afraid of him? Why do they still call him the Great Prince? Are they under his chain of command here on earth? Is there something I didn't know about him? Has he changed into someone I no longer know?"

There were so many questions I would have liked to ask him. It felt to me like I did not know a single thing about my Angel. After a long time apart, I wanted to know everything about him.

Infernal Marriage

Lilith

***

He took a few steps forward. Then his azure eyes locked on mine.

This harlot was being called to her owner. I could no longer walk slowly when he said, "On all fours, Lilith. Crawl to me bare of skin."

I could feel the stares of all the Leading Watchers. But I was never theirs to take. Obeying my Great Prince, my body was now uncovered before everyone. No matter how sore I was, I would crawl towards his mercy. I would not hesitate to show everyone how I kneel before him.

His caring hand cupped my jaw as if I were his sitting pet. His other hand lovingly combed my hair. "Were you being good while I was away, Lilith? Did you take care of yourself as I said?"

"I tried to. But I'm all right since you're here. I'm no longer in pain."

"Yes, you will be."

In starvation, my lips parted for a breeze full of his scent. Everyone in the hall suddenly evaporated into the air. At least in my mind they did. Samael never left. Only my Angel remained.

The kiss from the Angel of Death suffocated my lungs. Yet I was gasping for more of him. His aroma, his aura... I needed all of him to veil my bare flesh.

Handling me by my throat with his leading hand made my body shiver. The hair on my arms and shins had risen, just as my wings expanded. My hands were clinging to the layers of fabric he wore, begging for his bareness. A slight moan slipped out of my mouth in desperation.

He broke our kiss, watching me. His eyes locked me in thirst. He could feel my hand reaching for his hardening cock. "You want it, Lilith?"

"Yes. Please, Master."

"Then take it out."

I took off all his clothes while feeling his knuckles rub my cheek gently. My starvation towards him broke free. My thirst of his come sneaked in.

His thumb rubbed my bottom lip. I could not help myself; his thumb became my comforter. He lifted my chin to look straight at him. Leading and caring for me at the same time.

Him. Naked. Standing before me with his starlike skin. I had never seen him in such a bright place as here. With those many fireplaces in the hall, the fire made his skin a luminaire. He was indeed made of fire, igniting the arousal inside of me.

I stroked him a few times while looking up at him, waiting for his approval. My hair rested in his firm fist. My head was led closer to his cock. I licked the bottom of his crown, curling my tongue around his sensitive part.

His shiny drops of arousal made my pussy leak. It was ready to sheathe his sword. Caressing his cock, I did not want to miss any part of him. How had I missed him already? He was not away for long, but long enough for me to start longing for him.

I longed for his girth to fill me again. Taking his length bit by bit until he was entirely mine to swallow. How fulfilled I felt when he fed me this way!

He trusted me to lead until his needs were bigger than mine. Then he started thrusting at me vigorously. He grabbed hold of my hair and took the lead. Steadying me, he held my head still.

I could see that he enjoyed the feeling of me gagging. My tears begged for his mercy to give me more. It was not a mourning cry. It was a beggar's cry for more. I made sure he saw it.

He lifted me and laid me on the table. The very table the Watchers were sitting at. They were watching us get burnt by our flame. We let ourselves burn, so let everything else burn with us.

There was something in the way Samael drained my breasts. They were still full from bearing those departed babies. I had never done this with anyone before. He fulfilled my need to provide something for someone. But it was not just for anyone. I wanted to provide *him* with as much as I could.

I felt his fingers crawling through my inner walls. I let out a surrendering moan. "My Master's sheath missed your sword today."

It melted me weak to hear him growl with my nipple still in his mouth. My milk leaked down the side of my breast for him to lick it clean. I was sent to fly higher by his thumb rubbing the crown of my pussy while his two fingers hunted something inside me.

Massages from him reached into the part of me that I did not even know existed. The part where he flew me towards the seventh heaven. My dryness was no more. For the first time in my entire existence, it became a waterfall, bursting pleasure out onto his hand.

He pulled his drenched fingers out of me. The remnant of my fortress was cherished by his mouth. "I missed my harlot's taste as well."

After his mouth cleaned my come that had covered his hand, he filled my empty pussy. A moan of relief came out of me, knowing that his sword rested in the sheath. "Master is home."

"Have you really taken a good rest, Lilith?"

I nodded. Tears started running down my face again.

"Because after this, you won't be able to walk. My sheath will be sore tomorrow." He deserved to take away my ability to walk, but I still had my wings to fly following him.

If he wanted to carry me flying, I would snuggle in his arms. To feel the force of the lift that his twelve wings made would even be better than flying by myself.

"I don't mind. Please don't stop," I begged him.

He grabbed my thighs to hug his waist. This way he was sheathed deeper in me. His left hand pinned my throat onto the table. His right hand took the amulet off of his neck. He held it tight in his fist. His eyes started turning into flaming fire. Then the smell of smoke came from the table.

"That's it, Lilith. You're close. Come for me one more time. Harder this time." His movement became wilder and deeper into my hilt. His release followed mine right after.

Once I was undone, he lowered his body onto mine. There it was, something burning my skin. He pressed the hot amulet in his palm against my side.

Screaming my lungs out. Crying hard, I no longer saw anything or anyone in the hall. My Angel's face remained close to mine while my left side was on fire. I screamed until there was no more air in my lungs. It was chilling until there was no more voice to scream out.

Finally, he took the amulet off of my skin. "Here, I brand Lilith as my wife." He lifted his body from mine, saying his command to the Watchers, "I'm the only one who is allowed to humiliate and treat her as my filthy one. From this day on, you respect my wife more than you respect me."

The walls in the hall were echoing those voices of agreement. I was created to be lower than them. It was my Great Prince who put me in the place higher than them. It was my place that he built for me.

His hand caressed my face. "Shh, I'm right here, Lilith. I'll catch you when you fall."

Nodding to him, my tears were a pouring rain. I could not even let out a single word from my mouth. My entire body was trembling.

He asked one of the Watchers, "Would you please get me a cover?" He lifted me for a short moment and lay me down on the table again. This time, I felt a piece of fabric underneath me. He folded one side of the fabric to cover me halfway.

His fingers were rubbing my burning rib with something. Oil, ointment, or some sort of... honestly, I did not care what he was rubbing me with.

Cupping his jaw with my shaky hand, I gave him my gratitude. Then his kiss landed on my palm. This Angel of Death was my husband now. This was his mercy. He gave me the death of my old life.

He flew me straight into the married life that I had always wanted with him. He folded the other side of the fabric onto me. Once his body was covered, he carried me to his seat.

His knuckles were caressing my cheek. His thumb wiped my tears away from my face. I was still catching my breath and sobbing. Then I heard a Watcher pouring some water and handing it to Samael.

"Have some water, my love." He helped me drink since my hands were still shaking. He looked at that Watcher again. This time, Samael received a piece of cloth. "Appreciate it, Chazaqiel."

I felt better after he wiped my face with the damp cloth. I asked him with a shaky voice, "Why on my rib?"

"They replaced you with someone from Adam's side. It felt right for me, branding you on the rib."

If only I could slap him across the face, but I could not. What he said was right. He continued to clean my neck gently. He rinsed the cloth in the bucket of water. Never had I ever had someone clean me between my legs. This was my first time receiving such care right after.

With pouting lips, I said, "And you fold me like a baby with a blanket."

"It isn't wrong, though. You *are* my bundle of happiness. Is it all right with you if we continue our table here? We still have matters to discuss."

"I'd like to be nowhere but here."

He kissed my temple gently. "Take a rest. You will need it."

I nodded, obeying his caring words. As I was pulled closer to him, I could hear his beating heart. I had a place to live, but I felt at home in his arms. He was my home.

"As you all know, I've been doing metalwork. But it's starting to grow at the moment. They're a bit of a handful, with more apprentices coming to learn.

Not to mention, they're discovering more types of metals."

"I can help you teach them. The young ones are curious. They have more ideas than the grown ones. A lot more fun as well."

"Very well then, Azazel. I appreciate your help," said Samael.

"But first, I need to know what needs to be taught and the way you teach them—"

"Honestly, I never thought I'd be teaching anyone in the first place. What we did was simply show them how to do it. We—"

Their voices faded more and more. But I kept feeling Samael's fingers combing my hair. They were massaging my scalp lightly. Then my eyes got heavier under his care.

Nestling in his warmth like a little bird, I snuggled deeper into him. I felt another gentle kiss on my temple before falling into the depths of the night. I was no longer the night creature humankind afraid of. I was now my Guardian Angel's tamed little bird.

Detained
The Time After the Flood

Samael

***

The memory of our infernal marriage was constantly being recalled. It kept me alive in the moment, surviving through the darkness of the proto-earth.

To be able to ascend out of the abyss with that memory was the hope. Or other memories of her, as many as necessary to get me free. She would free me.

I gave these Watchers my Light every now and then, especially after the lashings. Not all the time, since I needed to be conserved well. Fifty have landed on me so far. It was necessary to take each one of those punishments, whether or not I was deserving of them.

After all of this was settled, I would be giving my wife fifty as the punishment she deserved. My Lilith was hesitant when I told her to retreat. Her being safe was my priority. There would be more lashing for her if I received more from them. Her pussy was always like a river stream each time I chained her like a dragon in our dungeon.

"Lilith had already grown her wings."

"What did you say?" He paused himself from writing our petitions. His face showed us that he heard my question the very first time.

"Are you still a man, Enoch?"

A frowning face with furrowed eyebrows was what he gave me. There were no words of answer that he let out.

"Eve came from Adam's side. Lilith was created from the same dust as Adam. Neither of them was the daughter of any man."

By pulling my bond upwards, its weakest chain broke free from the binding ground. Both of my wrists pulled the bond in opposite directions. The weakest chain between the wrists broke. "Lilith had already grown her wings when she and I became one flesh."

I walked towards him, locking my eyes on his. "So let me ask you one more time, Enoch. Are you still of humankind? Or should we call you Metatron already?"

***

To be continued in "The House of Alchemists"
and "The Guardian Prince of Rome."

Bonus Chapters

Rada Lyubomirova's "The Guardian Prince of Rome" contains the following chapters.

The Morning Star
The Time of Bronze

Samael

***

Last night was only the start of me having all of her for myself. As selfish as it sounded, she agreed to be my harlot. She was only allowed to ask for my come as a payment.

Her sleeping in my arms the entire night had got me a sleepless night. Not to worry, but to watch my wife. To watch how wonderful she was. *"I can refer to her as my wife from now on."*

This first morning of our marriage would never be forgotten. She would be the luminary star of my every morning for the rest of eternity. Cupping her sleepy face in my palm, I felt content. "Good morning, my wife," I said.

"Good morning," she said, pulling me closer. She did not let me go. How grateful I was that she did not. Not only this morning but since the time of origin. "Did I snore last night?"

Gently rubbing her back, I gave her temple a kiss. "You were sobbing in your sleep, actually. Don't blame me if I can't resist kissing you madly. It's closer for me when you start pouting like that. That was precisely what I did to her, devouring her lips.

She giggled adorably. "My plan worked then."

This small woman could be so adorable in the eyes of anyone who did not truly know her. Besides the Most High, I might be the only one who knew how powerful she could be.

"What is my husband fond of having this morning? I should get you some breakfast."

"I agree. You should serve me some breakfast." I released her from my arms, for I knew that my breakfast was already served. Tasting the delicacy between her legs. "This one I'm fond of having. My delicious sheath, perfect for starting my day."

The rhythmic sound of her moan sang in my ear as I lapped her pussy. Her sweet nectar was always available whenever I needed it. The crown of her pussy was always prepared to swell each time my mouth latched.

Hugging her thighs from underneath, I drowned my tongue in her nectar. Each part of her underworld took turns in receiving my attention.

Her thighs, her stomach, her breasts, and her nipples took turns for my hands to touch.

Her fingers ran between my hair, giving me a gentle head massage. Her touch on my scalp surprisingly relaxed me. Her gentle pressure worked its spells on me. My fingers returned the favour to her inner walls, massaging the inside of her.

She deserved to take everything from me. Everything about me was always hers to take. Yet she served me instead. "But how about mine? I want my breakfast, too. Please," she begged.

My arms pulled her thighs closer to mine. While keeping her pussy in my mouth, I turned around. My cock started to feed her. Her nipples were hardened, rubbing against my stomach.

"Take me all in, Lilith." There was something about her moaning that controlled my cock. "Take everything I give you. Are you going to be good?"

"Mmm... hmm," she hummed, nodding. That friction of her hum, her nod, and my cock in her throat, all at the same time, could be dangerous. They made me way more wicked. Deeper into the back of her throat, my sword went. Her throat was another sheath for mine.

She hugged me in her care. One gentle hand rubbed my back, starting from the base of my spine to my shoulder. Her other hand remained on my arse, with its fingernails buried in my skin. She touched me gently while being fed.

My finger returned to her inner warmth while I kept lapping her swollen crown. Adding another finger for her when she spread her leg wider, I said, "Come for me, Lilith."

She released my cock from her throat. "Yes, Master." Her tongue started lapping over my balls. I did not think she knew what she had done to me. Her moans became more raw when my fingers started to fuck her roughly. Her pussy became tighter. Then she got off easily under my lead.

I lifted myself from her. Her release on my hand was now licked clean. Kissing her lips, I let her taste herself in my mouth. "That's my good little bird, coming so nicely. You taste so good. From now on, I want my wife to serve me this delicacy every morning for breakfast. Whose sheath is it, Lilith?"

"Yours, Master."

I rolled her to her side, pressing my chest against her back. While whispering in her ear, my fingers crawled to her neck. "Remember that, Lilith. It's no longer yours but mine now."

"Please, Master, I need you."

"What do you need now? Hmm? Tell me."

"I need your sword sheathed in me. Please."

She screamed so loudly last night that it made the Watchers in the hall feel the agony in their ears. I tried to hold myself back from fucking her roughly this time. At least I was trying to be gentle with her after branding her last night.

"Then take it. Fuck yourself with it," I said while pinching her hardened nipple.

She took me in. She moved beautifully, pumping my cock. She licked her lips, reaching for mine right after.

My hand cupped one of her breasts and played around her nipple. Then it moved on to her other breast. She was so sensitive to my touch that I could see the hair on her arms rising.

"Look at you. Fucking yourself with my cock like a filthy one. To the outside world, you are my wife. But whenever you are alone with me, you're my harlot. When there are only the two of us together, you are my enslaved wife."

"Yes."

I was no longer able to keep myself gentle with her. My hand pulled her hair tighter. My other hand moved from her breast to her chest and eventually to her neck. "Yes, what, Lilith? Let me hear it."

"I'm my Master's harlot when we're alone. And never forget that you are the owner of this sex slave."

"Remember your place. You are my harlot to fuck. My slave to use."

Her lips parted open. Both of my hands held her neck from behind. I was thrusting at her faster than before. Maybe I was right that she was not only becoming my wife but also my harlot. "Now start touching yourself. I want you to come with my sword sheathed."

She was being obedient to my lead. Making herself come, drowning me in her release once again. Here, my release followed hers. I had followed her shadow for too long. I would follow her wherever she went from now on.

My Dark Angel

Samael

***

I said that she was mine, but truthfully, she claimed me to be hers since the time of origin.

"You were never created as an Angel. Yet I demand every Watcher respect you more than me. Because that's your place, Lilith. You deserve that place."

She turned around to snuggle in my arms. "What would we become, my love?"

"Everything. We become everything we need to be." I kissed her forehead gently. "Not quite sure about you, but I have everything I need here," I said, placing my hand on her beating heart.

She held my hand. Her face was wet again with tears. "I don't feel like deserving you."

"My little bird could make me fall into nothing when I lost you."

"Sometimes I don't know what to say to you."

My eyebrows rose, for I was not sure if I understood what she said. "Do you mind showing me, then? I'd like to see how you live, what you do, and where you go. I'd like to hear your stories. We had been away from each other for so long. I want to know about you. I want to understand you."

With that bewitching smile of hers, she was able to make me frozen still. The one who could keep my mouth shut. Not knowing what to say, I cleared my throat. "Lilith, last night, at the table, you fell asleep in my arms. I wasn't sure how much you heard—"

"Oh, I fell asleep immediately, my love. Your spells undoubtedly cast me. I didn't hear much of it, if that's your concern. I know I wasn't—"

"You weren't being lied to or kept in the cold darkness."

"Now I have a husband who is fiery. I'm sure he will keep me warm, even in the cold."

Each time I combed her hair with my fingers, I loved how smooth it felt in my hand. "We divided the tasks last night. I need to be away with you. Of course, I'll be watching how they're doing. Those younglings couldn't be left alone, even for a moment. They could be feral sometimes."

She chuckled. "Like father, like sons, I believe. Quite amusing to see you fathering them." She paused, and her hesitation became obvious. She kept playing with the hair on my body to conceal it.

"I saw it, my love, the Falling Flight, from afar. All of you looked like stars falling from the sky, granting everyone's wishes. I couldn't ask anyone, so I didn't know you were there. But then I overheard Serpent mention their Great Prince. Only I never expected that it was you."

"I never expected to be called by that name, either. To me, the name is in the past."

"If I were allowed to be selfish, at least my wish was granted that day."

"Tell me, my love, is it all right for me to bother you for the year ahead? You're important to me. I shall be with you for a full year."

"Bothering me only for a year? You can bother me for lifetimes ahead, husband. Would you take me with you when visiting the Watchers? I want you to share your life with me as much as I want to share mine with you."

"I'd love to take you to visit them. We shall travel over the land and seas." How much I missed the excitement in her emeralds. "Though we need to have rules about sharing, you see. I've been working here and there, so I have some belongings."

"Me, too, my love."

"That's my point. My belongings will be our belongings. But your belongings will be yours. It's important for me to take care of you. It's my duty to provide you with anything you need."

She cupped my face before kissing my lips. "But I want to cook for you. The kitchen in your house was well used. I thought at the time that either you lived with someone or you cooked. But I saw only your clothes in the wardrobe, so you must be cooking."

"I was aware that one of them disappeared. Still nowhere to be found."

"No, it isn't. Pretty useful so that no one could find me."

"Including me."

"I moved from one place to another. If only I knew—" Her words needed to be cut off with a kiss. It did not matter to any of us anymore. She understood it.

"The women taught me to cook. Different places have different kinds of food. I know that you can cook, but I want to do it for you."

"What did I say about getting everything I need? First, you serve me well in bed. Now, you want to serve me your cooking? Every day?"

"Mmm... hmm." She paused to shower me with kisses. Pouting her lips together, she shared her concerns this time. "Though I need to buy the ingredients, I don't have a well-grown garden. Your garden was well cared for. Mine had never grown. I thought that the seeds didn't go well with the soil at first. But, no, it wasn't it. Everything I planted eventually died. I think it was me."

This talk of planting started to be hurtful. "*Do I have the heart to tell her about the Tree of Knowledge of Good and Evil? It was Lilith who cared for it.*"

"No, it wasn't you. See the seeds inside me that you've nurtured since the first day we met? Obviously, they didn't die. Only growing." I started to nibble her pouting lips. "Also, you deserve every seed I have. I shall empty them inside of you as many times as I can."

Her hand was reaching for my half-hardening cock. "And is the '*as many times*' part including now, Master?"

"Only if you'd be my good little bird. Are you sore, my love?"

Shaking her head. She then lifted herself and fed me with her full breast. "Well, a little bit. I've been good, Master. Please, have me as you want."

I consumed every drop of milk her breasts served me. I moved her legs around my waist. "Take me home, Lilith. Inside of you."

Carrying her out of bed, I walked outside. With her legs locked around my waist, my sword was shoved into its sheath. I should have done this since the time of origin, taking off with our naked bodies exposed. It was still very early in the morning, but I would not even care about anyone seeing us.

By fucking her up in the air like this, she could moan and scream as loudly as she wanted to. Surely I deserved to hear the sound rushing in my ears. I would be fulfilled hearing them.

She expanded her strong black wings. They were beautiful and strong, as strong as she was. "I'll catch you when you fall, my love."

***

To be continued in "The Guardian Prince of Rome."

Bibliography

"1181 Lilith (Asteroid)." *In-The-Sky.org Guides to the Night Sky*, in-the-sky.org/data/object.php?id=A1181. Accessed 21 Apr. 2023.

Adamah, Benjamin. "Mountain Spirits." *Occult Blog*, 8 Nov. 2022, vamzzz.com/blog/mountain-spirits.

American-Israeli Cooperative Enterprise. "Samael." *Jewish Virtual Library*, www.jewishvirtuallibrary.org/samael. Accessed 21 Apr. 2023.

"Animals in the Bible." *New Advent*, www.newadvent.org/cathen/01517a.htm. Accessed 21 Apr. 2023.

Bar Yochai, Rabbi Shimon. "Bereshit 43." *Zohar*, London, Soncino Press, 1933, www.sefaria.org/Zohar%2C_Bereshit.43.432?ven=english|The_Zohar%3B_London,_Soncino_Press,_1933&lang=bi.

---. "Bereshit 44." *Zohar*, London, Soncino Press, 1933, www.sefaria.org/Zohar%2C_Bereshit.44.438?ven=english|The_Zohar%3B_London,_Soncino_Press,_1933&lang=bi.

Behind the Names. Mike Campbell, www.behindthename.com/names/search. Accessed 21 Apr. 2023.

Ben Asher, Rabbi Bachya. "Torah Commentary by Rabbi Bachya ben Asher." *Sefaria*, translated by Eliyahu Munk, 1998, www.sefaria.org. Accessed 21 Apr. 2023.

Ben Hyrcanus, Rabbi Eliezer. *Pirke de Rabbi Eliezer*. Translated by Rabbi Gerald Friedlander, UK, 1916, www.sefaria.org.

Ben Nahman, Rabbi Moses. *Commentary on the Torah by Ramban (Nachmanides)*. Translated by Charles B. Chavel, USA, Shilo Pub. House, 1971, www.sefaria.org.

Ben-Amos, Dan. "From Eden to Ednah—Lilith in the Garden." *Biblical Archaeology Review*, 2016, library.biblicalarchaeology.org/article/from-eden-to-ednah-lilith-in-the-garden.

Benner, Jeff A. "Satan." *Ancient Hebrew Research Center*, www.ancient-hebrew.org/names/Satan.htm. Accessed 7 Dec. 2023.

Beyer, Dominique, and Horst Klengel. "Syria and Palestine." *History of humanity: From the third millennium to the seventh century B.C.*, vol. II, UNESCO, 1996, pp. 499–528. unesdoc.unesco.org/ark:/48223/pf0000119150.

The Book of Enoch: Deluxe Edition of 1 Enoch, 2 Enoch, 3 Enoch. Bonus Apocalypse of Abraham. Sacred Scriptures Press, 2024.

Collier, Ada Langworthy. *Lilith: The Legend of the First Woman.* Canada, Devoted Publishing, 2016.

"Demonology." *New Advent,* www.newadvent.org/cathen/04713a.htm. Accessed 21 Apr. 2023.

Division of Christian Education of the National Council of Churches of Christ in the United States of America. "Deuteronomy 24:5." *New Revised Standard Version Bible with Apocrypha,* USA, HarperCollins Publishers, 1989.

---. "Deuteronomy 32:8." *New Revised Standard Version Bible with Apocrypha,* USA, HarperCollins Publishers, 1989.

---. "Ecclesiastes 4:9-12." *New Revised Standard Version Bible with Apocrypha,* USA, HarperCollins Publishers, 1989.

---. "Hebrews 13:1-2." *New Revised Standard Version Bible with Apocrypha,* USA, HarperCollins Publishers, 1989.

---. "Isaiah 34:14." *New Revised Standard Version Bible with Apocrypha*, USA, HarperCollins Publishers, 1989.

---. "Jeremiah 17:9-10." *New Revised Standard Version Bible with Apocrypha*, USA, HarperCollins Publishers, 1989.

---. "Luke 10:18." *New Revised Standard Version Bible with Apocrypha*, USA, HarperCollins Publishers, 1989.

---. "Matthew 16:23-26." *New Revised Standard Version Bible with Apocrypha*, USA, HarperCollins Publishers, 1989.

---. "Proverbs 18:24." *New Revised Standard Version Bible with Apocrypha*, USA, HarperCollins Publishers, 1989.

---. "Proverbs 28:1-6." *New Revised Standard Version Bible with Apocrypha*, USA, HarperCollins Publishers, 1989.

---. "Psalm 82:1-8." *New Revised Standard Version Bible with Apocrypha*, USA, HarperCollins Publishers, 1989.

---. "Revelation 4:2." *New Revised Standard Version Bible with Apocrypha*, USA, HarperCollins Publishers, 1989.

---. "Revelation 12:7-10." *New Revised Standard Version Bible with Apocrypha*, USA, HarperCollins Publishers, 1989.

Eliade, Mircea. *The Forge and the Crucible.* Translated by Stephen Corrin, Second Edition, USA, University of Chicago Press, 1978.

Encyclopædia Iranica Foundation Inc. "ḠUL." *Encyclopædia Iranica,* iranicaonline.org/articles/%e1%b8%a0UL. Accessed 21 Apr. 2023.

Esalawati, Nanda. *Astrology in Tarot Card.* USA, Alpha Eureka Edukasia, Inc., 2023.

Etheridge, John Wesley, translator. "Genesis." *The Targum of Jonathan ben Uzziel,* 1862, www.sefaria.org/Targum_Jonathan_on_Genesis?tab=contents.

---, translator. *The Targum of Jonathan ben Uzziel.* 1862, www.sefaria.org/texts/Tanakh/Targum/Targum%20Jonathan/Torah.

Ethiopian Bible in English Complete: Lost Books of the Bible. Apocrypha Complete. Sacred Scriptures Press, 2023.

Ford, Michael. W. *The Bible of Adversary.* Adversarial Flame 10th Anniversary Edition 2007-2017, Succubus Productions Publishing, 2017.

Gale, N. H., et al. "Alloy Types and Copper Sources of Anatolian Copper Alloy Artifacts | Anatolian Studies | Cambridge Core." *Anatolian*

Studies, vol. 35, Dec. 1985, pp. 143–73. *JSTOR*, https://doi.org/10.2307/3642880.

Gale, Noel H, et al. "Early Metallurgy in Bulgaria." *NBU/IAM*, vol. IV–V, 2000, pp. 102–68. *Academia*, www.academia.edu/10144854/Early_metallurgy_in_Bulgaria.

Gale, Noël H. "Metals and Metallurgy in the Chalcolithic Period." *Bulletin of the American Schools of Oriental Research*, vol. 282–283, University of Chicago Press, May 1991, pp. 37–61. *JSTOR*, https://doi.org/10.2307/1357261.

Gimbutas, Marija. "Gold Treasure at Varna." *Archaeology*, vol. 30, no. 1, 1977, pp. 44–51. *JSTOR*, www.jstor.org/stable/41706107.

Ginzberg, Rabbi Louis, editor. "The Birth of Cain." *The Legends of the Jews*, vol. 1:3, New York, 1909, www.sefaria.org/Legends_of_the_Jews.1.3?lang=bi.

Greenspan, Rabbi Mark, translator. *Marbeh Lesaper on Pesach Haggadah, Magid, The Four Sons 4.* 2017, www.sefaria.org/Marbeh_Lesaper_on_Pesach_Haggadah%2C_Magid%2C_The_Four_Sons.4.2?ven=Rabbi_Mark_Greenspan&lang=bi. Accessed 17 Dec. 2023.

Haight-Aston, Lady. *The First Sisters: Lilith and Eve*. UK, Moon Books, 2019.

Hirst, K. Kris. "Wootz Steel: Making Damascus Steel Blades." *ThoughtCo*, 24 Feb. 2018, www.thoughtco.com/wootz-steel-raw-material-damascus-blades-173235.

Horn, Trent. "Who Was Lilith?" *Catholic Answers*, www.catholic.com/qa/who-was-lilith. Accessed 21 Apr. 2023.

Horovitz, Rabbi Isaiah HaLevi. *Shenei Luchot HaBerit*. Netherland, 1698, www.sefaria.org.

Hunter, M. Kelley. *Living Lilith: Four Dimensions of the Cosmic Feminine*. UK, The Wessex Astrologer Ltd, 2009.

Innocity Ltd. "History Of Varna: 6000 Years In 1500 Words." *Varna City Card*, 24 Jan. 2019, varnacitycard.com/blog/varna-history-6000-years-in-1500-words. Accessed 25 May 2023.

Jewish Women's Archive. *Alphabet of Ben Sira 78: Lilith*. jwa.org/media/alphabet-of-ben-sira-78-lilith. Accessed 21 Apr. 2023.

Joseph, Dan. "Samael, Lilith, and the Concept of Evil in Early Kabbalah." *AJS Review*, vol. 5, 1980, pp. 17–40. JSTOR, www.jstor.org/stable/1486451.

Kadmon, Baal. *Samael: A History*. 1st Edition, USA, 2022.

Kimchi, Rabbi David. *Radak on Genesis 3:1:1.* Provence, France, 1235, www.sefaria.org/Radak_on_Genesis.3.1.1?ven=e nglish|Eliyahu_Munk,_HaChut_Hameshulash&lan g=bi.

Lambert, W. G., and Erica Reiner. "Babylonian Astrological Omens and Their Stars." *Journal of the American Oriental Society,* vol. 107, no. 1, Jan. 1987, p. 93. https://doi.org/10.2307/602955.

Lecouteux, Claude. *Encyclopedia of Norse and Germanic Folklore, Mythology, and Magic.* Edited by Michael Moynihan, Translated by John E. Graham, Canada, Inner Traditions International, 2016.

"Lilith and Algol." *Letters of Lilith,* lilithgate.atspace.org/essays/algol.html. Accessed 21 Apr. 2023.

Lumpkin, Joseph. *The Books of Enoch: The Angels, The Watchers and The Nephilim: (With Extensive Commentary on the Three Books of Enoch, the Fallen Angels, the Calendar of Enoch, and Daniel's Prophecy).* USA, Fifth Estate Publishers, 2011.

Mark, Joshua J. "Ancient Greece." *World History Encyclopedia,* 13 Nov. 2013, www.worldhistory.org/greece. Accessed 28 May 2024.

Mark, Joshua J. "Prostitution in Ancient Athens." *World History Encyclopedia*, 2 July 2021, www.worldhistory.org/article/28/prostitution-in-ancient-athens. Accessed 21 Apr. 2023.

Mars Communications Team at NASA's Jet Propulsion Laboratory. "BEFORE 1500 (the first observations of Mars)." *NASA Science Mars Exploration*, mars.nasa.gov/allaboutmars/mystique/history/early/#:~:text=The%20Greeks%20called%20him%20Ares,as%20shown%20in%20Homer's%20Illiad. Accessed 16 Dec. 2023.

McClure, Bruce. "Algol the Demon Star of Perseus." *EarthSky: Updates on Your Cosmos and World*, earthsky.org/brightest-stars/algol-the-demon-star. Accessed 21 Apr. 2023.

Metcalfe, Tom. "After many centuries, research suggests new facets to the blinking Demon Star." *NBC News*, www.nbcnews.com/science/space/many-centuries-research-suggests-new-facets-blinking-demon-star-rcna4813. Accessed 21 Apr. 2023.

Miller, Walter. "A History of the Akropolis of Athens [Plates XV-XVIII]." *American Journal of Archaeology*, vol. VIII, no. 4, 1893, https://doi.org/10.2307/495887.

Muhly, J. D. "The Copper Ox-Hide Ingots and the Bronze Age Metals Trade." *Iraq*, vol. 39, no. 1, 1977, pp. 73–82.

Orlov, Andrei A. "The Watchers of Satanail: The Fallen Angels Traditions in 2 (Slavonic) Enoch." *Marquette University*, www.marquette.edu/maqom/watch55.html. Accessed 12 Dec. 2023.

Pernicka, Ernst, et al. "Lead Isotope Analyses of Metal Objects from the Apa Hoard and Other Early and Middle Bronze Age Items from Romania." *Archaeologia Austriaca*, vol. 100, 2016, pp. 57–86. JSTOR, www.jstor.org/stable/44242704.

---. "The Development of Metallurgy in Western Anatolia, the Aegean and Southeastern Europe before Troy." *Western Anatolia before Troy. Proto-Urbanisation in the 4th Millennium BC?: Proceedings of the International Symposium Held at the Kunsthistorisces Museum Wien Vienna, Austria, 21-24 November 2012*, vol. 1, Austria, Austrian Academy of Sciences Press, 2014, pp. 447–62. JSTOR, www.jstor.org/stable/j.ctv5vdd0s.25.

Plovdiv Municipality. "History." *Plovdiv Municipality*, www.plovdiv.bg/en/about-plovdiv/history/#:~:text=It%20is%20believed%20that%20the,called%2

0it%20Evmolpia%20or%20Evmolpeida.
Accessed 11 Dec. 2023.

Rappoport, Jason, editor. "Shemot Rabbah 18."
Sefaria, 2022,
www.sefaria.org/Shemot_Rabbah.18?ven=englis
h|The_Sefaria_Midrash_Rabbah,_2022&lang=bi
&with=About&lang2=en. Accessed 21 Apr. 2023.

Regardie, Israel, and John Michael Greer. The
Golden Dawn: The Original Account of
Teachings, Rites, and Ceremonies of the
Hermetic Order. 7th Edition, Revised and
Corrected, USA, Llewellyn Publications, 2015.

Richardson, Christopher David, and R. H. Charles.
The Complete Books of Enoch: The
Apocryphal - The Watchers, Fallen Angels,
The Origin of Evil, and Cosmic Covenant.
2023.

"Satan Meaning." Abarim Publications,
www.abarim-publications.com/Meaning/satan.ht
ml. Accessed 7 Dec. 2023.

Sauter, Megan. "Lilith in the Bible and Mythology."
Biblical Archaeology Society, 26 Aug. 2023,
www.biblicalarchaeology.org/daily/biblical-topics
/hebrew-bible/lilith-in-the-bible-and-mythology.
Accessed 9 July 2024.

Sefaria Community, translator. "Hechalot Rabbati."
Sefaria, www.sefaria.org. Accessed 21 Apr. 2023.

Sherby, Oleg D., and Jeffrey Wadsworth. "Ancient Blacksmiths, the Iron Age, Damascus Steels, and Modern Metallurgy." *Journal of Materials Processing Technology*, no. 117, 2001, pp. 347–53. Researchgate, https://doi.org/10.1016/S0924-0136(01)00794-4.

Singh, Nihang Teja. "Taxila." *Sanatan Shastar Vidiya*, www.shastarvidiya.org/history/taxila.html. Accessed 23 Jan. 2024.

Smith, Josh. "What Is Damascus Steel? (And Everything You Need to Know About It)." *Montana Knife Company*, 13 June 2023, www.montanaknifecompany.com/blogs/news/damascus-steel.

Sofia International Model United Nation. "SOFIA History." *SOFIMUN*, 2015, www.2015.sofimun.org/?page_id=102. Accessed 18 Aug. 2024.

Stewart, Suzy. "The Algol Star – Features and Facts About The Demon Star." *The Planets*, theplanets.org/stars/the-algol-star. Accessed 21 Apr. 2023.

Taxila Museum. "History of Taxila City." *Taxila Museum*, 2021, taxilamuseum.punjab.gov.pk/node/78.

Thomas, Chan. *The Adam And Eve Story The History Of Cataclysms Uncensored Digital Version - Magnetic Pole Shift*. Edited by Sam Shadow, 2021.

Uzziel, Jonathan. *Targum Pseudo-Jonathan: The First Five Books of the Bible*. Edited by Tov Rose, 2016.

Vernor, E. R. *Lilith: The Mother of All Dark Creatures*. USA, Dark Moon Press, 2015.

"Why and when Athens got its name?" *Athens Insiders*, Insiders Travel Experiences, www.athensinsiders.com/blog/why-athens-named-athens#:~:text=The%20place%20has%20been%20inhabited,after%20its%20ruler%20%E2%80%9CAkteos%E2%80%9D. Accessed 18 May 2024.

Yakar, Jak. "Regional and Local Schools of Metalwork in Early Bronze Age Anatolia Part I." *Anatolian Studies*, vol. 34, Cambridge UP (CUP), Dec. 1984, pp. 59–86. *JSTOR*, https://doi.org/10.2307/3642858.

Zabel, Gary. *Demons: Lilith*. www.faculty.umb.edu/gary_zabel/Courses/Phil%20281b/Philosophy%20of%20Magic/Arcana/Kabbalah/demons02.shtml.html. Accessed 21 Apr. 2023.

About Rada Lyubomirova

Pen Name for Nonfiction: R.L. Zareva

Rada Lyubomirova writes adaptive fiction with medium-to-fast burn rate of erotic scenes.

Timeless narratives are being retold with the darker taste of romantic literature. Plots are twisted with morally grey characters. Classic stories are given a seductive passion that will keep you delightfully hooked deep into the night.

She is a travelling author. The nomadic life has been giving her opportunities to see how stories connect us through similarities. The pen name is to be the vessel to ship unheard speeches from the lands of restrictions and censorships. Her literary artworks are to cross the borders and travel beyond. The values within each work need to find their freedom.

Is there another myth, legend, or folktale that deserves to be reimagined? Your feedback will shape our compendia of unheard values and silenced voices. Leave your thoughts and reviews on her stories.

About the Publisher

Besides publishing fiction and nonfiction books, Compendia Publishing creates content for social media and online courses.

Scan the QR code above to see our portfolio of works.

Thank you for purchasing the original copy of this book. Your feedback will help both the publisher and author with future works.

9 781963 038071